An Offbeat Story

Siddharth Srivastava

FROG BOOKS

First published in India 2013 by Frog Books
An imprint of Leadstart Publishing Pvt Ltd
1 Level, Trade Centre
Bandra Kurla Complex
Bandra (East) Mumbai 400 051 India
Telephone: +91-22-40700804
Fax: +91-22-40700800
Email: info@leadstartcorp.com
www.leadstartcorp.com / www.frogbooks.net

Sales Office:
Unit No.25/26, Building No.A/1,
Near Wadala RTO,
Wadala (East), Mumbai – 400037 India
Phone: +91 22 24046887

US Office:
Axis Corp, 7845 E Oakbrook Circle
Madison, WI 53717 USA

ISBN 978-93-83562-08-4

Book Editor: Surojit Mohan Gupta
Design Editor: Mishta Roy
Layout: Chandravadan R. Shiroorkar

Typeset in Book Antiqua
Printed at Jasmine Art Printers Pvt. Ltd., Mumbai

Price — India: Rs 195; Elsewhere: US $8

Dedication

To my daughters Khyati and Alaynah: there is no greater happiness than being with them.

About the Author

Siddharth Srivastava is an independent journalist based in Gurgaon, National Capital Region. He has worked for *The Times of India*. Over the last decade his writings have appeared in reputed publications across the world. His other assignments include India-related consulting projects from clients based in America, Europe and Southeast Asia. This is his first work of fiction.

Siddharth has studied in St. Edmund's (Shillong) and Delhi Public School (RK Puram). He has a BA (Honours) degree in economics from Hindu College, Delhi University and a post-graduate in the same subject from Jawaharlal Nehru University (JNU). He represented Delhi state at the national level in water sports.

Acknowledgements

Happiness is about finding balance in life -- good health, professional progress, financial security, loving family and children. My two kids Khyati and Alaynah have given me unconditional love. Their smiles make my day.

My wife Ritanbara has kept me rooted and focused to keep the equilibrium. My mother has only thought about the good of me and my brothers all her life, advising and convincing my father accordingly.

I am still learning from my father qualities of staying positive while grappling lows and highs of life with determination, hard work and equanimity. My father-in-law tells me to stick to doing what is right, professionally and personally. He says it is important to always grow. My mother-in-law has looked after my kids as her own. I know I can count on my brothers Amitabh and Parikshet. I thank them all. I also thank Leadstart Publications for offering to publish my book.

Contents

Now that the serious portions have been done with, this is the real deal. This book is dedicated to cafes in Gurgaon where I wrote a bit in the evenings after work. I keyed in my thoughts over strong and bitter Cappuccino, enough to kick start the brain despite the large foamy portion in the cup. The loud music, bright lights, animated office colleagues, restless property dealers and frisky young couples in serious conversation formed the backdrop of my laptop screen and keyboard. Writing is a lonely and boring process.

The coffee shops removed some of the ennui, even if I felt I was inside a noisy airport lounge at times. There were also instances I wrote when I was very sleepy or drunk at night at home. So, please pardon the foibles, mistakes, abuses and obtuse language on occasions.

The following appear in the story, which is a work of fiction:

I (not the author, but the hypothetical narrator, referred as "Me, My, I" from here on): I am a Journalist, who can be self-righteous, corrupt, paupers, idealistic, hardworking, alcoholics and voluble. I got lucky with property investments and a consulting practice over the Internet that allowed me to service clients worldwide. My earnings were in dollars, pounds or Euros. My revenues multiplied several times courtesy a weak rupee due to an oil-import dependent Indian economy. I earned as much as a NRI based in India. My pay was like an expat, though I was not one.

Lata: My wife in the story. My real spouse may think I have built the character round her, which is untrue. I am very careful in dealing with my actual wife. If she is in a bad mood the nagging spoils my day. If I am in a foul space, I can ruin her time. This is healthy. This is marriage. It is about unloading, keeping things even or else one spouse turns into a garbage bin of the other's verbal vomiting. Both parties need to feel equally worthless, at times. Both should also feel good to be with each other, at times.

Pooja: The girlfriend, again imagined, whom I did not marry, unfortunately. There may be some who think it is them, but they are not.

Sushmita: My married lover with some philosophy to share about her being. She probably exists somewhere. I have lost touch. I think she was all in the mind though her physical appeal was phenomenal.

Seema: My girlfriend, while I was married. This complicates my life a bit, in the story. Again an unreal person who, like an *apsara*, takes a form of her own even as I envisioned more of how she could be. If she actually existed, I might have decided to be with her. It is not humanly possible to say 'no' to somebody imagined so pretty.

Alaynah: My daughter whom I love. Dads should wash their kids' potty when they are babies. It leads to the kind of bonding expecting mothers develop with the being inside. For males, pregnancy is ruled out, though this could be a future possibility given advances in medical science and other spheres. Whoever thought of space tourism or a half century in 12 balls in a T20 cricket match? Whoever predicted a Chris Gayle hitting the number of sixes he does? Watch Vicky Donor?

Still, until fathers can biologically carry babies leading to debate about men's abortion rights, cleaning kids' potty is the way to deeper spiritual meaning and purification as Gandhiji might have put it.

One cannot wash anybody's dirty bottom without inner emotions and attachments coming into play.

MORE ABOUT ME

As mentioned earlier, this is a work of fiction. Some readers may not believe the assertion, but that does not matter to me. As far as I am concerned this story is imagined. The locations, events and context in the narrative maybe real as they are derived from facts of life, like making love to a woman. But, the characters and events are fictitious with snapshots and vignettes from multiple daily experiences that can be illusory, ecstatic or completely fucked up.

Any resemblance to anybody that I know or do not know is incidental, though there will be some who may think it is them I have written about. They can take pleasure or pain from such deductions, but I intend to hurt nobody.

If somebody tries to sue me, including family and friends, I will choose to ignore unless the police are at my doorstep with court summons. The lethargic and inefficient constabulary in India is very efficient in delivering non bailable warrants. It allows them to exercise power, be rude and make money.

I don't believe in bribing cops, judiciary or any other authority. If pushed, I may even try and call the hyperactive TV people, maybe some chaps from an equally driven anti-corruption front, to showcase the high-handedness of state power.

I don't like to be disturbed at home. I may not be busy. I could be just passing time, maybe watching Sunny Leone online or Yuvraj Singh's six sixes on YouTube. This is despite the overdose of the un-gentlemanly game due to IPL and T-20. West Delhi bred youth icon Virat Kohli has taken Hindi sledging to new levels. Still, I don't like my personal space to be intruded.

I don't wield any kind of power or importance that people may need to pay me to get their work done. So, I have developed my own version of being an honest citizen – I don't pay any under the table money or across the car window bribe to the traffic constable. I pay the fine or none at all.

I personify middle-class morality that perhaps existed briefly post-independence inspired by ideals of Gandhi and Nehru. There has been some resurgence of truth in the recent past, with several sections of Indian youth taking to the streets to protest against corruption and crime against women. This is good.

A bit of the stubborn aspects of my character are derived from my father, a government officer, who never accepted any money on the side, though he could have easily. Sometimes, I feel he did wrong.

It could have made life of his children comfortable, like some of my father's friends (read batch mates) kids who live off rents from mansions built in prime localities in Vasant Vihar, Panchsheel or similar high profile addresses.

Still, I find it difficult to circumvent the inherent imprint of uprightness courtesy my father. My driving license has expired. I intend to stand in line at the secretariat for renewal rather than hire a tout, many of whom advertise their services online.

When my daughter was born the municipal clerk offered to leave her date of birth blank on the birth certificate for a few extra bucks. I could pass her off as younger or older as I wished, depending on the need. This is common occurrence, the clerk told me. I refused the offer. The irritated *babu* made me wait for a few hours before handing the document.

Sometimes I do break the law, like jumping a red light, in a hurry. I do say sorry when, say, a traffic cop threatens to fine a-hefty Rs 5000 for speaking on the cell phone while driving. I still don't offer a bribe. Though I have no qualms about apologizing, this usually does not work with lower inducement seeking *babus* in our country. My driving license has thus been confiscated a few times I was not carrying enough money to pay the actual fine.

I went to court, the ambience of which was a mix of a crowded railway station, government hospital and teeming unclean Indian market like Sarojini Nagar or Lajpat Nagar. Despite the cacophony, the judge was lenient and even smiled.

"You are not the sort who can be a nuisance to society," she said and ordered the DL back. I try not to cross some dividing lines though. I will not kill except in self-defence. That's how big game animals, tigers and lions are, unless they are hungry or pushed to a corner.

I sometimes perceive myself no less than a big cat. I am a fan of Animal Planet, Nat Geo and Discovery. I loved Steve Irwin. I feared he would be gobbled by a crocodile, but it turned out differently. It was unexpected. It was like an Army *jawan* surviving a war, but dying in a bus accident, though public transport in India can be more dangerous than battle gunfire, given India's high road fatality rates.

There are two aspects of my life that I would advise others not to follow -- don't be in multiple relationships, same sex or opposite. I am bringing in the gay aspect to be politically correct and maybe encash on a growing English reading market comprising guys who love other guys. Apologies for the sales pitch up front.

My second bit is -- don't live with in-laws, wife's parents to be specific or the other way round (husband's mother and father), post-marriage if you can get by without it. This complicates life.

It is best to be intimate with those one can naturally be close to – like kids when they are small, girlfriends, parents, pets, cars, bikes, cell phones, I-Pods, the potty seat where I spend a bit of my time reading newspapers, fiction and checking mails on my cell phone. Nature has not created a man or a woman and his or her in-laws to be proximate, just as homosexual sex does not seem to be a natural performance. So, why get into the wrong side of the way God created us.

My parents advised me against shifting to my in-laws house but, like all obedient children, I did not listen to them, while pretending I valued their judgment.

As my life turned complicated I enjoyed the unadulterated time with my daughter Alaynah. There is purity in a father-daughter relationship that no wisecrack can pollute. I noted down some of our interactions, in a blog.

Most people who read entries of my short online diary describe them as cute as father-daughter interactions are bound to be. I will get to them later towards the end of this story. This part usually appeals to women and maybe sensitive men, though this is a misnomer, unless we are talking about guys who happen to discover the woman inside them. This is happening quite often nowadays.

There are many other aspects about me that I would ask the reader not to emulate, but the above two stand out in particular for their absolute nuisance value.

At 40 today, I have experienced and survived both, but it should not be the preferred course in anybody's life, unless one is looking to learn and live the difficult way. I am one of the silly hard path varieties. Until I fall on my face and bloody my nose, I never get it right.

There will be many frustrations and challenges in life. Why add to misery? It is best to enjoy the little occurrences of daily existence by keeping it simple, as cricket commentators love to say – like spending time with your kids in the park, a Bollywood movie, coffee over conversation at CCD, playing cricket or making love to the same woman. I know the last bit sounds a little off track, but try getting under the sheet of your woman, and not someone else's, a bit more than you would like to. The tensions disappear, the warmth flows, the defunct prostate gland re-ignites and juices that you believed have dried up forever begin to stir.

When I was young, my elder brother Sid presumed girls dominated my mind, which was not totally correct as I thought about other matters too.

These included maintaining my scooter, keeping my body in good shape, sports, trying out street food, some reading and movies. Some time was devoted to porn in magazines, then video cassettes and finally the Internet, though I was much older by the time the last medium, the best and most efficient, happened.

In school I was never the chap outstanding in studies that are the teachers' favourites. There were occasional flashes of brilliance that surprised some competitive classmates and tutors who discounted me as topper material.

But, there were dips that worried my parents no end too. They debated endlessly about engaging expensive private classes. "We will have to spend a lot of money on you because you cannot study on your own," my mother told me.

"I will not fail. I will not top. I will do well enough without tuitions," I told her. I loved my parents too much to waste their money.

I knew if I worked upon a subject, I generally did well. If I did not put my mind to it, the results would show. Still, luck usually did not favour me.

Last minute slogging is no substitute to regular disciplined work that builds lateral knowledge that I usually lacked. Invariably, exam questions would appear from just the portions I did not study or forgot to revise.

I had a bit of a sharp tongue though. My school principal spoke to me following my class 10 results: "You have done better than I thought you would." "I never doubted myself, you did," I replied back.

Still, my life equations were pretty straight forward. In the crucial class 10-12 years, I managed to convert intelligence combined with a little less hard work than necessary to score high enough marks for admissions into a good college in Delhi University. Due to need for killer work schedules, I avoided the exacting IITs and medical entrance tests, which was okay by my father, who had visions of only the IAS exam for me.

As I grew up, I realized I naturally attracted girls. I am not being immodest here. The female species found me very cute and appealing. I was not the very handsome hard jaw line cigarette ad model Milind Soman variety; I was not the bad boy Salman Khan variant that girls want to reform.

I was not the glib, brainy and witty Aamir Khan type that talks their way into women's hearts and more; I was not the high on hygiene, designer underwear, perfumed armpits, chest shaved, tattooed, chewing gum and mouth sprayed metrosexual David Beckham genre either.

In my early 20s I was six feet tall, slim and athletic due to interest in swimming, soccer and cricket, fair by Indian standards, slightly reserved unless provoked and boyish looking. My smiles apparently were a lady-killer, producing shallow but noticeable dimples on both cheeks that girls never forgot to pick or mention.

This part of my anatomy was like a disguised Shane Warne Googly or a Muralitharan *doosra*. When females met me the first time, they did not suspect anything extraordinary about my looks, which is the correct assessment.

Then the smile and consequent dimples hit them. Most were bowled out, bamboozled, caught plumb in front. I turned into an irresistible male candy that girls could not refuse. Comments ranged from "he looks so innocent" to "even butter cannot melt inside his mouth."

I have spent some time of my life in front of the mirror trying to figure out the particular magic on the fairer sex. I could decipher none. Porn movies underline women dig size – biceps, triceps and further down. Nothing else matters.

X-rated films predictably highlight the inches. There is a vested interest here as big advertisers on smut web sites are makers of products that promise turning puny pricks into prized possessions. In my case the attraction was different, up front and not very large. God had created a contortion on my smiling face that made women want to take on a seductive role, somewhat like mythological *apsaras*.

I am usually polite with girls. They have reciprocated with their body and soul.

I see it as my destiny or luck, given that some of my friends and colleagues have spent a bit of their time, money, mind share and effort to score with girls. There are of course those who have done much better than me in this department of life that can sometimes subsume all else.

Yet, many were inspired and I suspect Sid too to make it to the IIMs, IITs or the IAS to rightly boast achievements, make money and hook girls. Sid converted his adolescent sexual energies into study hours that showed. I don't recall him not in top three in any class. I had to constantly multi-task between girls, sports and studies, which meant the probability of my making it to decimal point makes a difference competitive examination were remote.

There were times that I was in multiple relationships. I know there are moral questions that can be raised here. Yet, only people eligible to be with many women simultaneously should judge others similarly placed.

It is easy to preach refraining from "wrong" when there are no temptations. Activists in India speak against corruption while not in position of power. Once ensconced in establishment, they turn into selfish greedy hyenas moving around in red beacon cars surrounded by armed bodyguards paid by tax payers' money. They shun the very people who voted for them while short changing the system dry.

It is never easy to hold back when beautiful girls are throwing themselves at you tightly holding your backside the way only cheapies in public buses do to the fairer sex. Women are as fascinated by a man's bums as it is the other way round. They may not be as public about it as guys are about girls or gays about each other, but do express themselves privately.

To me, looks mattered but this was not paramount. What was important was that I was able to vibe well with the woman to be interested in her. I preferred women who are skilled in bed, though there can be no telling beforehand.

I like the voluptuous but generally avoid the fat or too skinny. Size zero is not for me. I don't like girls with acidic breaths who are perpetually psyched about eating less or overweight ones with thighs bigger than torsos that probably blow wind quietly. In any case, once in the sexual arousal zone, it hardly matters if the partner looks like an Aishwarya Rai, Vidya Balan or Katrina Kaif. It's the response of the senses that counts. Imaginations can take over tightly shut eyes. Most unbiased literature I have read emphasize size matters only up to point.

Moving on from women related analysis I have always liked sports, especially swimming, badminton, soccer and cricket. I made it to a couple of teams in school, college and Delhi state squad in water sports. As I grew older, I preferred to run regularly, mostly in the evenings as I cannot be up and about early.

My father disagreed with my late rising habit. He tried unsuccessfully to turn me into a morning person. "People active in the morning carry a shine on their face the whole day. They are more alert," he would say, peering closely into my eyes to spot the elusive "shine." He probably read sleepy written all over.

A few times, he forced me to walk to a nearby park but I dozed off on a bench or quiet grassy corner. He followed a few times to ensure I stayed awake but gave up.

The effort was too much. I simply could not be instantly out of bed to delve into an aggressive routine. My mornings needed to be slow over sips of tea, coffee, milk, newspaper, water, loo, a short walk and listening to birds.

Most of my movements, including my usual gait, easily qualified as slow. I do break into a trot if there is a bus to catch. Unless I am in a big hurry, I prefer to wait for the next one. In the evenings, though, I could run on any demarcated route until my calf muscles and hamstrings ached.

I would finish off at good speed, sweating and out of breath. It is important to be totally sapped during the run. Thoughts empty out of the mind as every ounce of energy is focused on extra physical effort. It is orgasmic, meditative feeling.

Over time I have picked and discarded vices. I don't drink regularly, but do enjoy getting drunk sometimes with friends. I like the numbness infused all over the body that shuts out every part of brain activity except portions that feel wild, happy and ecstatic. I don't drive rashly with horns blaring or pick up brawls or taunt policemen on the road when I am high. I think that is rude, irresponsible and dangerous if cops decide to give chase on motorcycles.

But, I do get raucous, loud and horny if in the company of the woman I am involved with. I smoked for a few years but gave it up.

Cigarettes attack the lungs, brain and ability to make love. I am against the stamina sucking erection busting throat cancer causing sticks. The need for tobacco shots to sustain nicotine levels in the blood stream can be very addictive. No amount of taxes can make cigarettes unaffordable. When I was short of cash I smoked *beedis*.

Dipping nicotine causes mood swings like that of woman about to begin her menses or a man whose hormones have gone haywire due to company of a pretty woman. It affects stamina and causes pre-mature hair greying.

It leads to bad sex which means erectile dysfunctions much earlier than struggling to make it last 40s and 50s. When I gave up smoking I left it for good and have never tried it again. If a friend happens to smoke in my presence, I bluntly tell him he is burning his performance in bed.

I am unsure about impact of smoking on women's breasts or bums, proportions of which matter to men. But, I am sure it affects the skin. I associate cigarettes with warty women and non-kissable smelly breaths.

Moving on from smoking, my other factors were mundane: when I am unclean, I smell bad, so I need to bathe every day. I believed my armpit odour was due to overactive hormones that make it difficult for me to resist women if they are available. But, I have been told quite often, especially those close to me, not to mix hygiene and hormones. They advise that I should spend some time under the shower every day using the soap instead of jerking off.

I often grew my hair long till they formed curls around my forehead and covered my ears. I also got them cropped short to avoid visiting the barber often. I like to explore multiple spa options in Bangkok, Ayurvedic massages in Kerala to knead the back, neck and shoulder muscles. Women masseurs are good.

The impact is due to right technique and training, not just strength. It is always more rejuvenating to have a woman working on the body. I have cultivated masseurs in Gurgaon, where I am settled with my wife and two kids, who do a good job of squeezing my body parts due to the healthy tip that follows.

ONE

Losing My Virginity

I lost my virginity in my mid-teens, which is quick by Indian standards, especially for guys. The scourge of girl child marriage continues to be prevalent in India. Frequently, much older sexually desperate men are married to girls below age of adolescence. It is a sad happening.

My first full sexual encounter happened at my father's home town Fatehpur in Uttar Pradesh we visited for many years during summer and sometimes winter vacations when school was closed for a shorter duration.

It was during travels to my father's roots that I appreciated the odds he faced as a kid. The open air school where he studied was still without chairs or tables. One teacher and scores of unruly kids meant no real work ever happened here. There was a constant cacophony of children that sounded like a plane about to land or taking off. There could not ever be any serious studies here. The only exception was my father, who excelled despite the odds.

My father told us there was no electricity supply when he was growing up, perhaps one reason he is unaffected by frequent power failures today, while others curse the government. He woke up every day at sunrise to revise his studies. Then, he undertook multiple trips to a nearby well to store enough water in the house for the use of his sisters and mother. Then it was time for school. It was his childhood routine that probably turned him into a morning person for good.

He made it on scholarship to college at Allahabad University, the hub of education and politics during his time, won gold medals for meritorious performances and qualified for the Indian Police Service (IPS) in his first attempt at the job.

There are innumerable such success stories in our country that should only make us proud as Indians despite corruption and moral decay around.

Lal Bahadur Shastri and Manmohan Singh come to mind, though the latter seems to have lost a bit of his credibility as Prime Minister due to his inability to check corruption in the rank and file of his administration. Indians don't like mute spectators as leaders. They like performers and positive thinkers.

Despite the apparent economic backwardness of Fatehpur, it would be incorrect to assume town and village girls are demure in any way. The women can be aggressive, raw, at peace with their sexuality and express it regularly and with abandon, even if they need to be secretive about it. This is partly due to high exposure to TV serials that thrive on bold portrayal of scheming ladies.

Bollywood movies that focused on women in daring and intrepid roles either donning little clothing or tight leather pants and jacket were also a hit in this rural belt of India. Then there were popular semi-porn video cassettes privately circulated. Many cast TV and movie personalities, before they made it big, some even in highly rated serials such as *Ramayana* or *Mahabharata*.

I can recall at least one Arjun and Bhim performing naked blue film acts, obviously selected for roles due to their large and muscular physiques.

My village girl, much older than me, visited my grandfather's house in Fatehpur as she was friends with my cousin sisters who too were visitors during summer vacations. Lazy afternoon were spent over *lassi* under guava, mango and lemon trees in the huge backyard. There were many sleepovers to watch movies on rented video cassette players.

We played cards and spent evenings at the local market gorging sweets and ice cream made from fresh cow milk and sugar cane juice. I liked the way my village girl smelt without any perfume – earthy, like fresh wet unpolluted mud after it rains. On windy days, we went to the roof to fly kites. It was idyllic. It was as if time stood still. Nobody was in a rush in Fathepur, unlike cities where everyone is in a hurry with an appointment, official or private, to keep.

Everybody had time for a gossip, chit chat, *chai* and *pakoras* anytime. Even though Uttar Pradesh was embroiled in one of its worst phase of caste and communal politics, it hardly mattered to us though we were aware of unhappy TV images linked to the issues, whether at Ayodhya or Mumbai, at that time Bombay, riots.

Like many similar locations in India, lovers in Fatehpur had to be wary about pervasive ultraconservative elders, probably severely sexually repressed during their youth, sniffing for mischief that they could never experience themselves.

As any other location was considered unsafe given the senior village and town population on the lookout to catch, castigate and even castrate copulating couples, most love affairs in Fatehpur were conducted on rooftops after twilight and carried on well into the night. As the houses were jammed together in *mohallas* (small colonies) and lanes very narrow, lovers hopped from one roof to the other to arrive at the roof top of the partners' home.

It helped electricity supply was uncertain. In the cover of darkness, couples could be wanton with each other, secure about the inadequate performance of the power department, as is the case anywhere in the country. Many collective curses emanated whenever lights came back on.

During my time in Fatehpur, there were some extremely frustrated oldies that seemed to have developed extra sensory perceptions when it came to young couples making out in the vicinity. They looked for signals, voices and odours, in their surroundings like scavengers seek carrion. Some formed vigilante groups to patrol roofs with battery-operated emergency lights or kerosene lanterns.

Lovers are never left at peace anywhere in the world. Luckily, one desperate or dirty great grandfather missed a step and fell off a roof and died on the way to hospital. He was carried in a rickety rickshaw in the absence of an ambulance service. That probably killed any remote chance of survival he might have had.

There were rumours the old man was deliberately tripped or pushed down. Anyways the snooping reduced considerably and everybody was at peace, for some time at least. I never imagined or suspected my father might have hopped roofs during his youth. Like Sid, who certainly carried forward our father's genes, his energies too must have dissipated in studies.

As I got to know my village girl better, I jumped over roofs to her house, crossing many others on similar missions as the sun set. She updated me about the local gossip that usually centred round couples fighting, making out, breaking up and daughters-in-law fighting with their mothers-in-law, with a few attempting suicide by setting themselves on fire or consuming rat poison. Mothers-in-law anywhere arouse incendiary reactions.

She asked me about life in the city and whether girls danced in micro attires in discos as depicted in TV serials. I told her that they did. "Do you go to discos?" she asked. "I do, but have never done so with a girl in a mini skirt. For that, the guy needs to be rich and we are not," I told her.

My village girl's father was a clerk at the local court while her mother looked after the house, the six cows, hens and goats that were treated like family members, each assigned an endearing nick name. An elder sister was married.

Her younger brother and sister studied in the local school, while she herself taught at a polytechnic for women in the mornings. She helped her mother look after the house and human, animal family, in her free time.

Her parents were very happy to meet me, the son of an IPS officer. My father was a legendary figure in Fatehpur, with many real and imaginary tales about his very high levels of intelligence in school that left teachers dumbstruck.

Not too many made it as far as he did. Nobody from her family disturbed me and my village girl when we were on the roof of her house. I guess there are some perks of being the son of a successful father.

"I am sure you also want what all guys want," she told me one day as we watched the setting sun over cups of very sweet tea and home-made *namkeens* that she carted up on a thin plastic tray. She was looking away from me and I was not sure how to react. I sort of motioned to put my arms around her when she turned and hugged me tightly. "Oh ma (oh mother), I love you," she said.

It was at her rooftop that I lost my virginity a few nights later. It was not an exceptionally exciting experience. It was over earlier than I estimated it should have. Despite long hours mulling about sex, ultimately the physical aspect were no different from self-pleasuring. The high was having the woman.

Some of my private areas were bruised and hurting under the foreskin that was not clipped at birth since I am a Hindu. Who says it is only virgin girls who may bleed post their first sex? For a while I feared I had contracted a sexually transmitted disease as I was not sure about the carnal antecedents of my village girl.

There was nobody to share my worries. I spent quite a bit of my time in the loo figuring out extent of injuries. Thankfully, the wounds healed and my anxieties subsided. I did not know whether my maiden partner was a virgin, though my hunch was that she was not.

Despite reading a bit of literature and hands-on experience on the subject I have never been able to figure out whether it is initiation for a girl I have been with. Rather, it is reactions later that can range from hysterical sobs to connecting the sexual act to marriage, that one can gauge the pre-sex physical status of the girl.

There has been only one instance of bleeding. The girl in question repeatedly queried me during the act. "Is this sex? Are we having sex?" I guess it was the first time for her, though I doubt every virgin spurts blood that soaks the mattress, sheets and pillows, the way it is portrayed in movies or music videos.

My village girl spoke no English, but I liked the mix of sensitivity and rustic, earthy, sometimes dirty humour missing in city girls. For example, she told me the key to hooking a guy for keeps was not by holding his "dick" but by having a grip on his "balls" as well. "One has to make sure his money is spent, his mother's influence is reduced to the minimum, and his energies are spent on work and looking after kids. Otherwise, like a dog he will run after other bitches."

"I can give you a blow jab," she told me once.

"Blow job it is then," I said, lying on a charpoy on the roof, watching the stars and the moon, even as she indulged me completely.

Like all girls and women I have known intimately, she too liked to ask about *Chhotta* Sid. Over time, the little fellow has been addressed variously -- "the violin" by musically inclined, "dwarf" by a girl who liked only white-skinned hunks invariably "hung long", India-view was an obvious coinage by a co-journalist and silly boy by another who liked sex but never admitted to the fact.

I guess women like to connect with a man's organ in their own unique way, just as men privately like to describe breasts and buttocks as jiggling papayas or pumpkins, as may be appropriate. My village girl was wise.

Although I called her regularly from Delhi, she knew there was no future between us given our social, economic, cultural and linguistic barriers. "I really enjoyed my time with you," she said, holding me tight, the last time we met before she married a businessman, selected by her family, dealing in leather products in Kanpur. I did not attend her wedding but heard she cried a bit during the "*bidai*."

One middle-aged housewife, gossip and caustic remarks the prime motive of her wretched existence, remarked: "Brides are supposed to weep at the *bidai*, but not so much. Is she missing someone other than her parents, siblings, cows and goats?"

For few years after her marriage I never visited my father's village house, making excuses of exams, sickness and some such to my family. When I finally went I was reminded of the time that we spent together. "These moments will never come back," she told me once. They never did. She was my first love.

I wrote about India's Noisy Fringe Elements that makes life difficult for young couples anywhere.

India's fringe elements have asserted themselves again. They have managed to keep away writer Salman Rushdie from Kolkata, held up actor Kamal Hassan's movie in Tamil Nadu, conveniently misinterpreted a piece written by actor Shahrukh Khan, virulently attacked sociologist Ashis Nandy's views about corruption by lower castes and backward communities and forced an all-girl rock band in Kashmir to quit.

The fringe elements (FEs from here on) in India can be broadly defined as groups claiming to represent sections of people such as dalits, Muslims, backward castes, Hindus, Bharat, India, NRI, whatever.

A more apt description should be that FEs like to disturb, disrupt and generally create a nuisance. They universally back their points of view with threats of violence, riots, arson and looting against those who don't listen to them.

The favourite targets of FEs are film stars, celebrities, intellectuals, artists and sometimes cricket or cricketers. What they utter can always be misjudged or misconstrued. Loopholes can always be found in movies.

Taking on personalities creates all-round impact and visibility that FEs seek. When there isn't much to keep them occupied, which is not often, the FEs pick on couples, women, vandalize an art exhibition or destroy a cricket pitch.

They beat up young boys and girls hanging out in pubs or parks for violating Indian sensibilities. In the land of Mahatma Gandhi, youngsters are taught a lesson about Indian culture by being soundly thrashed.

It is also fashionable to attack women, especially the ones that wear jeans and skirts in cities. Women in India are subjected to multiple crimes, all horrible — rapes, molestations, acid attacks, eve-teasing, murder, female infanticide, trafficking and female feticide, among others.

The solution, as per FEs, lies within the women themselves — suggestions include covering up, staying inside the house, no shopping, no watching movies, no going out with boys, not working, not earning. In short, women should stop living. Men will be men, so all women have to turn into nuns, is the view. The truth is, unless mind-sets don't change, women in India will not be safe.

The big question is how does one tackle the FE menace in India? Why is it that they periodically manage to bother and irritate us? Like dengue or swine flu, Indian FEs cannot be eliminated so easily. It is a virus that has spread.

One solution lies with the media. The Indian media, especially the national TV channels, love a FE controversy. It draws eyeballs normally addicted to cricket, Hindi movies, Salman Khan and TV soaps back to boring news channels.

News anchors scream, froth, shout, argue and quarrel in their quest to paint FEs as horrible, which is obvious to anybody.

Angry words fly about like fours and sixes in a T-20 cricket match. Self-righteous anchors pretend to be hurt and upset on behalf of the rest of India. It is a big con act. If they truly cared, the TV people could do the country a favour by blocking out versions of Asarams periodically popped into our consciousness.

Some may be essential to highlight, but too many could just be sidelights, unheard, inaudible. The media makes bigger monsters out the FEs that only feeds the frenzy. The uglier the FEs are portrayed the more one is playing into their hands. They love it when they are abused and attacked on TV.

It gives them sustenance for more. It feeds their irrationalism. They burn more effigies, cars and shops. The virus spreads.

A further irony is authorities in India like to side with FEs. By some perverse logic those in power believe that FEs mirror the thought process of the community they claim to represent. Politicians, ever the opportunists, think it is smart vote bank politics to back FEs.

They falsely connect mercenary FEs to Bharat, the poor, uneducated, illiterate and non-English speaking larger majority and thus voters. This is a fallacy as much as labelling Muslims as terrorists or dalits as corrupt or jeans-clad women invite rape or India's cricket captain should be changed after every defeat. The poor may have no money, but they are not brainless.

They value progress and education. They have been denied the opportunity. Truth is those in positions of power are equally wedded to the unreasonable.

Travelling in red beacon cars and surrounded by keen to use force bodyguards paid by tax-payers' money, they too, like the FEs, revel in muscle power – take out a Kamal Hassan or a Salman Rushdie, make them cringe and retreat, beat up innocent aspirational, better off, English-speaking jean- clad kids on the streets, representing little India as opposed to bigger Bharat, protesting against the Delhi gang rape.

Authorities, Mamata Banerjee in Bengal, Jayalalitha in Tamil Nadu or the Delhi police, acting like FEs are the worst case scenario. Draconian laws are invoked for piffling misdemeanours while usually slothful cops, more than eager to obey their masters, are set on the innocent. People and institutions in India need to change.

I wrote this piece about the right to kiss in public in India:

According to recent news reports, video clips of couples being intimate with each other while travelling in the Delhi metro have been uploaded on porn websites.

I use the metro whenever there is need. Mostly the coaches are jam packed compelling an orgy of intimacy with every passenger in the vicinity. It is similar to commuting in a crammed Mumbai local but for the air con and closed doors.

Like anywhere else in the world, one spots the high on hormones getting to know each other physically and more, young boys and girls in the crowded midst or when the coaches are near empty late in the evening. It is, without doubt, a heady period in their lives. Engrossed, for them, the rest of the world does not exist.

It is also easy to spot the married couples. They look the other way, are absorbed in their cell phones or the wife prefers to travel in the ladies compartment for comfort and time away from the hubby. There are the occasional middle-aged couples revved up by hormones like teenagers or those in early twenties. Probably, they are up to stuff away from their respective spouses that is not entirely above board.

I am not happy that metro clips of amorous youngsters have found their way to porn websites. It is an invasion of privacy even if the acts were conducted in a public place. The leak by authorities that have access to the CCTV footage of the coaches needs to be investigated. I am, however, happy that such clips exist.

This is because, in India today, normal folks are not allowed to express themselves, while the not so normal, abnormal, fringe, frustrated, powerful and those with vested interests get away with murder.

There are exceptions such as Sunny Leone who has uniquely combined a career as a porn star and Bollywood actress. MS Dhoni periodically expresses himself by winning matches in the last over shutting critics for a few weeks after which they start criticizing him again. Following his recent interview to Reuters, we know that Narendra Modi feels sad when a puppy dies. We don't know whether he feels sad about Muslims killed in Gujarat 2002 riots or Israt Jehan shot dead by promotion and power hungry cops.

I am not an advocate of couples crossing certain limits of decency unless they are in their bedroom or there isn't a single passenger in the train. However, a hug, a kiss, a pet, should be within the realms of accepted public behaviour and expression.

And, I am not talking about sexed up Page 3 parties where artificially made up women air kiss each other while trying to bed rich crony capitalists with knickers full of ill-gotten cash. I am looking at normal urban folks riding a metro, hanging out at a mall or a movie hall. Letting them be in my opinion, is a sign of tolerance, acceptability, respecting individual dignity, freedom and an indicator of an evolving democracy that is sadly missing in our society.

Unfortunately, as matters stand, the way we conduct ourselves socially or in public has been usurped by the moral brigades, fringe elements, khap panchayats, greedy cops and opportunistic politicians. They decide and the rest are forced to abide.

I believe those at the forefront of accusing young couples as morally decrepit should first try and fix some of the much bigger wrongs that afflict our society, apart from their own questionable views.

Too many unnatural happenings are ignored while a boy and girl being normal with each other is under unusual scrutiny. People stare, abuse, attack a young couple holding hands in public, while ruffians get away with drinking in public, creating a ruckus with nobody, including cops, daring to take them on.

I live in Gurgaon, a Delhi suburb. Liquor shops abound here. They can be found next to residential complexes, schools, hospitals, temples, petrol stations, anywhere. Adequate electricity and water supply is a problem, not alcohol. Soon I should be able to open the window of my house to buy a bottle of chilled beer.

Clearly, there are authorities that benefit by issuing as many licenses at as many locations. Look at the cops. Our cities would be much safer, should policemen pursue with the same zeal couples in parks due to a strict and inhuman reading of a law on public indecency that dates back to pre-independence.

The universal motto of the cops is to declare the guy to be a pimp while the girl is assumed to be a prostitute, even as a terrorist or a thief may walk by.

Our forefathers fought to ensure us the right to vote. There is need to exercise the right to hug, hold hands or kiss in public. I hope unlike the right to education and right to food, this one is a success.

TWO

No Bharat Ratna for Me

I did not make it to an IIT, medical college such as AIIMS or Maulana Azad, IIM's for MBA or the IAS, the top government job. This is very sad news for anybody living in India. It was particularly disheartening for my father who wanted me to become an IAS officer.

For many, especially the hard working, low on speculative gains and high on morality middle-class, the Indian population comprises those who carry one or multiple badges of above mentioned achievement like *Bharat Ratnas*.

The rest don't matter. They could be rich, poor, paupers, propertied, carpenters, electricians, shop keepers, cooks, politicians, maids, me and more. This entrenched caste system is not going to go away in a hurry. Only a few more make it to the list of recognized achievers -- cricketers and Bollywood stars who may or may not be educated, like an erudite Rahul Dravid or not very high on intellect Munaf Patel, the brainy Aamir Khan or the brawny Salman Khan.

My father was an ardent admirer of the *Bharat Ratna* emblems of success as he struggled up the ladder the tough and competitive exam way, his student life laden with gold medals, highest marks and citations of achievement. He made his parents very proud. It is said when my village-bred grandfather died he had a smile on his face as he was very happy about my father's stupendous progress.

My father made it as an IPS officer in his first attempt at the civil services exam; that is not a bad deal at all. But, as his career progressed he was probably rubbed wrongly by the higher ranked and more powerful IAS bureaucracy that controls policy, strategy and finance. Unlike police officers or Army men, IAS officers enjoy direct access to politicians, given the nature of their jobs, making them look down on rest of government functionaries.

My father wanted me to crack the IAS exam and make others lower in the pecking order suffer psychologically all their careers, as he possibly had, without much basis. As an IAS officer, he probably wanted me to badger the IPS cadres by refusing to clear their travel bills or disallow their wives to accompany in overseas trips. Government people can trouble each other in petty ways. They don't care about the rest of the population. They are not even worth troubling.

A few marks less scored by my father in the civil services exam meant a salary a notch lower than IAS counter parts. Though the disparity was slight, the symbolic gap is immense given the enormous egos of officials that include lowest level clerks, constables to top secretaries. If there ever was an instrument to measure the size of the egos of *babus*, they would be uniformly infinite, especially in interactions with private citizens.

I think my father was also keen after his retirement someone in the family commuted to office daily in a red beacon car that disobey driving rules with impunity and jump traffic lights in the name of security and terrorist attacks plotted in Pakistan. I was the chosen one to carry the legacy forward.

My father never openly approved or disapproved of brash VIP vehicles. He probably thought such an entitlement was okay in the context of much bigger crimes and corruption orchestrated by the state.

Also, at a more existential level, I think he wanted to avoid the hassle of standing in queues or approaching touts to renew a driving license or passport or gas connection or pay the electricity bill after superannuation. He expected me to look after these matters, the nuisances of daily Indian existence, the way he did for his immediate and extended family for more than 30-years in service.

The IAS is a tough exam to crack, statistically one of the most difficult in the world due to the ratio of number of aspirants, seats available and those who do not make it. Reading too much into this, however, would be misleading.

Anything vacant in India is potential Guinness entry, given the number of applicants for any job, college admissions, confirmed rail ticket, bus seat, gas connection or an empty parking slot.

I wanted to lead my life for myself, not for others, but had to give in to my father's persistence that I had to become an IAS officer. Like all good Indian boys and girls, harried about the virtue of listening to one's elders, I too fell in line, though not as easily as others. My problem during my younger days, even now, was I was not clear about my career path though I was certain I did not want to be an IAS officer, much to the chagrin of my father.

Youth is about being rebellious and not doing what you are told to do. Perhaps, I was disinterested in the IAS because my father was so interested. Maybe, ensconced in the comfortable South Delhi government accommodation allotted to my father, the burn factor was missing. Maybe, I wanted a life different from what approximated my father's. I am not sure that I still know exactly, though I have made up my mind never to be a corrupt person, inspired by my father.

My mother sensed my disinterest in the IAS but her views on my career choice did not matter to my father. He expected her to worry only about our food, clothing, health and hygiene matters. Still she did try to convince my father a few times that he should not force his ambitions on me.

Like most Indian husbands he did not listen to his wife. The environment I grew up in was, thus, not very conducive about my negative world view about everything in general and the IAS in particular.

During my childhood my father had his way as he was bigger and stronger. "Marks is all that matter," he would repeat as the only ticket to success.

When he was home, back from work in the evenings, I and Sid stationed ourselves at our study desks. I mostly pretended to read thinking about multifarious other unimportant matters but Sid was always serious about his time with the books. He studied irrespective of our father's presence in the vicinity.

As I grew bigger and taller, the physical threats stopped working. My father would clutch his heart in apparent discomfort if I disobeyed his commandments, including disinterest in the IAS. A few times we rushed him to a nearby hospital, where the nurses and doctors on duty had gotten to recognize us. They declared him to be all right without any tests.

"I wish I had never lived to see this day," he would speak loudly in bed with the medical staff, who knew about his high official status including direct access to the Prime Minister of India via hotlines called RAX phones. Today, telemarketers call up the finance minister when he delivers the budget.

The doctors and nurses would peer at my father lying on the bed fitted with drips on both arms. Intermittently they looked at me pointedly with disapproval and disdain. They thought of me as an unworthy basket case.

Lúckily, those were times when local TV and print coverage had not caught on in India. Otherwise, one headline could have read: "Son Refuses IAS Exam, Father Hospitalized." Maybe, I would have been verbally and intellectually mauled on News Hour by Arnab Goswami for being a disobedient son as a part of a series about vagabond boys in India who defy their honest and aging parents.

Noticing the media report, somebody might have filed a PIL or some court might have taken *suo moto* cognizance of my offense of troubling and torturing old parents and sent me to Tihar jail, that today offers living conditions better than many poor Indians can ever afford.

This is due to multiple reform models implemented by motivated individuals such as Kiran Bedi -- hats off to the feisty lady for turning a lock up into a lounge for criminals. The only undone bits are perhaps an air-conditioned café day kiosk, a south Indian fast food joint and spas offering free massages.

Maybe they already exist. I do not have the latest updates about the jail as I am not a criminal but I believe there are separate VIP enclosures. How can one differentiate between more and less important crooks?

It is no wonder that convicts like former telecom minister A K Raja appear rested and refreshed following time at Tihar. The knowledge that they have embezzled huge amounts of public money makes them feel happier. Even though my father feigned the heart attacks, I had no choice but to listen to him.

I attempted the UPSC entrance tests four times spread over four years. It actually turned out to be an all-expense paid holiday as my father made it a point to make life comfortable for me like never before so that I could focus on the exam.

I enjoyed a liberal expense account for car fuel, eating out, books, clothes and new shoes to attend the must enrol coaching classes.

Despite the freebies, unfortunately or expectedly I ended up belonging to the much larger numbers that fail to clear the IAS exam. Fortunately, I was a general category applicant, so was allowed only four shots to decipher the UPSC exam cramming code, as per the laws of the country.

If I was born a tribal, scheduled caste, non-creamy backward caste, disabled, handicapped, minority or some such concoction devised by our constitution, courts, lobbyists and politicians, my father would have made sure I appeared for the civil services exam many times as the statutes permitted.

Luckily, multiple attempts at the civil services exam is a possibility extended to the privileged sections of the Indian population otherwise considered as the underprivileged, like the propertied Yadavs of Haryana or UP.

I had disconcerting thoughts that I belonged to the reserved category, appearing for the UPSC exam till age 40, married with kids, with my father hovering about, well retired, but maniacally inspired never to stand in a queue again.

After I flunked the first attempt, my father believed I could still make it. "Be positive. Learn from your experience," he said in a demeanour that was more serious than I had ever seen him. On exam days, he took leave from office, which he never did otherwise even when he was very ill, to personally accompany me in the official car to the test centres.

He waited outside in the heat, under a tree or sitting on a bench. He would not sip any water saving it all for me during the break. The emotional overdoses did have an effect on me. I felt the pressure to study hard though the concentration levels were not optimum or else I would have qualified and by now written my memoirs about some district that I lorded over as DM or SDM.

After I didn't make it the third time, my father had no more advice to offer. He stopped escorting me to the exam hall. I felt bad for him and myself. It does not feel good to flunk any exam, small or big. I wish my father had not pushed me into a career choice that did not excite me, for no particular reason.

A friend, whose father sold property in Bihar to sustain his living and coaching expenses in Delhi, made it. He was soon hounded by marriage proposals sweetened by offers of property, cash and more.

If a huge economic cost rested on my taking the exam, I too might have coveted the IAS. My father waiting outside the exam hall with a water bottle was perhaps not enough to push me to work hard enough.

If my father had made a big sacrifice like selling our village house to pay for the IAS coaching classes, I might have hungered for the job, qualified and wooed by fathers on behalf of their pretty or not so good looking daughters. I think I am being very harsh on my father. Sid did not need any such incentives to work hard.

In order to clear an exam the competitive scale of UPSC it is essential to take the emotional leap of wanting to do the job or make money on the side, if one is so inclined or be blackmailed by family sacrifice. When I failed the fourth and last time, my father said, "You have belied my expectations. You did not try hard enough." "I did. I tried my best. Anybody can fail. I am human," I replied.

My mother was calm as usual. Like all mothers of Indian boys, she could never judge her sons harshly. "Don't worry, there are other avenues that you will excel," she said. Sid, in the process of accumulating all the traditional badges of success over time, had some views about my not making it.

"How could you make it in the IAS? You cannot work hard in a sustained way. You need to pepper your days and nights by interacting with girls. In between, you read porn magazines. This cannot work if you want to crack an Indian exam. You are too laidback. You should have been born in Europe."

Sid was always brutal in his assessments, a result of a very harsh 14-18 hour study regimen he followed to crack the IITs followed by the IIMs, the two Olympic gold medals for which middle-class India can chop off all their limbs.

My father was very proud of him, while I was the black sheep that failed to meet his expectations. In a way, I was grateful that Sid was the bright one.

He buffered the physical and psychological impact of my failures on my father. Sid was right in his reading about me. I did not think much about girls but was involved with them in a continuous and simultaneous way early in life.

In the absence of titles of achievements, my inspiration became Bill Gates, a Harvard drop out. During one's youth one is certain about making it really big. Today I would be happy if I made even 1% of Gates wealth. I don't think philanthropy would come naturally to me.

Studying Gates' life, I should have made it to IIT or IAS and then chucked them midway to qualify in the genre of successful people with associated romanticized tales of renunciation probably developed after they became famous. Still, I convinced myself that Gates would fit as my idol. I could make it big by following an alternate path without an associated *Bharat Ratna*.

I became a follow your dreams adherent, a message very nicely conveyed in the movie *3 Idiots*, starring my favourite actor Aamir Khan who makes good cinema that is also commercially successful. This is reflected in the choice of his second wife – not a stunner but the general intelligence adds to her beauty.

Over time I have discarded Gates as my hero. I have actually never been too excited about computers or software. I can spend some time surfing the Internet, marvelling multimedia and special effects. But, I get my high outdoors being one with nature -- a river, the ocean, beaches, wild life, mountains and women, though not necessarily in this order of preference. Maybe I will take up photography.

Mind you, I have great respect for my father. He remained an honest man despite the temptations that I am sure did come his way due to the powerful posts he held. He did his job well without expecting anything more than his salary. He believed in working hard to make as much of a difference as the system possibly allowed.

If he did not have a family to look after, he probably would have been happy to donate his wages to charity, cancer research or some such venture. I do not espouse any particular distaste for the IAS, either. The perks are good -- car, housing, free medical treatment for life, driver, servants and subsidized electricity.

Courtesy my father's profession we travelled comfortably across the country, South India, Kashmir, Rajasthan, north east, due to the free family travel allowance. My father's batch mates arranged for local lodging, commuting, free food and entry to zoos. These were times when amusement parks had not mushroomed all over India. Such a freebie would have been truly exciting.

It is, however, also a sad reality that many treat the government job as an instrument of corruption or earning salary for no work. The same *babus* could improve pitiable living conditions in India dramatically, if they wished.

The corrupt officials team up with political bosses, builders, contractors to form an unholy nexus that constantly short changes the country and tax payers' money, while pretending to be self-righteous during prime time TV debates anchored by Barkha Dutt, Rajdeep Sardesai or Arnab. Nobody makes as much out of corruption as the government people do.

The existence and insidious rise of such nefarious characters in our country has resulted in the emergence of new worshipped by middle-class anti-corruption crusaders such as Anna Hazare. Though the man has lost a bit of his charm due to his strong Leftist leanings in economic policy that does not gel with emerging India, his strong anti-corruption stance is still relevant.

I wrote this piece about Durga Shakti Nagpal (IAS):

The Uttar Pradesh (UP) government has suspended IAS officer Durga Shakti Nagpal as she dared to take on the sand mafia operating under her jurisdiction. Inspired by her, there are going to be some doubly divinely named daughters born here on, though I am not sure parents would encourage them to study hard for a career in the IAS that involves some serious grappling with goons, mostly garbed as politicians. Engineering, medicine or MBA could be safer options.

Durga has been rightly declared a real life heroine by the desperate to uncover corruption crusaders, the always angry national TV anchors, most of whom live across the Yamuna, residing in houses constructed by the illegally supplied sand. The middle classes too have been active on social networking websites.

My mail and Facebook accounts have been bombarded by online petitions, groups and pages, linked to liking, supporting and pleading for Durga. Sonia Gandhi has shot off a letter to Manmohan Singh that the centre should stand by Durga.

Apparently, she regularly writes such missives to Manmohan that are obviously treated as unofficial official orders to the PM. Many we do not get to hear about, like the one she must have penned about shielding a certain Robert Vadra. Given the urgency of the matter maybe she smsed – transfer Ashok Khemka right now. Some day we should have a compendium of the correspondence in the form of a book – letters and text messages from a super PM to her PM.

It is apparent reports that Durga lead a squad to demolish a makeshift mosque is as much hogwash as Katrina Kaif denying a relationship with Ranbir Kapoor. The politically powerful sand mafia wanted her out and so it happened, as is the case of thousands of honest officers in India and also many current and ex-cricketers who dare to question the rapacious money making policies of BCCI.

Akhilesh Yadav has again rubber stamped old world views of his uncles and father Mulayam Singh Yadav who don't care about the noisy middle-classes, English media, corruption crusaders and women. The Samajwadi Party derives its support from Muslims and backward caste voters of UP. The Yadav clan in power assumes that caste and religion based affiliations will override corruption, crony capitalism, absence of law and order and development. A certain Lalu Yadav thought the same, until he was kicked out by Nitish Kumar in Bihar.

The tragedy of UP is that there has been no leader of the stature of Narendra Modi or Nitish or Shivraj Singh Chauhan to take the state forward on a governance cum growth agenda. UP has been saddled by megalomaniacs such as Mayawati, obsessed with building statues of her own self and making a fashion statement of her sandals, purses and diamond drop earrings.

Akhilesh has been unable to move beyond the big shadows of his daddy and uncle-centric politics. His sole assertion has been distributing free laptops, the possession of which is a security risk in UP given the dismal law and order situation of the state. A few months back, one parochial-minded uncle prevented Akhilesh from speaking at Harvard, after he made the journey all the way to Boston. Not many young men I know obey their uncles the way Akhilesh does. He needs to learn to be a little disobedient.

Unfortunately, UP has also been BJP's playground of aggressive Hindutva, centred round building the Ram temple at Ayodhya. Given the violence unleashed across the country due to the supposedly disputed site, even Lord Ram would not want a temple at Ayodhya anymore. It might be a good idea to just make a park where children of all religions can play.

Meanwhile, Rahul Gandhi's interest in UP has been a few symbolic meals with the dalits and Muslims. For the Gandhi scion, like poverty, UP is a state of mind or rather only during elections state of mind.

I also have a problem with the way the government in our country functions, notwithstanding Durga's efforts. There is too much focus on blocking, removing, controlling, refusing permission to activities that may be legitimate or illegitimate.

It is a colonial mind-set honed by decades of the license permit regime of the 70s and 80s, when every petty babu was mai baap, due to the power he or she exercised over the common man. Today, the Indian economy needs to be unleashed into a rapid T20 mode, while our officials continue to operate in test cricket mode blocking all that comes their way, a la a Geoffrey Boycott, not even a Sunil Gavaskar forget about Sachin Tendulkar.

I would be much happier if our upright officers focused more on being pro-active like ensuring our kids do not die due to pesticide and poison laden mid-day meals or our roads are less potholed, especially during the monsoons.

Even in the case of the sand mafia, it is always easier to stop all activity rather than regulate in a way that the environment is protected. It is the same middle classes backing Durga that have invested their hard earned money into real estate projects that will be the most affected if the raw material supply lines are choked.

THREE

The City Girlfriend

My first city girlfriend was a very nice person called Pooja, who only wore sober hued green, maroon and pink *salwar kameez* and visited me in a Delhi Transport Corporation (DTC) bus following which we moved about on my scooter. There were times I cycled to a pre-determined location, while she walked. Girls such as Pooja make good and safe girlfriends.

They do not invite unnecessary attention anywhere which can be uncomfortable, irritating or even violent. They emanate an image that approximates the way most Indian men want their sisters, mothers and aunts to turn out.

One does not have to worry about them running away with other guys. There is no competition from other suitors. They do not ask for auto or taxi fare for hanging out, to and fro trips. They grow up watching their mother worship their father like God. Thus their subconscious selves eulogize any man in their life.

By myself, I often did not buy tickets in the government run bus service. I was caught red handed several times by the flying squads. I got away by using my close connection to my father, once I just ran while the pot-bellied, warty and very bad looking ticket checkers stood no chance. A couple of times I was made to do squats clutching my ears as I could not be fined as I did not have any money.

Luckily, there was no ubiquitous media, point and shoot citizen reporter mobile phones or CCTV cameras at that time or my pictures would have probably appeared in local news as human rights abuse by authorities on a minor or gone viral on YouTube as part of a comedy package.

It would be embarrassing. If I am on TV I would prefer to be portrayed in positive light or else make a lot of money to appear as a fool. Accompanied by a girl such as Pooja I always bought a ticket.

Firstly, she would not run as she would think that she is not fast enough or it was morally not the right thing to do. Secondly, she could cry. Thirdly, I would be expected to pay the fine for both. Fourthly, I was sure the ticket checkers would be extra-aggressive about collecting the penalty from me since I was with a girl.

It would bring back memories of their sorry impoverished childhoods when no girl ever looked at their ugly, pimpled faces. In their view a young boy and girl together in a bus or expressing themselves anywhere else is a crime as they never got to do such stuff themselves.

They could take away my watch instead or may be my shoes. The ticket inspectors can be desperately jealous creatures. Even a sober looking girl such as Pooja clad in *salwar kameez* would cause their tortured hearts to burn. They would insist on some form of payment, my protestations about my father notwithstanding.

They would make a pretence of doing their jobs, saying they are followers of Mahatma Gandhi, though deep down their distorted souls would be burning with envy wondering how it is to travel with a young girl in a bus and try and steal a kiss in the crowd. Pooja was the daughter of a professor in Delhi University.

Though she was a senior in college I spoke to her for the first time at the Karol Bagh area that is dotted with several coaching institutes that specialize in preparing unclean and unkempt students for various gladiatorial competitive exams.

Pooja was studying for the civil services exam like me and doing the mandatory rounds of the study circles considered essential to be fighting fit for extreme competition wherein half a mark could mean in or out.

Among the guys, I was the only bathed and clean student in our class. The rest, pass outs from various engineering, commerce and arts colleges from across the country, shuffled about like zombies in dirty undergarments, smelly armpits, broken *chappal*s, unshaven and unwashed. They were in the business of cracking an exam in India. Only marks count. Anything else is a waste of time, including perhaps cleaning backsides after potty to continue without disruption the process of devouring examination text books, notes and theorems.

Bits of scribbled paper that aspirants revised while shitting were strewn about the uncomfortable Indian toilets where the students lived. Lots of study material was pasted on the walls. Difficult equations that could not be solved in the mind formed the graffiti. Even the little time spent in the loo due to the awkward nature of the pot, was utilized for mugging up and revision.

Unlike me, the aspirants kept away from girls like the plague. For them, females meant distraction, distress and disturbance. Girls had to wait until they made it. Till then all sexual satisfaction, that was not insignificant, needed to be self-generated.

As Indians spend big on education, private study institutes that help students crack the exacting exam code do roaring business. It is unfortunate that teachers are lowly paid anywhere in the world, given their role in moulding future generations. At the Karol Bagh coaching arena, this was not the case.

Several professors at these study classes drove around in Mercedes Benz cars and expensive SUVs via money legitimately earned given good success rates of their wards making it big. Some openly boasted they were lucky not to have qualified for reputed jobs given the huge incomes they earned via the alternative careers.

In order not to miss out on what could have been, at least a couple of teachers fitted their car with red beacons and sirens to feel like ministers and bureaucrats that they could never be. With potential for such high earnings, some tutors at these centres were actually ex-IIM, IIT or civil service officers who quit their very cushy jobs to take up the new assignments.

Publicly they said they opted for the noble teaching profession to impart knowledge to young people who would be the building blocks of a new India. Privately, everybody knew that beyond the philanthropy talk there were deep mercenary interests. One does not bump into too many of such high flying graduates in regular schools and colleges where teachers earn dismal incomes and exercise power by bullying young kids, sometimes beating them up and making eager parents wait endlessly for an appointment or audience.

It can safely be said that a fair number of candidates that spend a bit of their family lifetime earnings at the Karol Bagh institutes do clear the exams. So, nobody can complain of being short changed.

Successful students who made it to the IAS, IIM or IIT were rewarded handsomely to endorse their rich experience at particular coaching institutes. Interviews were plugged in various high-selling career magazines due to the captive readership. Often this happened only in hindsight with managements of the study classes approaching winning candidates after they made it.

The money offered was too good to be refused by the erstwhile students, many from impoverished backgrounds steadfast in their drive to do well, earn handsomely and marry a convent educated jeans-wearing English-speaking girl whom they would fuck as often as biologically possible till she was well pregnant.

The pictures of students that made it appeared in the magazines that invariably showed them well-dressed, clean shaven, haircut and bathed, now that they had the time to indulge in such activities.

Some institutes paid for their multiple visits to the salon to make them look like human beings. Old time hair dressers boasted hosting several UPSC toppers, with pictures prominently displayed at the salon, before and after for effect. These are perhaps the only salons in India not plastered with fleshy posters of Bollywood stars Amitabh Bachchan and Dharmendra on the walls inside and outside.

"Toppers don't shave. I know one who did not for two years. This is the dedication required to make it to the IAS. I am sure you will not make it. You are with a girl. Those with girls never make it," I was told by one barber.

"Who is asking for your advice? If you know the trick of making it to the IAS, then you should have made it, instead of being a barber," I retorted. I made sure I did not use his services lest he chop off a bit of my ear.

As my study commitment levels were not so high, I chatted with Pooja over tasty *dosa* and fresh creamy cold coffee at the cheap, value for money, but reasonably clean restaurants in Karol Bagh. These outlets cater to the large multicultural student community from across India and shoestring budget foreign tourists housed in the area due to the cheap accommodation available.

The owner run eateries may not be making money like the fancier ones, but the foodstuff on offer is top class. The cold coffee is milky, not heavily diluted with water and artificial flavours that are usual fare at so many air-conditioned up market joints manned by broken English-speaking, uniformed waiters.

The *dosa* batter is fresh due to high turnaround, while the dimensions of the popular south Indian snack are bigger than most anywhere. Similar is the case with *samosa*s and patties, the other popular items served with liberal doses of chutney. Students can be picky about their food and value for money spent, given their usual tight financial status. A patty could well be lunch.

During our conversations over delicious nibbles that I could afford due to the liberal pocket money extended by my father, Pooja did all the talking while I listened. In no time she told me all that could be said about her mother and father, brother, best friend, aunt, her kids and their pets.

She also spoke about her burning desire to make it to the civil services. Unlike guys, girl's multi-task better. They can talk, eat, read and study at the same time. Or rather talk for a minute read notes next five minutes, then check the menu, order the food, go back to chatting, eat and then study again.

Guys are not tuned to operate in multiple spurts. They can do one thing at a time for some time, usually. This is why Pooja made it to the IAS while I failed.

I could not handle sex with a girl, long conversations, *samosas, pakoras* and studies sequentially, which she did. I was simply too pooped, physically and mentally, by the end of the day.

I proposed to Pooja on the phone after a few interactions at some of the Karol Bagh student diners. "Will you be my girlfriend?" I asked, expecting her to say 'no' as we barely knew each other. I can visualize those moments.

I had not taken a bath, was wearing worn out shorts without underwear for comfort and scratching my private areas, sitting inside the sunlit veranda of our South Delhi government flat. To my surprise, she said "yes" in a very determined way.

I was glad that she could not see me as high speed broadband laptops fitted with cyber enabled camera had not happened to the world yet. Even as I credited the impact of my dimples on her, she told me later that she wanted to experience a good looking man intimately. I had been called cute, sweet and silly by girls, aunties and mothers all my life. The good looking moniker sounded very pleasant.

I also needed to get my village girl out of the system as I could not help think about her, including her warm, strong, delicate, sinewy and slim body next to mine on the charpoy in Fatehpur. The blow *jabs* were exotic.

Just as smoking, alcohol, chicken, morning exercise, the emotional and physical companionship of a girl can be quite addictive and difficult to do without.

Every woman one has known intimately emanates a distinctive whiff, an aroma, like a supermarket does of fruit and vegetable or a garment shop of fibre and textile. She could be out of one's life but her essence endures forever. The only way I could fill the void following the exit of my village girl, was by being with another woman. I could sense that such dependence, like smoking, could be counterproductive in the long term. But, at that stage in life I was looking at short time frame solutions. I was young.

Plus, for a temperamentally laidback person such as me, a girl in my life was an important driving force to dress well, keep active, fit and even earn money. I remember my father ceaselessly remark: "The problem with him is that he lacks drive and ambition. He needs to get that into his system. Look at Sid."

When I kissed Pooja the first time, her body shook unusually as if she had caught a massive chill following sudden exposure to icy winds near the North Pole. Her mouth was dry and face turned into stone. For some moments I was worried she would faint. I guess it was her first time with any guy, though she learnt quickly to effectively use her tongue and lips whenever we kissed.

Yet, despite her desires to experiment in her personal life, deep down her sole ambition was to make it to the IAS. And she did. I call this the Delhi effect that impacts many who live in the city. In Bombay, the film stars are the real heroes.

Everybody knows and visits Bandra where Salman Khan and Shahrukh Khan reside or Juhu to glimpse Amitabh Bachchan's abode, like they do the Taj Mahal in Agra. I have tried spotting Big B in real life. The big gate of his house did open, but the Mitsubishi Pajero contained family dogs being taken to the vet.

A local told me that a highly paid nanny, who looked after babies of her previous employers, was attached to look after the pets. I made an attempt again later in life to sight Big B or his beautiful daughter-in-law Aishwarya. Unfortunately, I could only witness a smiling and waving Abhishek driving in and out, which is not very exciting. Probably, he was doing the groceries.

In cosmopolitan Bombay -- I don't like Mumbai just as I would not like it if Delhi is re-named Dilli by our unlettered and uncouth political class looking for easy votes in the name of falsely preserving our cultural roots -- everyone looks to be connected to Bollywood as directors, choreographers, fashion and costume designers, caterers, extras, car rental providers and more, if they can't make it as stars in their youth.

Down south it is the engineers that make it abroad and into software firms that set the benchmark for the youth to follow. The women look to be nurses in the Middle East contributing to the large remittance inflows. All of this is very healthy. It is about wanting to do well, provide for family and progress in life.

The national capital is liberally sprinkled with the dominant presence of the government -- Parliament building, Rashtrapati Bhavan and the heavily guarded Race Course Road where the Prime Minister resides. Security personnel regularly block traffic to allow convoys of VVIPs to pass.

The spanking clean leafy diplomatic area around Malcha Marg can match any location in the developed world. The well-maintained New Delhi addresses such as Chanakyapuri and Moti Bagh where top officials reside are neat and tidy.

This is unreal India where there is no shortage of water, no power cuts and the roads are not potholed. Burglaries, robberies and chain snatching are rare due to the large security deployment. The cops are polite as they know that anybody living here is a 'somebody'.

Spilled stinking sewage does not form ponds and puddles, offering perfect sanctuary for malaria, swine flu and dengue carrying mosquitoes.

The parks are lush green, watered and well looked after by the otherwise slothful government underlings who never bother about the upkeep of most other public places turned garbage dumps.

The pavements are perfectly paved by the municipal authorities without dark gaping uncovered invisible-at-night manholes found anywhere else in the country. This has caused many unsuspecting pedestrians to tumble and drown in the muck that flows underneath. It is the most horrible way to die worse than being shot by a terrorist or swallowed by a crocodile.

Yet, if one were to scratch the surface, the biggest thieves, looters and dacoits live in the New Delhi area. They are the many politicians and bureaucrats who embezzle tax payers' money to enlarge their illegal coffers in safe havens such as Switzerland and real estate land banks across the globe.

To be part of the New Delhi existence one has to crack the civil services or join politics or become a business tycoon like Birla or Mittal or Ambani.

Pooja and I, given honest service class background of our parents, did not possess indulgent fathers or godfathers. There was nobody to set us up in politics or business or movies or bequeath big bank balances or rent earning properties.

Pooja wanted me to clear the IAS exam as well. When she heard that my father had similar aspirations, she spoke to him and praised him for his ambitions about me. I think my father liked her a bit and had visions of her as his daughter-in-law and future mother of his grandchildren with similar facial features.

He believed Pooja was a good influence on me and due to her, my chances of making it to the IAS were brighter. He was sure she would make it, given her dedication to study. ``Two IAS officers in the family are better than one,'' he probably thought. "She is a good girl. I like her, straightforward. She has your interests in mind," he told me.

"She may be interested in me, that does not mean I am interested in her," I told my father. "You have to be careful about relationships. Don't play about with people's emotions," my father told me. "I won't," I said.

Emboldened by my family's acceptance and encouragement, Pooja pushed me to study hard. "I don't care whether you are fat or thin, good looking or bad looking. You don't have to take a bath. It does not matter. Just make it to the IAS," she periodically said as she probably sought our relationship to develop more depth than checking out looks and more sex.

"You need to realize that we have been together for some time. You need to take on more and think about us in a more serious way. That way you will also make it to the IAS. You need to take on more responsibility," she told me often.

"You will have to take on my responsibility. You know what to do with your life. I have no idea. I don't want to be an IAS officer. I am taking the exam on behalf of my father. I am barely serious about myself. How can I be serious about you? In any case, we have fun together, why complicate matters," I told her.

At 21, marriage ideas were very faint and distant in my mind. Still, I think Pooja meant well for me and my parents would have been okay if the two of us made it and settled down together, whatever that means as life is never a steady state.

But, in those pre-dotcom days my passion was to collect blue film videos from seedy parlours, to try out some of the difficult postures and positions. I admired the abilities of the very muscular protein shake, steroid injected, well-endowed porn stars and their equally flexible more than full-bodied women partners.

Looking back, I think I was quite mixed up, though some of the sexual innovations I attempted required extreme athleticism. These should never be performed by anybody sane unless they are advanced Yoga exponents such as Baba Ramdev, with the stamina of marathon runners and strength of professional gymnasts.

I tried to execute a 69 standing and ended up creaking my back and dropping Pooja. Luckily I was standing on the bed and my very good mother had chosen a soft mattress. Pooja would have certainly injured her head or twisted her neck. My village girl introduced me to the basics of love making. I wanted to take it to levels that were awkward to say the least. Currently, I like Sunny Leone.

I wrote about her:

Recently, two top Bollywood actresses Vidya Balan and Kareena Kapoor got hitched, which is not the most heart rending news for Sunny Leone obsessed Internet savvy sections of young India.

Importantly, both Balan and Kapoor declared that they would continue to do movies post-marriage. Would that be unusual?

It would be, if one studied precedents of Hindi cinema, though an exception would have to be made for Leone here.

There is no history of a top grade very sexy international porn star making it so big in B-grade Hindi cinema that whip the A-grade movies, in box office returns, though not intellectual film critic star ratings.

It does not matter if Leone is married, unmarried, mother, father, speaks, lip synched or remains silent as long as she does the stuff she does. She is still learning to speak Hindi, while her husband is the main protagonist in her eponymous porn website doing what he is supposed to do, but for others to watch.

Matters are not so straight forward for mainstream Indian actresses. The personal choices of these divas have always been linked to professional progress unless of course they choose to take the Leone leap of raw cinema. Nobody has as yet.

They are getting bold, like kissing and size zero bikini appearances to offer any age male audiences the big screen female body-fix, in keeping with competition.

The politically correct explanation to queries by the media is script demanded the stripping and smooching or it is interest of good cinema and a reflection of society.

One does not come across too many tiny bikini clad women in real life in India, excluding foreigners in Goa beaches.

Still, Indian screen beauties have struggled in the past to fit the supposed Indian male cinemagoer mental stereotype that obsesses about virgins and virginal women. The actresses needed to be single and available, in the mind of the Indian audiences, to be acceptable as heroines, was the definition.

Thus, most Hindi movie diva careers were done once married, as teens, twenties or thirties. Even if they wanted to act, the producers were reluctant to cast them as heroines or even accept a desperate offer for a skin showing item number.

They could, upon insistence and personal equations, play the role of dull and thus low paying whining, crying and often dying mother, younger sister or sister-in-law of the main hero, who could be much older in real life. Only, the gorgeous Dimple Kapadia could make a comeback after breaking off with hubby Rajesh Khanna.

Actors, of course have carried on forever, wrinkled, double chinned, though to take on current super star, the middle aged Salman Khan, the paunch probably needs to go. Marriage, families, extra-marital affairs have actually contributed to male actors aura transforming them into more desirable, dependable, attractive package that buttresses female following. This phenomenon of course goes to show that understanding psyches of women is not an easy process.

Amitabh Bachchan heroines regressed to play the role of his mother as well. The legendary actor successfully danced around trees with women he could grandfather, like Salman Khan does today with girls he could father.

In South India actors Kamal Hassan and Rajnikanth serenade women they could great grandfather. This brings us back to Balan and Kapoor or even the absolutely ravishing mother of a young boy Chitrangada Singh.

There is Kajol or the stunning comeback by the 80s siren Sridevi, mom to two girls now, and item number specialist Malaika Arora.

Today, Indian Hindi movie actresses, closely linked to men, married, with kids, think nothing of discontinuing their careers.

Have Indian male audiences changed? Maybe they have, maybe they have not. The female stereotypes in real life are undergoing transformation for sure, given emergence of working, career driven, economically independent, smart, educated women in our midst.

There could be a Leone effect. Having watched her and her online peers' innumerable times, movie goers probably appreciate meat in female roles, women who crack jokes, act, deliver good dialogues, dance well, emote, are part of a bigger story line rather than essaying a show of body parts.

Or else Balan would not have successfully delivered a Kahani or a Dirty Picture, Kapoor a pulsating dance item number for super hit Dabangg-2, Sridevi English Vinglish and Arora the Munni song.

Maybe the assessment is incorrect. But, it is very good to witness Indian actresses aspire for a longer career run while being mainstream, commercial and relevant. It is healthy, though it is still unlikely that Hindi songs will feature aging women prancing about with boys old enough to be their grandsons, unless it is Rekha.

FOUR

The Hack

I drifted into journalism. My writings began as chronicles of a civil services aspirant in a Mid-Day publication that daily commuters in Delhi chartered buses liked to patronize. The travelling, reading, office going population in the national capital today includes metro riders that mostly listen to music or play games on their cell phones. The era of reading and commuting is over for good. Rather, the habit of reading anywhere is over for good.

The biggest draw of the paper I wrote were semi-nude pictures of Page 3 models with absolutely private portions clouded as per censorship laws, but enough showing to keep the reader's imagination interested.

A cross word section appeared on the other half of the same sheet. The reader could fold the paper to pretend to work on the puzzle while surreptitiously looking at the scantily dressed girls. This was smart work by the newspaper management who knew their daily was mostly read with fellow passengers peering in.

This was the pre-Internet age. Online porn in the privacy of one's home did not exist. Surfing smut in an enclosed cyber café cubicle alongside a girlfriend who massaged the private areas was yet to take off. Semi-nude girls could only be seen in popular afternoon broadsheets and beaches of Goa.

Page 3 today chronicles those supposed to be jet set happening and successful. It is actually a forum of fraudsters, fixers, middle men and pimps who like to show off their ill-gotten wealth via money laundering, tax evasion, tinkering with real estate usage or some such illegality. The black money is splashed in glitzy parties that make it to paid Page 3 space. The late Ponty Chadha was a big party thrower.

I am not sure many people read my muses in the afternoon tabloid. The subjects I chose related to my situation as an IAS aspirant. The serious ones, of course, did not have the time or inclination unlike me to write for a rag for very little cash.

My stories delved into lives of diehard civil services exam candidates whom I got to know. A few of my subjects are well-placed in their careers today.

I wrote about quest to be DM, one of the three very important persons in India, the other two being CM and PM. I chronicled the girlfriend who made out, dated at a roadside *dhaba* over sugary cups of tea, rode pillion on an unreliable, polluting, noisy Bajaj scooter, given expectations of becoming an IAS officer's wife; about accommodating parents who loosened purse strings to enable their darling son to be an officer commanding high status in society; about supplicant relatives who congregated at my house to keep the networking alive to procure passports, gas connections and driving licenses, in future, after my father retired.

The IAS eluded me, but based on evidence of articles I wrote, I was absorbed into a National English daily as a reporter. The salary was pittance compared to amounts that Sid earned in his MNC job.

I misread my appointment letter, initially. The gross income was for the entire year and not for the month as I thought and smiled to myself. Divided by 12, it amounted to a negligible and sad number. There was no way I could graduate from riding a scooter to my own car. Sid was contemplating a three-box sedan.

My father was not happy with my career developments. For him education and vocation were subjects that needed to be determined and plotted and not drift into, as happened in my case and unlike Sid's.

My mother told him to let me follow my instincts and do as I liked. I think she was right. Despite disagreements with my father I do appreciate my old man a bit now. He meant well given the context of his upbringing and tough Indian competitive environment. It is due to him I have remained honest in most aspects of my life, except personal relationships wherein I have blatantly lied to cover up my follies, double standards and two timing self.

I blamed my dimples for a long time, though I must admit there must have been more to it than such slight anatomical reasoning. I think it was plain wanting to have more of the opposite sex, for company and in bed.

Journalism is a low paying profession for those who follow their conscience and like to do a good job. Hacks are cost centres for newspaper organizations and treated as such by revenue, profit driven, owner-backed marketing managers.

A newspaper, like soap or a film or Pepsi Cola, has to sell first. Everything else is secondary. The low payments for newspaper articles and dismal salaries of journalists are a reflection of power equations in media operations.

Top Indian newspapers pay Rs 1,500 for centrespread or oped opinion pieces in vaunted editorial pages that contributors have to re-write several times to satisfy enormously intellectual editors that oversee, discuss and ponder over such write-ups they believe makes a huge difference to the world. They also like to think the Prime Minister of the country is scared of them. We know Manmohan Singh is only afraid of Sonia Gandhi.

Usual staff writers and reporters in media earned monthly salaries in the range of Rs 15,000-20,000 with kids and wife to support. Drivers employed by the rich earn more. I read somewhere that Infosys boss Narayan Murthy's chauffeur owns shares worth crores given as e-sops.

Nitin Gadkare's driver apparently owns companies. Section editors are figureheads whose diktat extends to sanctioning leave to lowly paid copy editors. They are allowed to play around with limited left over expensive newsprint space after the ads have been accounted. With plenty of time in hand, a lot of effort goes into deleting prepositions to write pithy headlines.

It is never easy to predict the right age of an editor, especially male ones. Normal people wear wigs to look young. Balding, greying, weak eyesight are the brainy signs that editors aspire. Thirty year olds try to look over 40, those in their 40s try to look in the 60s and those in the 60s want to appear dead.

I know at least a couple of editors who wore glasses though they were medically not required to, just to portray an air of knowledge, reading and books. Most smoke cigars and cigarettes to convey to those around they are thinking hard. Many put on weight to look like uncles rather than young boys that they are biologically. An editor's job is opposite of a film star's. The latter are supposed to look young, fit and botoxed, while the former strive to look old and haggard. There is a similarity between the two as well.

Both the sets of people like to talk a lot, have opinions and solutions about every problem in the world. Like Shahrukh Khan, when an editor talks, he or she does not stop, unless there is nobody else in the room. I don't know what SRK does when he is alone in a room. Maybe he talks to himself or calls up Karan Johar to continue the conversation possibly underlining he is greater father than a superstar, even after the stupendous success of *Chennai Express*.

More universal principles, however, apply to women journalists. The older they are, the younger they like to look, as in any profession. The more powerful they become, the more seductive is their attire as they know they can flaunt their sexuality and get away with it.

Penury forces some journalists to turn into junket diggers to boast some national, international travel and justify their jobs to themselves, friends and family. Others realizing their pitiful existence pick up NIIT diplomas on the side to land an IT job, with opportunities to travel to America, Europe, a decent lifestyle and a small city-bred semi-English-speaking jeans-wearing wife, enamored by the idea of cycling in shorts in New Jersey, courtesy her husband's job.

Some never come back from their trips abroad. As illegal immigrants they struggle overseas hoping to provide better lives for their kids. Today off springs of such individuals are categorized as part of minority communities in America, enjoy full voting rights that propelled Barack Obama as President for the second term. The sacrifices of parents were perhaps worthwhile.

In order to retain sanity, some journos throw their weight around celebrities, politicians, corporate houses keen to feature in the news. Those who manage a lifestyle plug stories that favour the rich and powerful such as Mukesh Ambani, Vijay Mallya, Congress party or BJP bosses and lately regional political parties that have gained importance.

The Thinking Journalists

The thinking editors can be easily spotted sauntering around heavily lighted office floors with a halo of self-importance, enlightenment, double PhDs and enormous numbers of books read. They are the edit and opinion page staff that is happily oblivious of any monetary discrimination within the organization, subsisting in their own little world of high ideas, language and apparent old age.

They are invariably followers of Indian and Western Classical music and usually like to discuss Kafka, Rushdie, Ray and Chomsky. They look down upon Bill Gates, Steve Jobs, Bollywood, TV serials, Ekta Kapoor, cricket as mass culture phenomenon high on sensory, utilitarian appeal, crass and low in depth. Paradoxically, they use Apple I-Pods, not loaded with music but verbal recordings of literature that they like to listen during spare time.

Most are also in the process of writing a book that follows several others already written that look at deeper ways to solve global problems. The subjects can range from climate change to terrorism to India's diminishing role in UN to Kashmir and the north east.

They speak and write English in ways that is difficult to understand without periodically referring to a dictionary or thesaurus. Sometimes, I fail to decipher them despite best efforts, including consulting other people.

Such intelligence is usually tapped by liberally-funded think tanks around the world that seek out the highly evolved individuals to prepare papers and speak their mind on issues. It is a fallacy to think all views here comprise free thinking rationality.

The fund suppliers, that could range from pro-Pakistan to US lobbyists, big corporate houses, defence firms, ensure their interests are protected at every conclave. This further sets the agenda for the media and apparently lesser mentally endowed reporters and correspondents to follow in general.

The intellectuals, of course, are sharp enough to quickly figure the rationale that their arguments need to take to ensure the next invite from their sponsors usually at some exotic location accompanied by family and generous allowances.

Given their tremendously bright minds, they present convincing outlooks palatable to their ultimate hosts that remain mostly invisible to the uninitiated, newspaper readers and TV viewers. Minor versions of edit page writers abound among journalists with aspirations to transform into supreme intellectuals by turning in expansive PhD's, many books on contemporary subjects and finally air views and opinions on TV and at exotic conclaves across the world.

The Femme Fatales

The media profession attracts many women zealously inspired to crack stories, sniff for exclusives and make it big by making a difference to society. Like in any other vocation, some flaunt their sexuality to cultivate sources and build networks.

Given new age gay and lesbian permutations it could be anybody with anybody hitting the sack. The women have an advantage though. Due to pre-dominance of successful males that news gatherers seek, female journalists do gain better access points. This is not to suggest they go all the way each time.

Still, no politician, bureaucrat, film star, cricketer, corporate honcho minds or refuses attention of a pretty face on a dull afternoon. Somehow, it is also mandatory for women journalists in this country to smoke. Probably, it helps them think and behave like men – aggressive, abusive and hot tempered.

One needs to be all of this and more, given the fast-paced and very competitive media business nowadays. This was nicely portrayed in the movie *Peepli Live*, with the great Aamir Khan controlling matters in the background.

The Stars

These are the sprinkling of smooth talking and glib star reporters and correspondents from TV and print, paid well by their employers. Most are enveloped in self-righteous halos of self-importance due to professional habits of taking the higher moral stand on every issue. They have a view on every contemporary problem, some that others may not even have heard about.

A few popular names include Rajdeep Sardesai, Barkha Dutt, Arnab Goswami and Vir Sanghvi who think nothing of addressing senior bureaucrats, diplomats, minister and former and incumbent Prime Ministers or Presidents by first name or nicknames. They strut about like film stars and cricketers expecting everyone to recognize and acknowledge their presence, recall the prime time slots they occupy, their smart quips on air, latest article in a national daily. Many pretend to be their friends, but actually bitch behind their backs. It is due to envy.

The Pluggers

Unfortunately, this a rising category that promote openly or surreptitiously politicians and political parties, corporate houses, individuals, professionals, models, film stars, directors and fashion houses.

Given their clout, they are talked about in whispers. They have direct access and are on first name basis with every important personality as they act as gossip conduits the rich and powerful constantly like to use against each other, should the occasion arise. They are invited to the biggest parties and freely walk into the office of any secretary or minister, fixing bureaucratic posting and political deals that are important in the era of give and take coalition politics in India. Pretty girls are always found in their vicinity due to sniff of big money.

Some even become politicians, standing for elections or take the easy route by getting themselves nominated to Parliament. They make it a point to display the name and photograph of the important personality flashing on the screen of their expensive cell phone. They stand out in designer suits, big cars, boasting expensive club memberships, are appointed heads of cricket or sports bodies, afford fancy holidays and own apartments though their actually salary is measly.

They look down upon colleagues in the profession with contempt at their low class existence, laden with sweat and dust due to commutes in scooters, buses hunting for stories and leads. The high-stake pluggers move from the cool climes of their office cabins, to three-box chauffeur driven cars and big offices of the top notch that waits on them. Media barons and managements are wary of networked journos, keeping them happy while using their contacts for benefit, such as tax relief, duty free imports, diluted regulation laws and keeping out foreign media and new local players to avoid competition.

The Beavers

For some years I covered the mandatory correspondent beats. We are the guys who step out in the field, unlike the production staff, to report news, break stories, hunt for exclusives and take down copious notes at press briefings.

We get pushed around and beaten up by security personnel for intruding VIP space. We conduct sting operations, wait for hours outside offices and residences of dignitaries for an exclusive byte, refusing to relinquish our positions even if our bladders are about to burst urine.

At press conferences we take down notes like stenographers. Work pressure is high. Missing an all-important quote could mean the end of our miserable jobs, given breaking news coverage by the second. Most of us are unkempt, unclean, smell a bit and, like auto rickshaw drivers, liberally abuse in Hindi and also in English, given our primitive conditions of work.

We are also like construction workers out in the sun, emanating acidic armpit odours though donning slightly better clothing. Fortunately, we may have access to toilets, though we ease ourselves in the open quite often.

After a long-day out we trudge back tired to office, try to write good copy that is mercilessly chopped and re-written by the evolved editors who spend the day in air-conditioned chambers discussing and watching the big issues of the day on TV.

Later the editors proceed to the same TV studios to air their views on current affairs for some compensation. Correspondent stories and by-lines appear on the city, national pages and sometimes the front page which is always celebrated.

As we were too embarrassed to talk about our salaries, competition among correspondents is about by-lines, exclusives, where and how they appear, the length of a piece, the response of readers, via letters and mostly e-mails nowadays.

The positioning of write ups is determined by those who produce the paper under guidance of a resident editor who oversees a team of news editors, chief sub editor and copy editors. Like correspondents and reporters, they too are the slum dwellers of print media, doing night shifts, working till wee hours of the morning to put the paper finally to bed.

Along with many others, my area of operation focused over a small New Delhi zone that comprises the all-important Parliament,

Shastri Bhavan, North and South Block, foreign, home and defence ministries, BJP office at Ashoka Road, Congress party headquarters at Akbar Road, the Leftist parties and VHP.

The government briefings were frugal over cups of tea, coffee and cheap snacks such as *samosa* and Parle biscuits. The government people don't care about tax payers' money. They would rather have it all in their own pockets, including small change. Numerous minor Suresh Kalmadi clones thrive by falsely billing food items procured from cheap roadside stalls at five-star rates.

The business meets were lavish. Most corporate dos were held at up market and expensive hotels. Private entities know keeping a handful of journalists happy over butter chicken and above average booze, which is good Indian liquor served from Black Label bottles, is ticket to good press.

This is much cheaper than placing expensive ads. From mid-morning hundreds of hacks made the rounds of multiple press conferences at top hotels in South Delhi for beer, wine, whisky and non-veg platters. There weren't many teetotallers and vegetarians around. It would have defeated the purpose of availing the most frequently offered freebie in the journalistic profession.

Most pretended to write copious notes, but made it a point to lug commodious bags to collect free pens, watches, apparels and shoe vouchers that are then notionally added to the low salaries earned. Some journos boasted stationery collections that could be converted into a little store. These helped in soothing nagging wives and make children happier. Correspondents that worked for national media platforms were treated better with gifts especially reserved for them, usually hidden under big tables covered with thick opaque sheets of cloth.

Otherwise, it was first come first served basis. Many made it a point to arrive early not to miss out on the hand outs and beat the rush. I would drive around the city in my old assembled scooter that skidded on one side every time it rained due to the heavy imbalanced engine fitted on one side of the pillion.

Sometimes I borrowed my father's Maruti 800. But, I managed. I accepted the pens and watches that came my way, but did not make it the basis of my living. Given my childhood grounding of integrity, courtesy my father, I was naturally inclined towards doing stories I felt right about.

For example, I would not write about a doctor talking big about a heart cure medicine or procedure without cross-checking with several of his colleagues. I relied on my instinct to write about an issue of higher national or social import.

I believe there exists' many prototypes of the way I handled my job. As in any profession there are those who espouse the other side. We, the good ones are dedicated to our tasks and profession. Many label us as foolishly idealistic. Still, some readers abused me for favouring the BJP or Congress, being pro-government, anti-establishment. Comments on my articles criticized me as a "Sonia Gandhi stooge" or "L. K. Advani acolyte," pseudo-secular or anti-Muslim.

Even if there was any slant in my pieces, it was purely unintentional and without any benefit from any political or corporate outfit. Otherwise I would have been moving around in an Accent or a Fiesta instead of a battered scooter. So, I did get inspired by the Anna Hazare anti-corruption rallies later in my life.

When I began my career, typewriters were in use. Then, computers, with dial up facility and bullock cart download speeds were installed. The spell check feature made the army of proof readers redundant.

As they were heavily unionized, they could not be fired. They hung about the office with nothing to do but sip tea or coffee. Soon they formed groups that sang *bhajans* at night, when the paper is being produced, at various corners of the staircase, canteen, toilet and other common areas. It was a sorry sight. I resisted new technology but took to the desktop quickly when broadband, offering a smooth online interface arrived.

It eliminated the monopoly of video cassette parlours over smut. There were many free movies that could be viewed for reasons that need not be spelled out any more. It has been a while since I have written anything with a pen, but for cheques. This too has dwindled as I make most payments online now, except electricity as the government managed payment gateway is perpetually in crashed mode.

Over time I like gadgets. They are helpful. Unlike cars, better configurations cost lower over time. I have bought a 300GB notebook with Wi-Fi, DVD player and higher RAM cheaper than an earlier 20GB laptop with fewer features. It took ages for technology in sectors such as automobiles or aviation to re-invent itself.

Mobile phones and computers have evolved much faster to tablet touch screen versions that approximate a laptop and vice versa. It creates confusion about the purpose of buying a particular gadget -- word processing, playing games, mailing, chatting, making presentations or watching movies.

It is not easy to type on a tablet. Laptops have less battery life and are heavy to carry. Netbooks are no good for movies, they charge longer and are easy to transport. By the time one figures this, one is poorer by a few lakhs of rupees.

I wrote the following piece on Indian politics, called Rahul Gandhi takes the plunge:

India's reluctant prince, Rahul Gandhi has finally taken the full political plunge, anointing himself the Vice President of the Congress party. This effectively makes him the main party mascot for the 2014 general elections.

Though Rahul has been the second most powerful person in the Congress after his mother Sonia Gandhi for some time now, the appointment officially makes him so.

The rest, of course, do not matter in the party, unless they toe the Gandhi line. For long, Sonia has been criticized for belittling the office of the Prime

Minister, by being the real head of the government and not Manmohan Singh.

Rahul too was being castigated for following the same model – of wielding absolute power in the party, without being nominated to exercise such authority. Officially Rahul continued to manage the youth wing of the party, though he is in his forties when all cricketers, except Sachin Tendulkar, retire.

It is not yet clear whether Rahul would be the Congress party's Prime Ministerial candidate. Indications are that he will again follow his mother's footsteps of running the government without being part of it. This, of course, can happen only if the Congress party wins the elections again or has enough allies to support it.

The Congress will not be able to count on Mamata Banerjee for sure. She recently threatened to beat up Manmohan for not releasing enough funds for the state of West Bengal. The beleaguered Prime Minister is unlikely to have said "theek hai (okay)" to Mamata's statement.

Rahul's elevation happened during a Congress brain storming at Jaipur (January 2013). It was obvious that the move to elevate him was pre-decided, though Congress party members, imbued by total sycophancy to the Gandhis, tried to pretend that they had no clue about the move.

Clearly, they had been advised to act surprised in front of the media, but made a hash of the acting, though politicians generally do a good con job, especially when they are lying about corruption.

The only person who seemed genuinely astonished at Rahul's new position was Manmohan. He probably did not know, an indication of his status in the party, when even those hired to burst crackers and beat the drums had been briefed about the celebratory moment. Clearly, Manmohan's best days are past him now.

The Congress party won the 2009 elections portraying him as their Prime Ministerial candidate. Corruption scandals have tarnished his image. The Gandhi's, meanwhile, have moved on, letting Manmohan handle the corruption bogey. They have instead focused their attention on being popular with the "aam aadmi" broadly defined as illiterate poor folks by announcing gargantuan doles involving tax payers' money that they consider theirs to play around with.

As a result, the educated hard-working middle-classes are disenchanted, probably making the younger lot question their parents' approach of making them study so much to be eligible for jobs, but disqualifying them from the aam aadmi status, reservations and freebies, including direct cash payments from the government.

Rahul marked his elevation in Jaipur by making a speech, which was high on emotion and eloquence. Prior to this event, many said say he was unfit to lead the country due to his apparent low IQ and overall mediocrity due to which he did not even complete his college studies abroad.

Given the extremely low expectations from Rahul by the whole of India, except Congressmen, he scored a few points just for the delivery. He proved his detractors wrong by managing to deliver a speech that was clearly not written and perhaps not fully understood by him.

The enigma about his thoughts and solutions about the country's many problems remain. The main Opposition, BJP, meanwhile is competing aggressively to be worse than the Congress.

Senior leader Sushma Swaraj recently had her Mamata moment when she said that India should behead 10 Pakistani soldiers for the one Indian killed. Maybe it would be a good idea to send Sushma and Mamata, itching for a street fight, for time on the Indo-Pak border, giving our overworked soldiers a break.

If the Congress is in bad shape, the BJP makes it appear good, by being in very bad shape. The BJP leaders continue to bicker and fight. They say that such in-fighting and airing of views is a sign of true democratic functioning unlike in the Congress where nobody has the guts to say anything except the Gandhi's.

But there is a limit to which the intrigue and quarrels can be considered healthy. Besides, like the Gandhi's for the Congress, nothing in the BJP moves without the blessings of the RSS that controls cadres, logistics and hard-line Hindutva ideology.

The RSS, like the Gandhi's, is wary of any popular BJP leader emerging that could threaten their position. It likes to prop up leaders such as the reluctantly removed BJP president Nitin Gadkari, who fancy themselves as national leaders due to the opportunity to appear on TV. By similar logic reality show contestants in Big Boss could hope to be Members of Parliament.

Currently, the RSS is apprehensive of being subsumed by Narendra Modi. Given such a fragmented opposition, it is no wonder that the Congress sees a winner in Rahul Gandhi now that he has delivered a speech.

FIVE

Cheap Dating

In pre-Internet, pre-liberalized India the money I earned from my newspaper job met my needs. There was no need to show off. I was as comfortable smoking a *beedi* or a branded cigarette, Gold Flake or Classic or Wills Navy Cut. My rooftop village situation was easy on the wallet. The oldies smelling for sex could also be dealt with as I have talked about earlier.

There were no traffic jams in Delhi. Nobody travelled to Gurgaon for work. I never heard of the place till college. The salary cheques piled up in my drawer as I never felt the pinch. Petrol was cheap. My scooter ferried me and a companion miles.

I drove without the spare pillion tyre, so the girl held me close. Punctures happened, but it was worth the risk, given breasts firmly pinned on my back due to fear of toppling. It was a sexy sight, young lovers on a two-wheeler with the girl's bare-arms wrapped around her man.

It attracts attention. I spotted envious harried older successful guys in imported vehicles stuffed with nagging wife, boisterous kids, toys, diapers, baby food, vomit and maid. I was lord of the roads on a decrepit two-wheeler.

That was a comparatively innocent age to achieve materialistic well-being and sexual highs with little expense. Girlfriends were frugal. As opposed to fancy restaurants they settled for cheap roadside orders such as spicy *aloo chaat* at Sarojini Nagar or spicier Indian style chicken Manchurian at JNU.

This was regular middle-class dating. Sex naturally followed, often at home when parents were not around. Physical intimacy was not weighed down by money spent doing exotic stuff. If you made the girl laugh and she kind of liked you, it happened without fuss, for pleasure.

The money calculations were minimal; the worldly expectations of females were low. High credit card bills did not determine making out sessions. In any case, there were limited shopping choices, expensive Sunday wine brunches or holiday options to Bangkok or Hong Kong, Srinagar or Shimla.

Some of today's usual dating expenses were simply not accessible. There were no organized retail outlets peddling touch screen cell phones, netbooks, laptops, I-pods, fancy cars, branded shoes and apparel in the tightly controlled license permit Indian market scenario.

Air and rail tickets needed to be purchased over the counter after long waits in winding queues. The insolence of rude airline officials matched the cashier at the national bank. There were no low cost airlines while online booking could not even be imagined. The ugly arguments at ticket counters happen today in a different context, like Kingfisher Airlines going bust due to focus on flamboyance, paying brand ambassador Yana Gupta, high salaried fair-skinned model air hostesses, free flying hours extended to Deepika Padukone by beau Siddharth Mallya.

Thrift hardly mattered to the promoter and his son. Dating is a different ball game today. The malls are packed with things to buy. There is a sale on always. Expressions of love are measured by the shopping list. The proverbial G-spot exists. There is only one way to hit it.

Guys need to spend big on their muses, an impact of a growing Indian economy, liberalization, high income, aspirations, expectations and keeping up with the largesse of other men to impress their girls. With money multiple girlfriends naturally follow. I think I can never earn enough to keep even one happy.

An all food, drinks, cruise and sightseeing holiday to Goa and Istanbul is mandatory. This was the kind of break that most could not even dream about when I was growing up. Today quality time involves spa treatment and perfumes that cost as much as a car and zipping about in SUVs priced more that an apartment.

Then there is the permanent life tattoo to show real commitment to finally coax the girl to bed. More than an engagement ring, going down on knees to profess love, the forever body tattoo is a must to convey eternal love that may not last. David Beckham and closer home Saif Ali Khan with Victoria and Kareena embossed on their bodies have raised the bar for other lovers to follow.

Later, multiple painful skin grafts are needed to conceal the same tattoos linked to ex-girlfriends. The drawing could be on the neck, shoulders, biceps, buttocks and even more private portions. The removal process is worse than paying alimony.

There are positive aspects of change too. There are affordable options for young couples to move about without being bothered by frustrated and oversexed cops, touts, pimps and bystanders. Coffee shops, plazas, new and swanky movie halls, malls and more have mushroomed.

The one big plus is cops usually stay away from such locations. The urban air-conditioned and glitzy malls are an antithesis to what cops stand for -- uncouth and unkempt wild hyenas looking for easy prey -- amorous couples, infused with sex hormones that induces uncontrolled making out sessions.

If our security personnel in cities look out for criminals, robbers, burglars and Khalistani (and now *jihadi* terrorists) with the same zeal as they scout for young physically permissive lovers, our country would be a much safer place to live. When I was growing up and even now, cops made it a point to eye couples as if they are porn stars about to perform for an audience.

This is a strict, inhuman, callous and insensitive implementation of an archaic Indian law dating back to British times that punishes couples for public obscenity. Physical assault is always an option for the recalcitrant reluctant to part with their money and valuables as bribe.

The cops scavenged for couples in cars the anytime bedroom of young love and lust-stricken couples without access to privacy at home or hotels. They waited for the boy and girl to shed inhibitions. Then they harassed them to part with belongings including wallet, watch and any jewellery items. Nowadays they snatch cell phones and credit cards.

Still passions regularly ignite in the open, among shrubs, uncut grass at parks, monuments, green areas, forest clusters in the national capital. Nehru Park and Lodhi Gardens in South Delhi remain two couple hot spots.

It is never easy for young lovers. Fear of parents, money issues and age prevent minors, otherwise sexually active, from checking into a hotel that tend to refuse teenage or early twenties couples as a business segment.

They prefer singles, travelling executives, oldies, families or foreigners as customers. Many teenage couples try to fake their way through, adorning *sindoor* and armfuls of crinkling traditional maroon signifying marriage bangles.

But hotel managers, obsequious outside but slimy inside, are generally alert about such instances. They are very sceptical about allowing in adolescents given legal complications of having minors as guests.

Cops in any case keep a vigil on hotels being used as prostitution dens. This is not to prevent the trade, but to thrive on their cut that could include some time with the women on sale illegally.

I was cornered by the Delhi hyena cops several times during my initial high testosterone years, including the trouble some teens. In the absence of money to book a room in a good hotel, the family Maruti 800 often served as the tiny cramped bedroom. I was never certain about the quiet zones in the otherwise unsafe Delhi environs, given prying eyes of cops.

I learnt to keep the car engine running to make a quick getaway if needed. I ensured the doors of the Maruti were manually locked. There was no central locking. A pack of eunuchs seeking quick money surrounded my car, once. Trouble can hit lovers on the road anywhere.

It was a misty winter night, when a dark-complexioned warty transvestite, with heavy powdered pink make up, chunky yellow jewellery and betel red teeth, a few of which were missing, peered inside from my side of the window. The dark gaps between the teeth made the effect worse.

The man as well as woman tried to pull open the door which was fortunately locked. It was a scary sight, versions of which movie directors have re-created with much effort, re-takes and employing top makeup artists.

I could hear many eunuchs hovering around, chatting amongst themselves in distinct voices that are neither male nor female. Fortunately, my partner, who I was to marry later on in life, was pleasuring me with her mouth and did not realize the impending situation until I drove off a little distance. She continued with her good work, blissfully unaware.

The eunuchs gave chase and threw stones that luckily missed the rear glass. The small Maruti was not an easy target in the dark. They would have hit a big car. I think they did not hear the engine running and did not expect me to drive away so quickly. I heard shrieks and abuses. I might even have knocked someone.

Another embarrassing instance was when I was striding Pooja again inside my father's Maruti 800, a very useful possession at that time. I had pulled my pants down while my bare backside pointed towards the sky, on the front passenger seat. Although my car was parked at a secluded by-lane, the cops had it covered. There was no chance of escape as I was in no position to drive away.

Three hyenas peered through the front wind shield. I couldn't see them while Pooja could as I kissed her ravenously. For some moments I mistook her violent body movements, pinching my buttocks and pulling my hair as signs of her sliding into the big orgasm zone. I thrust harder, hoping that she would ease up and stop hurting me, but she unlocked the door of the car and threw me off.

"Was he trying to rape you?" one hyena asked Pooja as she tried to smooth her crumpled clothes and cover herself.

"No, he was not," Pooja replied firmly. I was proud about the way she supported me. "Sirjee, *thane chalo.* I think we will need to interrogate you (which in cop parlance only means shoving unpalatable foreign items into very sensitive portions of the body)," one gleeful hyena said in Hindi.

I got on my feet, zipped my pants, with the bulge still prominent. I expected a slap any moment or worse somebody would kick my box area.

Then, began the usual blackmailing process ceaselessly repeated across the country by the second like rape, road accidents, robberies, eve teasing and female infanticide. The words "Third Degree," spoken in English, liberally littered the conversation amongst the policemen present.

It was to create an instant impact of scaring Westernized people such as me expected to be familiar with the coinage and language. The idea was to evoke images of being hung upside down with chilli powder liberally sprinkled around the bottom, often described graphically by the press and also portrayed in Hindi movies that reflect reality of Indian living directly or obliquely.

How can making love be a crime in any country? Weren't those cops born out of the same process by parents? Or was it something else, or the other way round? Anyway, this was not the most opportune moment for such a debate.

This is best left to the TV channels and their list of usual wizened participants to rationalize. Logic does not work for boys and girls subsisting at Ground Zero. They are forced to bribe.

Luckily, I had an escape route. "My father is in the police," I told the hyenas in Hindi before they could cause any further damage. This is the one time I am always grateful of my father's position.

"IPS? Retired or in service?" I could sense the hyenas already backing off.

The IPS connection always scares off the lower level constabulary that thrives on petty corruption backed by physical violence on supposed perpetrators of crime, usually innocent.

"IPS and on deputation to Delhi, in the Home Ministry. All policemen are brothers," I shook their rough hands, liberally used on many of our less fortunate population, even as they limply offered theirs.

"Phone number?"

I gladly offered it to them. Dealing with parents is easier than corruption-stricken cops, though I was sure the hyenas would never call to check.

It was a ruse to test my reaction. This category of cops prefers to eschew any attention, happy to carry out their shady extortion business quietly, undercover, in the dark. "Ok sirjee, but don't do such things here. We will be in trouble if our SHO finds out," one hyena said.

This should be interpreted to mean the SHO would be angry an earning opportunity was lost or that the hyenas should be careful about choosing their victim lest it caused them trouble from higher ups.

More than suspension or dismissal the cops dreaded being transferred to police lines to train young recruits. There was no scope of making money on the side here. "Ok, sorry, going." I sped off with Pooja, who kept quiet for some time, perhaps a little overwhelmed by the events.

"You handled the situation quite well," she told me, clinging to my arm, her breasts moist due to sweat, almost bare against my skin. She was in love with me. She probably thought I would be a good father to our children and protect her.

In an Indian situation Tiger Woods' brawl with his wife (now ex) perhaps would have been a little different:

Firstly, if he crashed his vehicle outside his house, the police and ambulance would be the last to know, given the sorry state of such services in India. Nobody would have bothered to call or inform them as they never arrive when needed.

No one wants to be involved in a "police case" in any case that could drag on for years, with innocents harassed the most. Woods would have been carried back home by the otherwise usually helpful and also very nosy neighbours. "He is having an affair/s so problems with the wife," they would speak in whispers as such matters are never spoken about loudly, in public, to the media and never in front of the wife.

Secondly, riots would soon threaten to break out outside Woods' house, presumably in congested Delhi or Mumbai where roadside pavements are home to millions of homeless. It would soon emerge that Woods, in a state of intoxication and in order to escape his wife, drove his big vehicle over beggars and construction workers sleeping on the pavement at night. Some would have died without knowing what hit them.

Thirdly, after sometime the police would arrive sensing the accident involved a rich man, who is not a politician or bureaucrat or an affluent businessman with connections. They would wonder how being a golfer could be a profession. Over cups of tea, they would wait for Woods to regain consciousness and ask him to breathe into a dirty, bacteria and infection-laden instrument to test for alcohol levels. Then they would threaten to take away his driving license (which are never easy to procure, given inefficiencies of the system) and SUV unless he took care of them. Bribe and booze bottles accepted they would step out and fire in the air to disperse the crowd. The log at the police station would read: 'no alcohol traced'. The accident would not be mentioned.

Fourthly, the media, seeped in middle-class sensibilities, would have sniffed out the story as it has a very powerful and saleable peg -- the rich and famous driving big cars over the poor. Only top reporters with experience of covering events such as the Mumbai terror strike that provided first hand live visuals, including to militant coordinators sitting in Pakistan, would be selected for the assignment. The top reporters would station themselves outside Woods house 24/7 and others would fan out to hospitals and push and shove their way and mikes on the half-dead or dying accident victims for the elusive byte, against all medical advice in the name of freedom of press, democratic rights and bullying.

Fifthly, the case would go to court. By now much money would have changed hands, involving Woods' well-placed friends, relatives, lawyers and police officials. Handed more cash incentives, the cops would discover that the SUV that Woods was driving was not registered in his name as it was illegally imported to escape duties and taxes. The court would accordingly be informed that the entire case was fabricated as Woods owns no SUV so he couldn't be driving one. The accident probably happened due to a rashly driven truck that escaped in the cover of darkness. Witnesses could not be believed as they were too sleepy. The number of killed and injured would be reduced by the cops as some would be illegal migrants from Bangladesh with no record of their existence in India. Media reports about the actual casualties would be dismissed as mere hype and hyperbole.

Sixthly, some of India's top personalities who love to appear on TV on any occasion, also known for multiple affairs, multiple wives, would support Woods publicly. They could include film stars Aamir Khan, Saif Ali Khan, Vinod Khanna, Amitabh Bachchan, Kabir Bedi, Shekhar Kapur, Boney Kapoor, Mahesh Bhatt or cricketers Mohammed Azharuddin, Sourav Ganguly or Yuvraj Singh.

Seventhly, Mrs Woods would be extremely sorry for what happened to her husband and hold herself responsible for all the problems in her family because under Indian conditions, the husband is God and can do no wrong. She would undertake a gruelling fast, visiting temples all over the country to cleanse her sins. *Woods' mistresses would disappear from the scene. For the unmarried ones who presumably had a good time (in bed and otherwise), there would be no question of talking to the media to protect their family honour. They would have been taught by their mothers to keep intact the virginity tag, the ultimate gift on the night of their marriage to the Indian husband Gods. The married mistresses would keep quiet for obvious reasons.*

Eighthly, *the labourers and construction workers who survived the crash would regain consciousness to discover that one of their kidneys had disappeared from their body, to be sold to the organ trade mafia. They would be told that they were lucky to survive as both their kidneys could have been taken. Soon, they would be packed off by hospital authorities and police.*

Woods *would go back to playing the PGA, wife and mistresses, if he happened to be an Indian, that is.*

I wrote this piece, India Cheers More Coffee

Sensing a big and growing market Starbucks has launched in India. It was Mumbai first and recently the national capital New Delhi that witnessed a beeline of people seeking their first taste of the American cafe chain.

Not an extraordinary happening as Indians usually like a new experience, especially when they spot a queue for it. The struggle to get there makes it special. That is why queues in India never get shorter, over time. They only get longer.

Starbucks will add to the Café Coffee Day (CCDs), Costa Coffee, Barista, Gloria Jeans and others already in the market. Due to competition some players have shut down, others are struggling, but overall, doing coffee is good business in India, though it takes a little while for patrons to figure out a Mochaccino from a Cappuccino from a Frappucino.

Cafes are lifestyle for many in Indian cities now. They are good venues to conduct office meetings, work on a laptop while young couples and friends hang about.

Most coffee shops are brightly lit unlike the dim pubs that like to approximate night during daytime. The marketing people probably link darkness to Old Monk and Black Label and radiance to Latte and Cappuccino.

Conversely, the music at pubs is loud compared to lower volume at coffee kiosks, though the numbers could be just the same, David Guetta beats for one.

Boozing is linked to raised voices and hence the higher decibels in general. Coffee is associated with quieter, subtle, peaceful and more civilized conversation with no eager to jump into brawls bouncers in the vicinity keeping guard.

There aren't reports of girls being harassed or people beaten up at cafes unlike the frequent free-for-all at pubs. The coffee kiosks around Delhi and suburb Gurgaon, where I live, are usually brimming with customers through the day till late evening that obviously prompted Starbucks to take the plunge here.

Indian food outlets are either empty or choc-a-bloc with customers. Business is never steady. It is roaring or none at all.

Popular eateries and sweet shops in areas such as Bengali Market, Green Park or Chandni Chowk in Delhi have been around forever and only growing. Multiple generations visit the locations to experience what their grand and great grandparents savoured. Similarly the employees also speak about grandfathers or mothers working at the same jobs.

The CCD combos are good value for money – coffee, with sandwich and a chocolate mousse shot – more the merrier for the same amount of cash.

Barista usually has an online one-on-one offer running. Costa Coffee is priced higher, but offers better ambience and couches.

Young uniformed waiters struggling to speak English fuss about, though they could do equally well by sticking to Hindi. No point trying to portray what you are not unless one is dealing with a foreigner with local language issues.

A sign of success of Indian café's is the gradual disappearance of couches and love seats. At the most popular value for money CCDs, that have proliferated to almost every city in India, the settees have been replaced by slim wooden chairs with little tables that occupy minimal sitting space, to raise the bum count.

In travelling by Indian Rail terminology, this could translate to a shift from first class to general compartment. Next table conversations are easily audible while e-mails or power point presentations of an adjoining coffee drinker are very readable, if one is so inclined. Yet, middle-class India, the main patrons of coffee shops, do not mind the clutter and hubbub as long as basics are met — a place to meet, air-conditioning that works, reasonable cleanliness and fair pricing.

In India, there is fierce competition for everything in any case – parking, school and college admissions, making it to a job, rail reservations or standing space in the metro. Most are used to being stuck in traffic jams.

Many are thus content to make it to an empty coffee table. It is an achievement. Young couples, getting to know each other better, obviously abound at the Indian cafes. They are much safer here than public places such as parks where they can be hounded by cops, vigilantes, right wingers, touts, the moral police, cell phone and bag snatchers and others.

A boy and girl out in India are targeted by vested groups desperate to seek attention, make money, exercise muscle power, vent their frustration and envy.

Still, coffee shops do not provide the cover of bushes and trees at a park or even a shrouded pub, should the need arise. But, undisturbed romance can be good at the cafes without risk of being beaten up or mugged.

Given predominant conservative mind-sets, Indians shirk physical intimacy in public, though quick pecks at the cafes are common now. Maybe there will be some smooching too, despite the bright lights. Hope it happens soon.

I wrote this piece, An Air Ticket to Goa

Will air travel in India become cheap again? Will typical Indian middle-class families comprising noisy unruly kids and carting food neatly packed in multiple tiffin boxes, be able to afford a plane ticket again?

Just a few years back this was possible.

The thrifty train travelling population of India that likes to pack homemade Poorie (oily form of bread) and Pickle to save money at restaurants could afford to fly to exotic destinations such as Goa at rail fare budgets.

The offerings were from low-cost no-frills airlines such as Indigo, Go Air, Spice Jet and the erstwhile Air Deccan. If one got lucky online, the air fare could even be cheaper than the to and fro airport taxi expense.

Swarms of itinerant Indians clicked themselves for the first time inside aeroplanes proudly displayed in personal albums or later Facebook alongside the must do moments in front of the magnificent Taj Mahal or the Qutub Minar.

Planes turned into noisy picnic spots. This writer remembers couple of instances of kindly aunties happily distributing their home cooked food stuff to any passenger that cared to partake the victuals like it often happens during Indian train travel.

Even the crew joined the party. Only the state-owned Indian Airlines, comprising forever in a bad mood crew, continued to lose customers.

To take on competition the carrier changed name to Air India for whatever reason, while heavily losing money even as the unionized staff aggressively fought with the government for better salary and perks. The flying experience, however, was overhauled, courtesy the private players.

For those who could afford it, there was full fare Kingfisher Airlines, named after the popular beer brand, usually patronized by the snooty suited corporate class, travelling on company expense with access to free booze at business class lounges and added attention of very pretty and leggy hostesses for the feel good factor.

Kingfisher's extravagance included gifts to each passenger and a personal message on individual screens, another novelty for a domestic carrier, delivered in style by diamond earring-studded king of good times Vijay Mallya exhorting "guests" to live life king size.

The gorgeous Yana Gupta in a micro mini explained the life jacket process. All passengers listened and watched for a change.

There is something electrifying about a very pretty girl, otherwise clothed, wearing and taking off a life jacket. Still, even if everybody could not afford the Kingfisher experience, at least air travel was.

Until, it all came crashing down due to high fuel costs, taxes, government mismanagement of air routes and Kingfisher selling a dream beyond its means.

If one happiness index is measured by the shorter length of the mini skirt, the Kingfisher girls, selected personally by Mallya, have completely disappeared and so has the airlines. The flying business is not another free flowing beer party, it is about keeping costs in check, Mallya realized, or maybe he still hasn't.

The high-flying company executives have since occupied low-cost airlines seats now priced much more than the erstwhile full fare rates.

The corporate tickets continue to be packaged with free meals on board to keep the envy factor alive. Those paying from their own pockets obviously do not shell out Rs 200 for an extra-spicy, extra-oily sandwich, just because one is mid-air for a couple of hours. Sadly, the friendly flying aunties dishing out delicious Poories to spread all round happiness have disappeared.

The budget traveller, already struggling with rising inflation, except cell phones that only seem to get cheaper, has been pushed out. There is only so much that one can do with a cheap hand set, with almost-free roaming facility, if travelling is unaffordable.

Flying to Goa is a middle-class dream once again, the sublime beaches accessible only on post cards. One can actually visit Southeast Asia at similar fares, with the added label of having visited a foreign country.

The Poorie and Pickle travelling section, described infamously by the eloquent Shashi Tharoor as the cattle class, are back to rail and bus holidays, given limitations of absolute travel budgets.

This brings back the original question? Will the rail travellers again graduate to flying? Changes are happening in India's struggling aviation sector following amendments to foreign investment rules.

A new low-cost domestic carrier backed by AirAsia, the indefatigable Ratan Tata and Tata Group is in the offing.

Foreign players such as Emirates and Etihad are looking at investment options in Spice Jet, Jet Airways and the grounded Kingfisher infusing much needed capital. A price war is currently underway, though cheap tickets are still very difficult to come by. Will India's aviation sector sustain?

Will the cattle class be able to occupy planes again? Will the pretty model hostesses of Kingfisher airlines be back with their life jacket performances?

One can only hope for the best.

SIX

Hit by Sushmita

It was while doing the journalistic rounds that I met Sushmita. Her eyes were beautiful, lips sensuous, body ravishing in a sari that she wore usually. If ever a woman was created for naval gazing, it was her. Her cleavage could mesmerize men with access to the best women.

I was close witness to many top politicians and business tycoons, who enjoyed company of exceptionally beautiful white and Indian women, lose it with her. Even those bedding Central Asian chicks with sharp Caucasian features and strong athletic bodies that dotted the Delhi social scene given the flush of new Indian money, could not have enough of the opposite sex, once smitten by Sushmita.

Her presence impacted male hormones instantly that went haywire, mutating even the most controlled gentlemen practicing and preaching regimented routines, including following Baba Ramdev, a celibate by choice.

They simply craved more of her. Like cocaine, she blew minds that sought stimulation caused by her again and again, hovering around her to be jolted and electrified by her presence. Such was the impact of Sushmita on the male species, maybe she affected females too.

Well-known national political names, suave party spokespersons, analysts and ministers seen on multiple TV news channels every evening for their verbosity and ability to twist any debate in their favour, maniacally called Sushmita.

Always keen to be on TV to fan their massive egos, they were as desperate to know Sushmita a bit more to douse the unnatural sexual turbulence that she created in every man's body, soul and mind. Usually it is the journalist who has to make multiple phone calls for a quote or appointment or TV appearance by a guest. In the case of Sushmita it was the other way round.

Every male politician, in 20s to the 80s, sought an appointment to be interviewed by Sushmita. Initially the secretaries and other lower staff called incessantly, then the bigwig personally. The one's that had already met her sought her for special insights. They devised every excuse to interact with her -- lead, interview, one-to-one, help in formulating party manifesto, advice on taking over a steel plant, prepare a speech to be delivered in Parliament, strategy to topple the government.

Proposals were positioned in ways that her inputs and views would determine the course of India's contemporary history.

Such was the exalted level of her suitors whose names I cannot mention to risk defamation cases and physical assault by henchmen. Politicians are known to live long as absolute exercise of power, fame and money creates a heady life enhancing concoction that also makes them natural women seekers.

Many ladies do not mind responding positively to avail multiple favours such as allotment of DDA flats, petrol pumps and coal mines. If I were an attractive woman, I don't see myself refusing some of the lucrative offers, though I cannot say this with absolute certainty unless actually faced with such a reality.

My estimate is that the success rate of the rich and powerful making it under a desirable woman's sari or skirt is quite high.

Politicians thus have every incentive to keep limbs young, kicking and alive, unlike normal folks who pick up ailments as they age due to absolutely boring lives with nobody sparing time to acknowledge them. Given the collective wish of near and dear ones that they die and stop being a burden, they do.

Sushmita was a smart, grounded lady who knew what she wanted and usually got it. Given her years of doing the political beat for national dailies, she had learnt the art of utilizing her magnificent assets to her advantage.

For example, she remote controlled the *pallu* of her sari. Her mind body eye hand co-ordination was perfect like an accomplished cricketer, similar to triple century scoring hitting a six over third man Virender Sehwag at his prime.

The flap of covering slipped off just the right moment for the big shot whose attention she was seeking to get a good estimation of the most gorgeous breasts ever seen under any blouse. Any man could never be the same again, married, unmarried, old, young, sane, insane.

Sushmita understood very well the high profile invitations to penthouse, party, farmhouse, resort, exotic foreign locations such as Bali or Hawaii was intended to cajole the *pallu* to slip more and what might follow. Everybody, like Duryodhan, wanted to disrobe her sari. That was not so easy or so I believed.

I could barely take my eyes off her when I first saw her at the daily briefings at the headquarters of various political parties that abound in the New Delhi area. Journalists hung about till she arrived to be seated in her vicinity, same row or behind or if they were lucky, on her right or left that always was an opportunity to strike a conversation or steal a peek-a-boo under the *pallu*.

There was an unhurried scramble for a vantage position next to her. Nobody made it obvious. It was subtle. A news breaking quote from Sonia Gandhi or L. K. Advani was sought with as much zeal as a seat next to Sushmita.

She smiled at her few favourites and conversed with a very select lucky lot. I had the opportunity to speak and sit next to her a couple of times. Just like anybody in the political beat I too craved for such exclusive interaction.

Given hordes of desperate attention seekers, our interactions were sporadic and I was among everybody else whom she said "hi." I produced my biggest dimples when our paths crossed. She never noticed.

She took copious notes of briefings in her notebook, a sign that she was diligent about her work. Many beat reporters take the easy way out to jot down broad points relying on cut pasting and re-writing the agency copy later.

For obvious reasons, Sushmita was always picked from among many to ask a question during any important press conference.

I finally got to ask her phone number. "Please don't call unless it is really necessary as I receive too many calls," she said. She rang me first. I closely observed her number flashing on my cell phone for a while to be sure it was her.

"Can we meet at someplace before the Congress briefing? I need to discuss something urgent," she said.

"Absolutely, certainly," I said. There was no point pretending I was not excited.

It is usual for journalists to exchange information and notes about press meet timings, conferences, news pegs without letting out the exclusives.

I never expected Sushmita to make me her sounding board given the easy access she had to anybody, including knowledgeable greying hacks, too old to score in bed, but more than keen to impress younger women with their smooth talk, knowledge and experience.

The aging verbose journo gets an opportunity to stare and smell a young body up close, while the lady in question gained new insights, no doubt without making any covert sexual compromises. It is a win-win situation.

I met Sushmita at Bengali Market, a convenient location next to our respective offices. We shook hands which was an electrifying moment in itself.

"I like the way you write. There is a certain balance and neutrality about your pieces," she said, over delectable high calorie chicken *shammi* kebabs and extra sweet vending machine coffee, though hers was low sugar that is still high by most diet conscious standards.

"This happens when you don't get close to any particular party or politician. Or rather, none of the important people feel the need to cultivate you. I argue my points the way it appeals to me and not twist it to suit a particular vested interest cloaked in fantastic English and logic, including some of the big by-lines," I said. I was being matter-of-fact as I felt no need to impress her. I stood no chance.

She nodded in approval. We discussed more political happenings in the country, including the pros and cons of coalitions. As I had guessed, she was quite clued into the beats she covered.

Before going her way, she asked. "Why did you take up journalism?"

Since I was not a MBA degree holder, despite my private school trained by Irish brothers spoken English, Sushmita was perhaps curious to know about my professional intentions. I wish I knew.

"No particular reason. I sort of like the process of writing and became eligible for this job. If I knew about the pitiable salary beforehand I would have considered other options. I am still open to the idea. Many of my school and college friends made it to IIT or IIMs. The rest have gone abroad to collect degrees and international jobs. I am just floating around figuring out what is best for me. I have no advisors as my father wanted me to be an IAS officer, nothing else."

I told her I did not take up the low-paying journalism profession driven by a higher desire to cleanse the system or expose the wrong doings in society, like some, though as I grow older I feel a trifle more concerned about public interest matters. "I was okay with anything that is not IAS," I said.

"I like the intellectual feel about journalism. Money matters, but that is taken care of in my case. You look more the management sort though, you would look good in a uniform also," she said.

Although she hardly ate and I finished most of the kebabs, she insisted on paying. "Remember, I called you," she said. "You can still be my guest," I replied. She paid, shook hands that shocked my body again, and left.

Sushmita was perhaps right to typecast me as a smooth-talking MBA-type high on inter-personal and communication skills that fits well into the corporate bureaucracy of big companies such as Coca Cola or a Pepsi.

After slogging my butt for a few decades, I could retire happily rich to be able to educate my kids abroad and also afford treatment of lifestyle ailments picked up along the way such as high cholesterol, blood pressure or worse, heart disease.

My professional highs would include attending multiple conferences and brainstorming sessions at luxury resorts across the globe, figuring out ways to entice thrifty housewives to purchase instant noodles or pasta or high calorie bad for health fizzy drinks for children and adults alike.

When I died, my contribution to make the world a better place would be an army of unbearably obese kids whose flabby tummies formed tsunami waves under their shirts as they sluggishly moved about.

Sushmita called often to discuss news pegs. We met over cold coffee in the afternoon or over a couple of drinks after work to discuss our impressions about some of the personalities the media swarmed around like pests for an exclusive quote -- Sonia Gandhi, L. K. Advani, Atal Behari Vajpaee, Arun Jaitley, Narendra Modi, Pramod Mahajan, Mulayam Singh Yadav, Mayawati and more linked to ideological Left Parties, the VHP and RSS.

She told me that she and her spouse, a MNC rat racer selling a global chewing gum brand, had decided not to have kids to focus on their careers.

He, an IIT-IIM badge owner, led a very busy life and seemed to be the only person in the world disinterested in physical proximity with his wife to experience the excitement of being jolted irretrievably by her presence.

Sushmita's husband travelled ceaselessly all over the world to fulfil his ambition of being a global CEO and dollar multi-millionaire before he turned 40 by convincing populations around the world to chew more gum as a one-stop solution for digestion, strong teeth, longevity, emotional stability and high IQ levels.

Beyond, his aim was to turn into a venture capitalist-cum-philanthropist, the latter part probably for image and wider acceptability. I could never get myself to think so long term. I admire people such as Sushmita's husband.

But, if I was her lesser half I would have coaxed her to accompany me on all my travels or postponed the top job ambitions a little. It would have been difficult to let a night pass without making passionate love to a woman like her.

I would have researched every porn position possible. As a wife she could not say no, I believe, even legally. Sometimes, our conversations veered towards the inter-personal. "There is an interesting fact about you. You are the only who had my number but I was the one who called first," she said.

"I did not know what to call you for," I replied. There was only one reason for a guy to ring Sushmita which was to bed her. In my estimation, I stood no chance given the competition, assuming she was inclined to cheat on her husband.

"There is no point in calling a woman like you. You can call anybody and the guy will be more than willing to speak to you and run around you. You have to exercise the choice of interacting with me, not the other way round," I said.

"Apart from your work, I like you for a couple of more things," Sushmita told me a few weeks since we met for coffee the first time.

"I can be myself with you. You don't challenge me and are not overwhelmed by my presence. You don't pester me about meeting or talking on the phone unless I want it. Plus, I like your dimples."

I was surprised she had noticed the most useful part of my anatomy as far as impressing girls on first impact was concerned.

There was not much more to me – no money, power, fame, success or *Bharat Ratnas*. Snatches of the conversation with her did turn interesting.

"They just want to get under my bra and panties," she would tell me over puffs of cigarette smoke referring to some politician or senior bureaucrat.

"Why do you drop your *pallu* if you do not seek the unwanted attention?" I asked her. She was a little taken aback that I had noticed.

"Somebody is being very observant. I need to get the exclusive stuff through the one-to-one interactions. It helps," she said.

"Do things go beyond the *pallu* falling?" I asked.

"Depends on how I feel about it. But, I never mix work and pleasure. I will never sleep with my boss or a politician for a story. I think that is unethical. If somebody excites me, then it is another matter," she said.

There was more to Sushmita than just her overpowering sexiness. She wanted to be good at her work. "You okay about extra-marital affairs?" I asked.

"My brain is divided into compartments. My husband occupies one, but there can be others. I don't mix the two," she said.

"What about your husband's feelings? What about the loyalty factor? If he finds out, then what happens?"

"Every relationship is a universe of its own. I give my time and effort to each. They don't inter-mingle. I am never in conflict. But, I cannot go for a man for his money or some favour. I like to fight my battles. I go for a guy I like."

"How many guys have you liked?" I asked.

"You will never know," she said.

I was fiercely attracted to her. We met more often. The venues and nature of our interactions turned more informal. I figured why she did not like people calling her. She rang me when her husband was not around which was quite often.

Going out with her was easy on my limited finances. She had no qualms about spending at a fancy restaurant or pub that she knew I could not afford.

She held corporate membership of an expensive gym, swimming pool and spa at a five-star hotel, courtesy her husband. I tagged along when she was alone. She knew the lot of parking attendants, waiters, managers who made it a point to acknowledge and smile at her. She was a head turner and big tipper.

At the pool I put my arms around her, rubbing her back and massaging her shoulders. On occasions we splashed water on each other. Approaching under water I pinched her thighs or patted her bums to which she reacted with loud guffaws and chased me trying to pull down my trunks.

Following such events, I embarked on freestyle rounds of the pool for the bulge to settle down inside my swimming costume. Doing the back stroke would have been very embarrassing unless I covered myself with a float.

On another occasion she told me, "I think that my biggest assets are between my ears, but most seem to think they are a bit lower down," she pointed to her *pallu* that covered her cleavage and beautiful boobs.

I instantly felt wild stirrings. I shifted my bums to push my hard on back inside my undergarment. "Are you farting?" she asked. "No, just a little uncomfortable and you know why. I need to be a robot not to notice them," I said staring at her breasts. She looked away and smiled.

I made myself believe she was a little embarrassed. This was a good sign.

She knew her breasts impaled men's minds turning them into a mass of confused jelly. She did not mind my noticing or commenting about them.

Maybe I could caress them someday, I thought for a second, but banished the notion as a farfetched possibility. There is no point being pushy with a woman such as Sushmita. One has to just take it as it comes, allow her to lead hoping for good things to follow.

"Do you think you could like me?" I asked when she was high at a South Ex pub.

"I am still checking you out." She blew smoke into my face and smiled. I was enthused her reply was not an outright "no" that I expected.

"I was a *Geisha* in my previous life. I was born to give love," she said.

"My cup is empty," I replied. I wanted her to sense a bit of my rising attraction towards her without being boorish about it.

"What about your girlfriend?"

"I have two cups like you have many compartments," I said.

She laughed freely, full throated, loud, raucous, throwing her head back. She was absolutely sexy and was driving me insane.

I wrote this piece about India's VVIP's culture

We have yet another instance of a VVIP, this time Uttar Pradesh minister Azam Khan being questioned by security officials at an American airport.

Apparently Khan was gently quizzed by a lady official for ten minutes, the time normally taken by disembarking passengers to visit the loo, if there is a bit of rush.

Usually, when they take you aside in USA, they strip you to the very minimum and beyond, without peeing, that can be uncomfortable after a long journey.

But, Khan suffered no such indignity, though he should be happy he now belongs to a long list of more distinguished Indians who have been double checked at American airports many times. They include Aamir Khan, Hrithik Roshan, Shahrukh Khan, Abdul Kalam, among others. Most have quietly carried on with their itineraries, except SRK, who once timed his very public airing of grievance to the release of a movie, which was good marketing strategy.

Azam Khan could have easily headed to Harvard along with Akhilesh Yadav, the chief minister of UP, India's most populous state, whose hand is full managing egocentric uncles, relatives and father Mulayam Singh's rabble rousing pals like Khan.

Harvard University invited Akhilesh and Khan, to speak about handling the Kumbh Mela, a logistical nightmare involving millions of God-fearing devotees who believe that a dip in the heavily polluted Ganga and Yamuna will cleanse them of sins for eternity even if they have to deal with sores and skin disease in the immediate future.

The students of Harvard instead got to witness a first-hand case study of a pure bred narrow-minded vote bank seeking middle-level Indian politician at his rabid best. This will be helpful to anybody wanting to do business with India. They will need to know how to deal with law makers such as Khan. They abound.

Indian politicians, as we know and probably Harvard found out the hard way, thrive on any opportunity for free political mileage. Khan sensed a global audience from Boston, an occasion to be on CNN, BBC and Times Now at the same time.

He went ballistic linking the security episode to America's imperialistic designs, specific anti-Muslim profiling at airports, a weak Manmohan Singh as Prime Minister due to which he was targeted. Khan's equally demented supporters joined the chorus deriding US authorities and Singh.

Manmohan, for once, reacted rightly by keeping silent. President Obama, already caught up handling deranged kids in America, probably thought Khan was a supporter of former Pakistani President Pervez Musharraf seeking asylum.

Narendra Modi probably thought it was a stupid idea to fly all the way to America when 3-D video conferencing could have worked better. Rahul Gandhi probably feels Khan should undertake a train journey to know the real America.

Though there is some truth about Muslims being targeted at US airports, Khan clearly went overboard in trying to kill 10 political birds with one stone, including cancelling the Harvard lecture. Ideally he should have lodged a formal complaint, used the toilet and carried on with his program.

Instead, the students of Harvard, luckily or unluckily, also got a glimpse of India's overbearing VVIP culture that is very touchy about having their way, including walking in and out of Indian airports and aircrafts unchecked and unhindered as if they are visiting a restaurant in a mall or a movie hall.

Common Indian citizens, of course, have to submit themselves to a physical rub down at these locations by semi-literate, ill-trained, lowly paid security guards derived from impoverished areas such as Bihar, who spend most of their day scratching private parts, smoking and chewing tobacco. It is not hygienic.

The Indian VVIP culture reflects an attitude of superiority, invincibility and treating common citizens like dirt. It thrives on trampling rule of law, abuse of power and treating of tax payers' money as a personal savings account with free unlimited withdrawals. The VVIP could be ministers, bureaucrats, police officials, Mukesh Ambani, goons protected by the state due to connections or money.

One manifestation of high handedness is witnessed on Indian roads everyday wherein any travelling VVIP is accompanied by an entourage of SUVs stuffed with heavily armed security personnel who menacingly weave their way through heavy traffic at high speeds.

They jump red lights, don't line up at the toll and expect everybody else to quickly move aside or else abuse and assault with impunity. In India, ambulances get caught in traffic, never a VVIP convoy and Domino's pizza home delivery.

SEVEN

Riding Realty

.

I bought two plots in Gurgaon with the money I saved from the meagre newspaper job, help from my parents, including living with them that can cut down expenses such as rent, food, domestic servants, car fuel, electricity and phone bills.

Anything located within the purview of national capital Delhi was unaffordable when I and my family scouted for property, at the insistence of my mother.

Though my mom was married off to my father at 16 she retained a practical and sagacious side that could only be matched by top professionals in any field. Maybe I am being biased, but that is the way I felt deeply.

"The biggest mistake your father made in his lifetime is not to invest in property. I will not let my son make the same blunder," she said. My father did not believe in the concept of accumulation, including realty.

"Learning is the biggest asset. All else is of no use," he would say.

"One has to be practical in life. There are some basic material needs that should be fulfilled apart from building knowledge," my mother retorted.

We went about assessing properties in our well-maintained Maruti 800 on the very bumpy Gurgaon roads that cows considered their rightful ground. The resident cattle population was very unhappy with our irritating presence due to incessant honking that interrupted their grazing and lazing.

City bred people can never drive without being noisy, even if not required. It defines us, given the rough, overcrowded and unruly road travel conditions in metros. Psychologically, we are tuned to blow the horn while driving in high gear due to messy traffic and road situations.

We had the government Ambassador with attached driver available and allotted to my father that most would use for a journey to Gurgaon. But, we were a different lot due to the path of utmost honesty chosen by my father, especially when it concerned a cause backed by my mother.

My father thought nothing of using the official vehicle during my IAS exam process as it was his idea. We did not insist on travelling in the Ambassador during our multiple visits to Gurgaon lest my father feign another heart attack for not listening to him. "All the nurses and doctors know he is faking the heart attack. God forbid, if it really happens, then nobody will know," I told my mother once.

"Keep quiet and never talk like this about your father again in your or my life," my mother snapped. Despite her abundant logic, foresight and forbearance, for her, husband was God. He was a matter of faith.

No power in the world could change the position he acquired in her life. Like all good wives she did criticize and nag my father at times. But, she would never tolerate anybody else assailing him. I and my brother had to treat him with utmost respect, even though we argued a bit with our mom.

My mother never called my father by name. He was always "sahib" to her. I wondered whether I would ever manage to marry someone who would call me "sahib" with the same dedication.

The likelihood was remote given the rising numbers of aggressively driven career women often earning salaries much more than the husband.

There is a growing category of married men in Gurgaon today who mind the house while the successful wife earns the big moolah working up the ladder in big MNCs such as Coca Cola, Pepsi, Nokia, Nestle, Microsoft and more.

Given such a scenario, several male spouses have imbibed soft skills such a potty training the kids, nappy changing and bottle feeding, to remain relevant in the family unit. If men had breasts they would probably have to deploy those to feed the babies and sexual gratification of the other half.

Still, if one can set aside the definition of dominant male head of the family rooted in patriarchal mind-sets it is not a bad life for any guy. Deposit the kids in school in the morning to be followed by golf, time at the gym, swimming, lunches with cousins and friends, reading, gardening, watching movies, TV and later in the evening attending the big corporate do with the high flying wife.

Most such activities are part of anybody's utopian retirement plans after a lifetime of accumulation and hard work, in the process picking up diseases such as blood pressure, hyper tension, weak heart or high cholesterol. One can superannuate early, if lucky to be married to a successful woman.

After scouting about a bit, the land that I finally purchased in Gurgaon, as per advise of my mother, was part of a bigger inhospitable territory that sustained wild animals, snakes, scorpions, leopards. A male tiger seeking to mark out new territory had been sighted in the area. Two plots in a corner were the only ones I could afford.

As an extension of lower Aravali Hills, Gurgaon was a desolate land with large expanses of barren space leading to the semi-deserts of Rajasthan. There was an abundant sprinkling of temporary mud and straw huts inhabited by nomads in colourful red, yellow, pink hand woven attire and turbans.

They moved about with their entourage of animals, large extended families, many children, half-naked, sparsely clothed and dripping nosey. The Gurgaon shrubbery proliferated fertilized by the extensive organic droppings of human and cattle poop courtesy the buffalo-goat-sheep-camel-cow rearing local inhabitants.

The lowest in the food chain were armies of hefty looking pigs, similar to the soon to be bacon animals in American farms, that also thrived on the abundant potty in the area. Like their well-fed US counterparts, they too never starved.

My to-be plots were being utilized as natural toilets by a couple of big nomadic families with kids and cattle freely defecating in the area anytime of the day or night. They were unhappy when the newly acquired land was cordoned off by barbed iron wires, with only a locked iron gate for entry.

They saw us as intruders that gate-crashed their personal dwelling shutting them out of their own god given lavatories. Most plots in any case were technically out of bounds, sold off to other spill over Delhi population looking to invest in property. The centuries-old local occupiers could continue to use the plots till the actual construction of houses began in the area.

Though the barbed wire was deterrence to animals, humans could clamber over them when the owners were not around.

For some time that we inspected my plots regularly, the nomads had to shift their shitting to other pastures already in use as open air urinals by neighbouring families. The bigger message was, however, clear to the long-time residents.

Their common land was gone, acquired by a private real estate developer then sold off to individuals such as me for profit. The local denizens could glare and fart as much as they wanted, but they could no longer freely defecate on the land that they considered for ages their personal loo and grazing ground for their livestock.

"I feel as if I am buying two toilets," I told my mother as we made final progress towards buying the land, including a close reconnaissance by foot of the area strewn with rotting excreta, like it is with any river sidewalk in India, whether Rishikesh or Benaras or Allahabad.

"One day you will remember and thank us for the decision to buy these plots. These are pots of gold not potty," my mother retorted.

Though it was her idea that I invest in property, she always used the word "us" to include my father. She could never imagine any individuality separate from him.

It was not easy for my mother to hop over piles of human waste in a sari. I considered it a major achievement that my mom, and so many others like her, could be so nimble despite her attire. She refused to wear pants or jeans despite our insistence. Sid bought her a couple of Levis but she never wore them.

I think she sensed that my father would not like it as he never verbally supported any change in her sartorial style, despite our prodding. Deal settled the sellers of the land were thrilled at the couple of lakhs of profit booked.

The value of their common toilet turned plots had remained stagnant for a while. Yet, as destiny and my luck would have it, the economy of Gurgaon was meant to change. The former owners lost out big time while I gained enormously.

In a couple of years the two plots located among lazing buffaloes, jackals, *neelgai* and other wildlife, turned into gold as my mother had predicted, set amidst glitzy malls, high rises, MNCs offices, big cars, golf courses, international schools, state-of-the-art hospitals and later a world class metro service.

The arrival of the big earning professional class employed by slew of top notch companies led to spiralling real estate price. Pretty girls wearing expensive shiny high heels backed by very rich fathers, sugar daddies, godfathers or husbands swarmed pubs, gyms, spas, five-star hotels and retail outlets.

The government, as usual, has failed to keep pace with the private sector driven growth in Gurgaon. The roads, power, law and order, water supply, garbage and sewage disposal systems under the administration continue to be abysmal, third class and third world. A CEO sitting inside his plush office in Gurgaon could be a scene from anywhere in the first world, including America or Europe.

Outside, the broken roads, traffic jams, overflowing muck, cows ambling about, can only be India. Despite the shortcomings, as matters emerged, within six months of possession of my plots, BPOs, software companies, MNC's set up shop in Gurgaon. The trickle of companies quickly transformed into a wave and then a tsunami, all driven by massive prospects of making profits in the emerging India market. My net worth zoomed.

The value of land became million times the salary I earned. It was the kind of money that successful NRIs with IIT or IIM badges managed to save after decades of hard work in America or Mumbai. My mother, as usual, was right. The multiplier effect of property investments is unmatched.

Gurgaon brought me luck. My father retired from his highly respectable government job with a total corpus of Rs 7 lakhs and a small DDA society flat in West Delhi, a reward for honesty and hard work for over 35 years.

My plots quoted Rs 2.5 crores each within a couple of years of possession. I am no votary of undiluted capitalism. Private schools and hospitals can fleece customers. Healthy competition needs to co-exist with independent regulators that keep everybody in check, in terms of tariffs charged and quality of service offered.

I remember my first few visits to the malls that came up in Gurgaon, their inaugurations amidst much fanfare and media coverage with politicians and film stars in attendance. I wrote about it:

Lifts in order, escalators moving, friendly security guards, organized parking, clean urinals, plenty of space to fool around, cool air-conditioning, no litter, no betel-juice splattered walls, no graffiti such as 'Indians love Pakistanis' or 'Sachin is God', clean floors -- this cannot be India, I thought.

It was a novelty for sure. At that time, in Delhi, the only decent public urinals one could visit were located at five-star hotels that deputed alert guards at vantage areas to shoo away suspicious looking young men looking to relieve themselves. I guess when you got to go, it shows.

The rest of the badly maintained public utilities left an odour on the body that lasted till a change of clothes, perfumed soap bath and conditioner. Thus, innumerable Delhiites relieved on the roadside while women had a bad time holding their bursting bladders.

Similarly, the only locations with free air-conditioning were the American and British Council libraries, where retired civil servants on complimentary lifetime memberships and sundry others without work, snoozed and snored in cool comfort during the afternoons.

The rest of the unemployed, especially the youth, overawed by libraries, spent peak summer time at cheap movie halls showing equally low value movies. The one last bastion of coolness was the underground Palika Bazaar at Connaught Place where there was no space to walk given the crowds, while a fire or bomb scare, courtesy the Khalistan movement, happened every other day.

That is until the malls happened. No family outing or dating itinerary is now complete without a visit to one of these. The same people who lined up outside temples or India Gate in the evenings, the most popular family entertainment for a long time, now visit the malls.

There is equal space for elders to take a cool siesta while the youngsters can just hang-around doing nothing without paying entry fees or being hassled by cops or be obliged to buy anything. Couples can move about without being bothered.

Initially there were three malls, Sahara, City Centre and Metropolitan located in urban Gurgaon, the satellite town of Delhi, and was described by Indians who had not visited Singapore as the Singapore of India.

This is because the new buildings were plush, while the rest of infrastructure, including roads, public transport and traffic leading to the malls were in an appalling condition and they still remain so.

There were gaping manholes formed every monsoon even as the currents sucked in animals, people, cars, scooters, and sometimes also trucks. Thankfully, the story was different inside the air-conditioned shopping complexes that easily approximated those in Southeast Asia.

And, herein lay the paradox. The glitz was for real.

Multi-storied air-conditioned buildings housing restaurants, multiplexes, clothing and electronic shops, coffee kiosks, fast food, girls in short skirts and tank-tops meshed to create an un-Indian scenario, seen only on television and events such as an Indian fashion show, wherein all women's bodies are heavenly, prêt wear includes microminis, everyone eats chicken in small bites and sips the whisky and wine instead of gulping it down.

I decided to check out the malls personally, to know for sure that the outward look did not conceal a whole lot of muck inside as happens in the case of every other Indian project.

Having used the toilets, the cleanliness can be vouched for, the flush was working and even the toilet paper was in order.

As a matter of fact an attendant waited outside and entered immediately after my exit to crosscheck for spots and clean if required. This can be slightly disconcerting for the user.

I sniffed around for dark dank corners that are usually visited by more normal denizens to ease their bladders, but found none. A friendly security guard, not a regular specimen, came up to me and said, "That way is a dead end, sir." The words were broken, but they were English all right.

I scoured every lift to check for graffiti, the 'I love you forever' types – 'Rohit loves Sharmila till he dies'. There were none. A friendly liftman, he was actually there, said, "Have a good day sir," as I stepped out.

This is not India, I told myself. Talking of lifts, the one that was not working had a warning placard announcing the same. Generally, when lifts do not function, the authorities find out last.

So, there are usually people stuck inside who bang and scream as if they are running out of Oxygen and short of time to attend to an emergency, although all of them must have been stuck in a lift sometime or the other in their lives, given the poor condition of such service in India.

Even the escalators were working. An escalator was installed in Delhi at the Railway station in the 1990s even as India moved into the first flush of economic reforms, liberalization and taking over of market forces.

It never functioned; at least nobody saw it move.

Finally, I had to check whether the one bastion of Indian-ness was transcended -- litter. Littering is a post-independence Indian birth right. Many parents feel proud when their children eject toffee bites and potato chip bags everywhere.

It gives them a sense of power and choice, of being able to do what one wants to, of freedom and democracy that great people such as Mahatma Gandhi and Jawaharlal Nehru fought for.

Sadly, there was no litter at the mall.

Given my sharpening journalistic news sense, I tried to ascertain the behind-the-scene story that had resulted in the neatness and organization.

The corporate office of one mall was a venue for such answers. The manager on duty was patient and heard out my woes.

"Where has India disappeared?" I asked.

His explanation was simple. Indians per say do not like to be the first to do anything. Only if one does it everybody does it and if no one does it, nobody does it.

"Just as we had one Miss Universe and now we have so many. It is the same syndrome," he explained.

The critical issue over here, he further added, is to ensure that the first of such happenings do not happen.

"If one person spits in a corner, within minutes there will be 50 more spitting at the same spot, which will turn into an impromptu permanent spittoon. Similarly if one person writes on the wall of the lift, 100 will follow in 20 seconds and the entire mall will be a big American graffiti," he explained.

"The key is security, and we are very tight, though polite about it. But, at the same time apprehensive as one slip up (quite literally) means things will go haywire."

I did not agree with the manager.

More and more Indians have been exposed to systems abroad and know of their spotless functioning. Perhaps, it's a change of heart and mind. But, one could also be jumping the gun. As they say, we are like this only.

I wrote this piece about road rage:

A Pakistani diplomat was recently assaulted in Delhi when his car bumped a motor cyclist. Although Islamabad sees a larger conspiracy, this gives too much credit to India's intelligence agencies which, unlike Pakistan's dreaded ISI, are incapable of executing such a delicate operation – getting a lowly paid agent to ride a bike, bump a diplomat's car and then land a few effective punches.

In all probability the Indian agent, chatting on the cell phone while driving, would have tripped his bike without denting the car or got beaten instead of beating.

This is understandable. Most IB and RAW officers hone golfing skills while plotting their next prime posting in London, Geneva or Washington. The focus is not tit for tat out manoeuvring of Pakistan. Unlike an Indian agent, the Delhi bike rider was no push over, thinking nothing of assaulting the Pakistani diplomat.

He is among the millions of short-fused denizen of congested roads of India's national capital that resort to violence at the slightest provocation, imagined or real, irrespective of fault. While the ISI devotes time and military resources to train jihadi terrorists, on the roads of Delhi and adjoining suburbs of Noida or Gurgaon, individuals are naturally inclined to assault and fight.

Those with guns shoot. Like easy to detonate improvised explosive devices (IED's), vehicles are manned by human bombs waiting to explode into paroxysm of rage. Traffic in the city is a chaotic cauldron of buses, cars, auto rickshaws, pedestrians, cattle, motorcycles, scooters, window-knocking beggars, carts and unauthorized peddlers of fruit, vegetables and apparel. As rules are mostly flouted, space limited and not demarcated, there are bound to be infringements, enough to ignite a fight, especially with summer temperatures raging.

I have been driving in the national capital region for over two decades now. So far, I have survived. Road rage and accidents abound. Nobody cares about the injured, but everybody is inclined to quarrel, judge and combat.

A crowd accumulates at the accident site at a pace that can only be equalled by viewers assembling in front of a TV set in an office or market, during a cricket match, fixed or otherwise. The extremely rash and wild drivers include youngsters who believe bikes have wings. Many more suffer the same mentality.

These include call centre and BPO cab drivers, auto rickshaws and super-rich young brats who are convinced their big and powerful SUV's, BMW's and Audi's can take off from any tarmac. The results are often horrendous.

Fast moving VVIP convoys comprising big red beaconed vehicles are another hazard. This is perhaps the only instance that anything linked to slothful governments show some kind of speed, though it is inappropriate and unsafe.

My impression is women drivers have an easier time on the road. Most patriarchal Indian men mistakenly think that women are dumb.

So, a lady crashing her car is seen as an extension of her inherent stupidity. She is allowed to drive away while the crowds giggle and the injured fend for themselves. Even cops seem to espouse the same mentality when a woman driver brazenly jumps a red light, flashes a smile and accelerates away.

For male drivers, it is best to be prepared for the violence as much as the avaricious cops. Often, diplomacy does not work. Aggression has to be matched by even more aggression. There is no point being a sitting duck in a lake full of crocodiles.

It is prudent to let an IED know that you are RDX material, letting off a few Hindi or English expletive as the case may be. As I have read in the papers, the Pakistani diplomat tried to reason with the bike rider who was driving on the wrong side. Rationality hardly works on Indian roads.

Mental preparation is needed to hone the street fighting spirit given increased existences in sanitized environments of gated communities, well protected air conditioned homes, offices, malls, airports and movie halls.

I like watching Sachin Tendulkar take on Glen McGrath or Sunil Gavaskar in his prime eye West Indian pacers to ensure some aggression related hormones settles in the brain. Discovery or Animal Planet clips of belligerent lions and buffaloes perpetually locked in the fight to death also helps.

Over the recent past, the road rage situation has worsened due to exponentially rising unruly traffic, more powerful bikes, cars, crazier kids, cabs and VVIPs in even more hurry. I watch clips of gory MMA cage fighting involving use of bone crushing elbows and knees to keep the mental tension going. There is no choice.

EIGHT

The Future Wife

There was no reason for my relationship with Pooja to not work out. It just didn't. I guess we were destined be apart. Matters began to cool between us when she joined officer training at the Lal Bahadur Shastri Academy in Mussoorie and was allotted the Bihar cadre. She underwent her district initiation at Chhapra, another town where young couples probably jumped roofs to meet and mate.

Long distance relationships are difficult to sustain due to new distractions that can spring up in one's local environment. I don't have a deep voice, biceps, triceps, shoulder blades, calves that could snare me a woman.

There was no extra cash or extraordinary achievement to compensate for physical short comings, only the dimples that turned me into a minor lady killer. Some friends whose lives were parched of female company except sisters, mothers, aunts and grandmothers labelled me Casanova.

Pooja's constant goading me to do well in life, especially making it to the IAS, was wearing me down. There was nothing wrong in her prodding, except she reminded me more and more of the way my father was with me. I was sure if Pooja had her way she would try to wake me up early in the morning.

There was nothing unnatural about that either. But, at that stage I wanted to be left alone to do my own thinking and pace my life. Pooja was a determined girl who wanted us to work out. There were times I was rude. I told her she should focus on poverty alleviation and flood relief operations in Bihar rather than wasting her time and effort on me.

"The country needs you more than you need me," I told her, recalling a famous speech somewhere in the world. Still, she called me long distance often.

She chatted for hours, coaxing me to study hard for the IAS exam, although I was settling into my newspaper job. "You should worry about your phone bill. There could be a vigilance inquiry if you are passing it off as official," I told her.

She ignored my words. "Put on weight, become fat. It does not matter. You can lose all of it later. Right now focus on study and make it."

"I can't stop myself from going for a run. I like it. I will try and not exercise then I will surely put on weight, like you wish," I said, irritated.

I could never figure out why she connected making it to the civil services exam to obesity. Her assertions remain an enigma to this day. Probably, it was her version of the mythological Arjun-Dronacharya interaction in the epic Mahabharata -- of focusing on the aim and nothing else. Maybe this was her philosophy of life due to which she made it, though she continued to be slim.

Exercising an hour every day to keep fit could not be cause for not making it into the IAS or muddling one's brain. There were deeper reasons such as my inability to slog like a horse and thinking too much about sex, my primary drawbacks.

****

My Gurgaon plots played a part in my marriage. Lata was the daughter of my father's batch mate from Punjab, another honest officer, who, however, reasoned in ways similar to my mother

Based on premonitions about Gurgaon he bought plots across the desolate land following the lead of property developers operating in the area.

"They have foresight," he would say to which my mother nodded in agreement while my father looked away.

Eventually he quit his low paying government job to set up a real estate entity. My mother also believed in parking capital in property but was set back by my father's distaste for speculation and quick money.

He did not expect or want her to think beyond the daily healthy food and washed clothing needs of the family. My mother's upbringing was rooted in regarding husband as God. She could never oppose or ignore his views completely.

But, she made sure that I invested in real estate. She did not pursue property for Sid. She was sure he would make it on his own steam. I was the one that needed support, or so she thought.

I knew Lata since childhood. We met at the usual batch mate dos and birthday parties organized with much gusto by our mothers. These involved the use of a bit of government machinery at their disposal -- cars, servants, venues, attractive discounts from sweets, cake, pastry suppliers and more.

Over time even my father believed such liberties and entitlements were acceptable given massive corruption at all levels of government functioning. "Hundreds of thousands of crores of tax payers' money goes into pockets of politicians and their sycophants," he would say.

I and Lata began to click as we grew older. She did not carry badges of achievement, extraordinary 98% average marks in class XII, 100 % in two subjects and still not securing admissions in St. Stephen's Eco Honours or SRCC B-Com due to others that score more hundreds.

The problem is with the system, not the bright kids. There is an artificial scarcity of sufficient seats due to mismanagement of quality higher education in India.

Lata was not mixed up about her ambitions like me. While Sid wanted to scale the corporate sector, Pooja IAS, Lata knew the business of real estate was her calling. It was anybody's guess how she developed the interest. She got it from her father.

"So, you own two plots in Gurgaon? You could sell one and live on tax-free interest forever. You can continue to struggle with whatever you want to do with your profession, but money will never be an issue in your lifetime," she told me.

"Who will buy the plots? The sub soil is full of pig and human potty," I said.

She brushed aside my comment. "The plots are worth more than gold. We own land in Gurgaon. I know," she said.

"You will soon forget about Gurgaon. In a couple of years you will be married to a software engineer in California or investment banker in New York. Your final destination is America, for the dollar earning NRI, Green Card and elusive US citizenship status for the yet to be born next generation."

"The foreign returned guys will not be able to afford what we have. My father is sure about this and I agree with him. Land in Gurgaon will cost more than New York," she said coolly.

"Your father and my mother seem to think alike," I said.

"You should respect their views," she said.

"Why do you think I bought my plots?"

Lata's predictions were right. The prices of my plots zoomed to unimaginable levels. Almost in synch with rise in my net worth, Lata called more often.

She wanted to hang out with me. I was open to the offer, naturally. "You have become a crore-*pati* with no effort. Congratulations. You are a man of destiny. You need to take me out for dinner," she said.

"I think such big words and phrases should apply to people such as Gandhi, Nehru and our fathers, not me. As for dinner, it would an absolute delight."

My father too dreamt of congratulating me the way Lata did after I made it to the IAS. Making money without effort due to escalated property valuations did not fit into his worldview of any achievement, unlike Lata, her family and my mothers' thinking. Anyway, what is not to happen does not happen.

I dislike beating around the bush with the girl I go out with especially if I am attracted to her. That is, unless the person happens to be somebody such as Sushmita with whom I discussed work, was not technically dating, though attracted. Sushmita was also married.

Otherwise, I express my feelings quickly, clearly and early. It ensures entertainment expenses are well-invested or the little money I possess is not spent. I am not over eager about mechanically hitting the proposal button the moment the second date is done with. To take matters to the next level the chemistry, passion and inner stirrings need to be sensed by both individuals.

I usually hold back till the third or the fourth time I go out with a person when I perceive meaning in a future relationship, which generally involves dollops of physical pleasing of senses.

It is not as if I am right all the time. I do go horribly wrong. Still I arrive at a decision either way. Luckily, I have never been slapped, reported to the police or chased by desperate folks that 'honour kill' any guy who propositions their daughter.

I know of guys who hang out with a girl for years never speaking their deep desires fearing a rebuff. They think revealing inner feelings usually of carnal nature could cheese off the female with opportunity of intimate interactions at some future occasion lost forever. I disagree with such a hypothesis and could never suffer long lonely nights of fantasy, make believe passionate love making to the girl I professed platonic love in her presence. Lata was a very pretty girl and she wanted to date me. I conveyed my feelings to her in good time. She was okay with it.

These are moments that one can never be comfortable about. One rehearses it in the mind a few times. The adrenalin is high. It is like taking an important exam or playing a pulsating tennis rally at set point or scaling a Temple Run high score.

One tells the girl about the attraction bit, those deeper emotions that can only be sealed with a kiss. I think, for her too, it is important to imagine the guy as physically proximate and feel good about it. She could say 'yes' or 'no' or convey in different ways she needs more time which usually also means a 'no'.

"I don't earn much, be warned," I told Lata.

"It does not matter. Do well in your work as you enjoy it. Importantly, you have the plots. I know you for so long. You are cute. I could even marry you," she said.

"I am not sure about marriage, but I surely can kiss you for the rest of my life," I told her. She blushed. I liked that. I also liked Lata's honesty and probably she was not averse to mine too. I was relieved she did not suffer an IAS obsession. Too many people in my inner space seemed to be bitten by the IAS bug.

I was not absolutely okay with the concept of marriage though the inevitability of the happening did occur to me. I guess the 'M' word was hammered into my being by Pooja, who spoke about the subject as often as my father did about the IAS.

I think she was under pressure from her family to add the wedded badge to her achievements. Modern day girls' parents have it tough. They have to doubly worry about right career and then right husband for their daughters.

Fortunately, with Lata, our intimate moments were in safer zone and we did not run into cops and other peripheral beings. The only time we were in some kind of risk was with eunuchs. I have narrated that episode earlier.

Lata's father worked out of an office in Gurgaon, two nicely furnished rooms with a pantry, bathroom and a fridge well stocked with beer, sparkling white wine, Thumbs Up and Sprite. Though her father did not drink himself, he understood alcohol played an important role in any property transaction being pushed to fruition. Booze eased the process of a client making final commitment to invest in real estate that always involves a lot of loose money.

There were servants who kept the office spotlessly clean. Lata brought the duplicate keys whenever needed at night or during the weekend when the office was shut. I don't know how she managed the keys with her family, but she did.

Although I did continue to be inspired by porn videos, my love making did develop some finesse with time. I had gotten over the "woman is piece of meat" obsession to take it gently initially for my partner to climax before beginning the countdown to ejaculation. "Should I?" I would ask Lata sometime into our love making. She would ask me to wait or say "Ok, make it hard now."

Earlier, I would get into the final "rapid" mode instantly oblivious of the partner's situation. I realized sex was not a hundred metre dash but a longer race that both parties needed to enjoy and feel fulfilled.

However, I never appreciated the elaborate oral sequences in porn movies. I was unable to probe excretory and menstrual areas with my mouth.

I don't expect or pressure any of my partners to go down either, though there have been exceptions. Some females like to do the guy. I don't have any problems with that, but cannot reciprocate the kind gesture.

Still, some habits die hard. I tried several porn positions with Lata, including one on the computer chair with wheels, used by her father in the daytime. She held the armrests with both hands while her body was swung around, tummy pushed against the back rest. Her bums faced me standing upright behind the chair that rolled around the room, while I held onto her thighs with both my hands.

These circus-like attempts at sex were mostly unsuccessful. Ecstasy was attained via regular missionary, doggie or woman on top positions on the sofa, study or conference table. "I wish you would stop being funny and keep it simple," Lata told me often while also constantly updating me about the value of my plots as informed by her father. His staff maintained detailed graphs and charts about real estate price trends prominently displayed on the office notice boards.

"Love and lust go together. If I did not lust you, you will think I do not love you," I told her, ignoring her pleas for normal sex.

The blue-movies exposure was useful on one count. My initiation about sex was courtesy such films. Our father did not sit us down one evening to explain that it was not the fairy that brought us home but our mom and he making out.

I never used contraceptives. That's the way porn stars do it. I tried condoms a few times purchasing the prominently displayed Kamasutra brands with bold Pooja Bedi packaging sold at chemists, but never liked the reduced feeling.

Prostitutes, susceptible to disease, were thus ruled out as bed mates, while I needed to be careful about pulling out at the right time. I immodestly admit I have never spilled at the wrong time, except when my wife asked me to.

Someone told me women with broad hips do better in bed and later as kid bearing wives. Examples of such forms are easily visible at Khajuraho, *Kamasutra* coffee table books, or the South Indian temple architectures.

I hardly gave such thesis any importance even though Lata's hips were narrow by traditional standards. In my opinion if the woman has feelings for you, the love making can only be ecstatic. They know how to make their man slide into them deep. During initial stages of a relationship it is men that usually make physical overtures while the women are hesitant to let go.

However, with time the woman slips into a comfort zone with her man. It is she who wants physical intimacy more than the guy who loses steam and sometimes interest with the chase over.

The charm further dwindles as the guy has to attend to mundane matters of keeping her happy, dealing with mood swings, purchasing truckloads of flowers, promising marriage, getting along with her family, being on friendly terms with her pet dog and earning money. Given such circumstances, the mojo can fizzle out a bit. This can lead to double existence for guys who score easily with women.

I wrote this piece about banning of pornography in India:

India's Supreme Court is deliberating banning Internet pornography. The trigger has been the brutal sexual and physical assault on a 5-year old girl in Delhi by two perverts, allegedly after drinking alcohol and watching porn.

Interestingly there is no call to ban sale of alcohol, which is a much greater social evil due to direct linkages with domestic violence, attacks on women, road accidents, brawls and more.

Will perverts, psychopaths, abnormal creatures stop raping and killing girls once access to porn is snapped, if that is technically possible?

The connection, in my view, is simplistic. For the mentally deranged, violent triggers can be anything – billboards, short skirts, TV ads, jeans, movies. Do we stop living due to the perverts in our midst?

Assault on fairer sex is a deeper social problem linked to education, upbringing, unchecked consumerism, objectification of women, patriarchal mind-sets and scant respect of laws.

It is not going to disappear in a hurry and needs to be tackled the right way at multiple levels. If there has to be a shutdown, then ban sale of alcohol and cigarettes, castrate policemen who don't register a rape case or hang politicians who loot tax payers' money. What about violence in movies?

The impact of porn on the human mind has been blown out of proportion. Perfectly normal people can watch porn with no side effects, while completely abnormal people can have no access to porn and be a nuisance to society. At the same time, perfectly normal people could get drunk, crash their cars and cost lives. Perfectly normal people can smoke and die of lung cancer.

An absolute ban on online porn does not sound all right, as consensual sex is not unnatural human behaviour to begin with. Curbing individual spirit and natural feelings does not work in India, elsewhere or any sphere of life.

We saw it with the erstwhile license permit raj that created India's black and hawala economy. Will it work if Chris Gayle is asked to score a century off singles or Virender Sehwag is told to cut out the lofted square cut?

Banning porn will simply drive the industry underground, as it used to be earlier, to seedy parlours and illegal DVDs that nobody can control. The desperate online search for Sunny Leone will translate into brisk sale of offline hard copies.

A healthy interest in sex is not bad. Watching porn for entertainment is not bad, even if it involves two or more people steroid or silicon induced to turn private portions to resemble enlarged genetically modified vegetable or poultry.

Porn can be therapeutic, especially during a lonely spell in the day or night, if one can ignore the steroid bit and focus on the silicon bit, assuming that it is men who are the largest consumers of porn as multiple studies prove.

The bigger question is about regulation of porn. That is required, like censorship in movies. Access to porn by children needs to be strictly monitored by parents and schools. There are aspects about child porn, bestiality and subjugation that cannot be tolerated and must be weeded out, the perpetrators caught and severely punished. The Taliban have got everything wrong except summary treatment of those accused of sexual crimes on women and children.

It is necessary to form a group of independently appointed evolved people to decide what is right, wrong, permitted or should be banned online, like the Censor Board for movies. Obsolete characters that link misbehaviour with women to consuming noodles and suggestive looks need to be strictly kept out of such a panel.

Ideally they should be doomed to a life of abstinence from here on, with no access to even porn. Decisions on publicly consumed content also cannot be left to the whims of over-stretched, desensitized, easily corruptible beat constables, as demonstrated by the case of the arrest of two girls in Mumbai for innocuous comments on Facebook.

Statutes to deter rape can always be strengthened further. While there are those who seek hanging and public flogging, I suggest that parents be culpable for such crimes committed by those under 25. They need to be responsible for the demons that have created. Make the parents also accountable for related crimes linked to alcohol abuse and driving crashes due to over speeding.

Delhi's Police Commissioner said he would resign a thousand times if rapes don't happen by his quitting. I say he should be made to resign a million times for having personnel under him who tried to shoo away the poor 5-year old's parents when they went to report the crime. Only when the chief is directly responsible for the behaviour of his staff, will the working of our security forces improve.

This should apply to other departments and private sector. There should be a culture of accountability, not hiding behind Z plus security, bodyguards and red beacon cars.

NINE

The Overlap

There was a period that my relationship with Pooja and Lata naturally overlapped. Sushmita had inducted me to her theory of compartments though the concepts were still a bit hazy in my mind. Yet, complications linked to two wives or girlfriends did not stress me out or trouble me much.

I prepared myself, researching the subject probably with more interest than preparing for the IAS exam. I procured, borrowed, Xeroxed literature on polygamy, monogamy, divorce, extra-marital, two timing from the British Council Library. I knew about the second marriage of actor Dharmendra to Hema Malini, cricketer Azharuddin to model Sangeeta Bijlani.

Luckily, at that time I was reading existential and similar philosophy that I interpreted as living the moment, optimizing immediate short-term experiences rather than worrying about longer-term aspects of life and living.

I don't know whether I understood the concepts of Hinduism or Buddhism, but I sort of mixed up *Maya*, momentary existence, cause and effect principles to be in a steady mental state and importantly sexual high. This reasoning gelled well with the situation I was facing. It was important that I did not delve too much into my double existence, to try and form a higher meaning.

That was needed. I defined my life to be a stream of multiple experiences with two successful desirable women that could not continue for long. It had to snap somewhere. At the same time, making love to two women on the same day is interesting. No number of theories can make up for such a practical pleasurable experience. I needed to be very careful not to mix up names during love making, as unfailingly happens in movies. It can happen in real life too, surely leading to disastrous results. My twin relationships transpired over a year.

During weekends Pooja would catch an overnight train from Patna to Delhi. She stayed at Bihar Bhavan, not her own house in North Delhi, so I could visit her without feeling constrained in the presence of her family.

Rooms were available unless occupied by the chief minister's big family, loud obsequious cronies and accompanying officials. Pooja was no longer comfortable moving about in DTC buses. She was an officer. A dedicated Bihar government car fitted with a red light was usually at her disposal.

When the CM was around, we used autos. We took long walks in Nehru Park or Lodhi Gardens. I liked to pin her against a tree or rock face at Nehru Park for a kiss. I was bolder at the Lodhi Garden monuments providing fulsome free entertainment to the many severely frustrated males that slyly observe lovers at such locations to avoid spending on porn videos.

"We need to be careful. It will be embarrassing to be caught by the police. I am an IAS officer. It will be a scandal," Pooja would say after kissing back, which is a completely different experience from the occasion when a partner does not reciprocate. It is important for any couple to be involved with each other beyond just the physical to enjoy sustained intimacy. I hardly listened to her.

"Don't tell them you are an officer. I will tell them my father is in the police. That will be enough." "Okay," she would say, even as I continued to ravish her. At Pooja's insistence, I visited Chhapra to stay with her at the gleaming white official bungalow that stood out like a palace in the area. Even junior most IAS officers can boast good perks and living conditions due to the elite service they belong.

I took leave from work lying to Lata that I was off to my village to manage the agriculture produce. Unlike Pooja, who liked to interact with my mother and father to discuss ways to improve my personality, Lata kept our private matters to herself maintaining a deliberate distance. As our parents knew each other, she probably did not want family involvement at that stage of our relationship.

Luckily, the cell phone industry was at infancy in India at that time. Women in love can be quite obsessive about calling every two minutes 24 X 7. It would have been difficult for me to take Lata's call with Pooja in the vicinity or vice versa. I did not own or could afford a mobile phone unlike Lata, given her affluence. She kept it switched off, most of the time, unless she really needed it. Handsets were expensive and incoming calls were charged.

Pooja told me there were moves by the government to permit free mobile phones to officers for better co-ordination in administration, but that was still to happen. The ability to be in touch with a person whenever was limited when I was seeing both Pooja and Lata, which suited me fine.

Today the telecom revolution has everybody in its fold. It has created a nation of poor and rich alike forever engrossed in texting or conversation due to cheap call rates, throwaway handset prices courtesy China's low priced and exploited labour.

In Bihar, Pooja sent over her official red beaconed white ambassador to pick me up at the Patna Railway Station, where the train tracks are a regular shitting area for the local population. Rail drivers know from past practise to slow down and blow the horn. Sometimes, they shout, spewing abuses, at the blockage ahead by leaning out of the window, to clear the path for their far away destinations.

With experience the occupiers of the tracks wait till the last moment when the engine is almost onto them. Then they hop off, mouthing expletives and pointing an abusive middle finger at the driver, then the passengers in the coaches. It is never comfortable to be disturbed midway doing potty.

The shitters stand shamelessly naked with their fronts or unclean backsides visible, leaving a not very healthy image of Bihar to those inside the train. It is best not to be having a meal while crossing Patna by rail.

The crappers get back to their routine uttering more curses once the train has passed, irritated by the intrusion. At the Patna Railway platform, Pooja's driver and armed bodyguard saluted me as if I was the chief minister of the state.

Thinking I was somebody important, a small crowd of beggars, hangers on and passengers whose trains were indefinitely delayed, followed me to the car.

I waved and smiled at them as we left the station feeling like a minor TV star whose serials are obsessively watched in far-flung locations nobody has heard about. The drive to Chhapra from Patna was dusty, uneventful and back breaking due to extremely poor road conditions. It was a mistake not to wear my tight gym underwear to prevent injury as my balls perpetually bounced around my navel area.

It soon became evident why cheap labour, including rickshaw pullers, coolies and security guards, anywhere in India originates from Bihar. The extent of poverty is pitiful. Cities such as Mumbai or Delhi do not seem to belong to the same country, just like New York, London or Singapore, are in a different league of development.

Pooja had taken the day off to pamper me. She personally prepared my favourite dishes -- butter chicken, fried fish, mushroom *matar*, *jeera* rice, salads and cut fruit in cream. She scrubbed the dirt off me in the bath, undressed to join me in the shower. She ordered the servants to leave the house.

"I really miss you," she kept whispering into my ears. Naturally, we made love. Thankfully, the balls seemed to have survived the jarring journey.

A lot of Indian women can spoil their man. They take pleasure in developing expertise in food and sex that guys love the most. The trait is inherited from mothers who dedicate their lives to their fathers and later kids.

Unless the moms change the daughters won't. Guys obviously need not be hassled if the transformation does not happen. Still, in today's context, it is never easy to know beforehand which way one's woman is going to turn out.

There are the toned bodies addicted to massage and cardio routine social butterflies or the husband is god variety. Some are ambitious initially and then lose it, while others could get even more career oriented than one might have bargained; some begin by showering a lot of attention, but change later.

Many modern-day housewives are not the way our mothers were. They don't wait on their husbands in the evenings. That is handled by servants while madam drives about town indulging in multiple activities, including kitty parties, gyms and spa time with chosen favourite masseurs, including sweet-talking males.

If the spouse is working late they party out; many travel and holiday alone or with friends if hubby is too busy. An affair or two on the side is no big deal.

Guys are simpler to define – they are usually a combination of booze, sex, money, career and food. A new category, however, is mushrooming -- those who don't mind women wearing the pants and take over the earning.

The working woman also naturally worries about the upkeep of the house and children's home work later. Life cannot be too bad for sit-at-home males with plenty of leisure time while money matters are taken care of.

In my opinion, it is best to experience a woman as she reveals herself. Pooja was more the old-world genre the way my mother was. I did not mind the mollycoddling. Who would? Plus she was in the IAS that made the love making infinitely more pleasurable.

I spent my time in Chhapra watching Harrison Ford movies on VCD (even pirated DVD's were too expensive at that time), episodes of MASH, or reading Jeffery Archer in the daytime while Pooja was away at work.

I joined a group of youngsters playing soccer at a local school ground nearby that was bare due to absence of grass, but skirted by trees that was ideal for a run or walk in the unpolluted evening air with Def Leppard, Queen, Brian Adams, Jim Morrison or Pink Floyd blaring on my Walkman for company.

I-Pods had not been invented yet. Steve Jobs was still to happen and unfortunately die of cancer. Pooja's official residence was comfortable despite being a government accommodation that can often be badly maintained. According to an orderly attached to the household, the previous incumbent spent a bit of tax payers' money to do up the place. This was to impress his bored city-bred pretty young wife suffused with some attitude.

The orderly told me "madam" roamed around the house and Chhapra in shorts and thigh-length skirts, attracting a bit of attention in the local vernacular press due to her bold appearances in a conservative set up. A couple of editorials derided her bad influence on other young school and college girls in the area who were also sighted in minis, showing plenty of skin that was driving men crazy.

"The chief minister made many official visits to Chhapra when madam was here. Everybody knew he was enamoured by her," the servant told me. I was not sure whether the head of government visited her when her hubby was away on important assignment cleverly designated by his boss. That would be a delicious scandal that happens all the time.

I think the lady in question could have been better off married to a MBA, MNC dude like my brother posted in a big city like Singapore or London or even Gurgaon. She could spend her time at malls, spas, gyms while the husband slogged to maintain her upkeep. In the evenings the duo could party, get drunk and make love. If the hubby got too busy she could always rely on her group of friends, male or female for company, like Sushmita.

I got the ready to please me orderly to massage my body, especially the lower back, thighs and buttocks that were being put to a lot of use at night with Pooja.

"Young boys on motorcycles would follow the official car hoping that madam would step out flashing her very sexy legs including her panties," the factotum, who was clearly trying to be extra friendly to win favours and rewards from Pooja by pleasing me, whispered while pressing my shoulders.

Soon I formed an obscenity brotherhood with the servant that was useful. I asked him about the local porn VCD market. In no time, he plied me with many blue movie videos smuggled from Nepal, starring Americans, Germans and Russians.

I specifically told him that I would pay nothing to watch Nepali maids making out with skinny famished Nepali boys with penis like pencils that barely sustained while the extremely dissatisfied women almost slumbered during the process.

I think I was charged more than market price, but did not mind. The videos were still way cheaper than in Delhi and got me sufficiently horny for the evening action. I tried to put in a good word about my porn movie supplier-cum-masseur to Pooja. She told me she never liked him. "He has dirty eyes," she said. I ignored the comment. I did not want to ruin the good time I was having by persisting with his case and putting Pooja in a bad mood.

Some of my time at Chhapra was spent soaking inside the large ivory coloured bathtub with bubble facility installed by previous occupiers of the house that could have easily fitted with the ambience of a Maharaja Suite at a super luxury hotel. I imagined "madam" using the tub while her husband was away on work.

The warm water was soothing. My bums and her thighs probably settled at the same locations. I read, listened to music, and dozed off following a big meal of river fish or jungle fowl imbued with natural juices and flavours.

These can never be found in the farm produced variety sold in cities, high-end restaurants, abroad and star hotels. I tried to make love to Pooja in the tub, though this is not very easy, despite millions of porn skits in such a situation. It is slippery and dangerous.

Although Pooja's household staff included a full-time cook, apart from guards, gardeners and orderlies, I discovered a couple of good fresh fish and chicken eating joints for lunch usually brimming with Bihari families out to have a good time. Butter chicken anywhere is popular, with rich and poor congregating for the same experience.

Small town India, especially in the North, is the same everywhere – narrow broken lanes, little shops, overflowing gutters, stink, blue State Bank of India hoardings, abundance of rickshaws and cycles, piss and spit splattered everywhere, women in shiny saris and naked impoverished kids with noses running scampering about. Nothing much has changed even today, except a few additional signboards of telecom companies such as Vodafone or Airtel as the only sign of development.

In the evening Pooja personally cooked my favourite non-vegetarian dishes including fresh-river prawns she picked herself on the way back from office. Intermittently she massaged my head using a concoction of special locally made oils, while I chilled over some wine or beer.

Fully relaxed after the afternoon tub bath and body kneading by the servant during the day, we made love through the night. I don't know how Pooja managed to stay awake or alert in office the next day. I slept late while she slipped off to work without disturbing me.

She tried to convince me to get married to her. I told her I needed some more time as I did not feel settled in my career. Pooja was prepared to come to terms with my failure, disinterest, and inability to make it to the IAS. She told me she was happy I was working hard at my newspaper job even if it was low paying. "I am sure you will make something big out of it," she said. Like my father, she did not attach any value to my plots. "Career is much more important," she said.

Indian women or maybe others too when in love are prepared to accept anything of their boyfriends and future husbands. I could have been a security guard Pooja would still have married me.

Unfortunately, by now I was deep into my relationship with Lata. If she had not been in the picture I think I might have said 'yes' to Pooja. There were some piquant times in Delhi when I commuted to work, met Pooja and then Lata.

Youth is about levels of physical and sexual energy never the same with age. I ensured Pooja and Lata did not know about each other's intimate existence in my life. A woman can hate a man infinitely more if there is another woman involved. This I figured out without any reading or research. That is why married men involved in affairs are always vulnerable to vicious physical, emotional and financial attacks. The girlfriend always knows about the wife.

It would have been more complicated had I wanted to be with both Lata and Pooja. Or, I was married and either of the girls was not. There are innumerable stories of married men messing up their personal lives. The wife can sue the husband for adultery should he try to walk away from the marriage. The girlfriend can accuse the lover of rape should he chose to stay wedded. Either way the guy is fucked and destined for some time in jail or huge monetary loss or both.

Such a man is also an ideal candidate that hyenas among cops and lawyers look to fleece and milk to build their own mansions and educate their children abroad. To put it a bit crudely, a few extra dips of the "dick" does cost dearly -- the wife, girlfriend and system have the guy by the "balls".

There could be children to be raised as balanced individuals. The needs of modern-day kids are beyond the financial. They grow up on concepts of sensitivity, emotional support, caring and conversation with parents to share adolescence issues, including the lure of drugs, drinking, porn and sex.

For younger kids, there is mandatory fun time at the three Ms -- mall, multiplex and McDonald's interspersed by annual overseas and domestic vacations to Disneyland, Orlando, Honk Kong and other amusement parks. This is not how it was when I and Sid were growing up. We would be caned by the teacher or beaten up by a parent for any mistake.

Today, such events are a scandal though I agree corporeal violence should be illegal and abolished as such forms of discipline can cause lasting physical or psychological harm. Still, I hardly remember chatting with my father as a kid. Fun time was when he was away. We were too scared to be in his presence. All messages, if at all, to him were conveyed via our mom.

The only face to face was when exam results were announced -- we were either admonished for bad marks or he grinned for once if we did well. Our father smiling at us was the biggest prize, not McDonald's burgers. Sid was the recipient of many such awards. I think I managed one or two in many years.

Getting back to my two women situation, sadly my time with Pooja was up. She said there was pressure from her family to get hitched.

She acceded to her father's repeated requests to meet potential grooms. I don't think he was happy with her choice of me, in any case. She called to say she liked a colleague from the Bihar cadre. They had decided to get married. I could barely say 'ok' on the phone when she hung up.

Either she was angry or emotional, but she had moved on for sure which was the right thing to do. I searched her new guy on the Internet. He was not a great looker, but must have made his family, village or town that he belonged infinitely proud of his IAS *Bharat Ratna* achievement.

His folks must have paraded him around streets on a donkey or horse to celebrate the success. They would expect him to return the happiness favour by ensuring his brethren government contracts, ration cards, driving license, passport, water supply and electricity in the village.

My life could have gone either way. I could have married Pooja or Lata. I was okay marrying both, as long as everybody was earning well, responsibilities were dispersed, sex and food was good, the kids were taken care of sensitively and most importantly both the women were happy. Unfortunately, this can only be wishful thinking as I am no Dharmendra, equally hunky, rich, good looking and successful. I believe my hero Aamir Khan also manages both his current and ex-wife well.

TEN

Marriage Pressure

It is never an easy process to get hitched. Men and women can be choosy about a life partner. Every Indian parent passionately collects CVs of potential brides and grooms to explore the arranged marriage option. I was born under a set of planetary configurations that turned my girlfriends into wedding mode with me.

Women are genetically trained to be futuristic – they subconsciously check out the man's potential as a good father, his emotional stability, good hygiene, financial security and protector from the big bad world. He has to be tall and strong, preferably endowed with gym honed biceps, shoulders and triceps.

He has to be loyal, excite her in bed, explore the right zones, not necessarily with his hands, take her to exotic holiday hotspots, make her laugh as sense of humour counts. The man has to be sensitive about buying flowers and perfumes and get along with the girl's family, including pets.

If the girl is not a dog lover while the guy owns one, the poor doggie's future suddenly becomes very uncertain. Many are bumped off to a relative's place or left for adoption at dog homes. Some are abandoned at far-flung areas as street dogs. Unable to fend for themselves given their pampered existences, many die.

In the current ambition-driven independent working-woman scenario, the man has to know how to change nappies, teach, write out homework on behalf of the kids, bottle feed the baby and clean potty. These are aspects my father never pondered about as they were the exclusive domain of my mother.

Young men today are burdened by multiple performance pressures to call a woman their own. India's declining sex ratio does not make the process easy. In a way, the men have brought it onto themselves.

The difficult permutations have borne the metrosexual man personified by celebrities such as footballer David Beckham who doesn't think twice about riding pillion to wife Victoria. I can never imagine my father riding a bike with my mother on the driver's seat. Beckham shifts continents, Europe to USA or vice versa, to enrol in soccer clubs depending on Victoria's fashion business and socialising interests.

Some men find solace in male company and alcohol. A rising number develop deeper emotional bonds with same sex partners that are legally recognized in many countries. There is emphasis on the sexual aspect of homosexual relationships that ignores the emotional side of companionship and realistic expectations. Thankfully, my inclination so far has been for the opposite sex.

Thoughts of marriage, seriously thinking about a future together can diminish sex drive. There was a time I made out with Lata three times in an afternoon, during the weekend at her father's office, over beer, movies and chicken rolls. The zeal dipped as I could sense her wish for wedlock, an event that was not very palatable to me, but looked inescapable at the same time.

I was wary about the inevitability of marriage. I was inclined to stray, given deep attraction and time spent with Sushmita. We were not in a relationship but I knew that I would not be able to say 'no', if she decided to take matters between us to another level. It was up to her.

I was open to the idea. This was not a healthy sign for anybody contemplating lifelong commitment, sacrifice and acceptance of every idiosyncrasy of the partner such as my father freely farting in the presence of my mother.

She never complained despite the obvious stink. I think she felt good that my father could do as he pleased in her presence. I still controlled my farts with Lata lest she construe them insulting.

I was not comfortable with the idea of letting myself go. I never like to persist in a conflict and consequent stress causing situation for too long. Earlier in my life I had decided that the IAS was not for me. And, that is how it remained despite immense pressure from my father.

If a scenario arose that I had to see two women at the same time, I was confident of arriving at a steady mental state in some time. Given my readings of Philosophy I felt I could deal with aspects of morality and integrity as per my convenience.

Still, such overconfidence could boomerang as logistics of handling simultaneous relationships was different and difficult now due to arrival of ubiquitous mobile phones that allow anytime time access to anybody.

I was apprehensive about new technology and apps that could track a person's physical movements such as unzipping that could set off an alarm ``pants down, check if target in loo or otherwise via Skype.''

Suspicious spouses would be a big market for such gadgets. Also, e-mails, texts, social networking websites can be giveaways, even if one is very careful about leaving no e-prints. Technology has an in-built anti-cheating code that is never easy to circumvent.

Lata was sexy, fair and attractive. She attracted attention anywhere. Her family and social background matched mine. The vibes between her and me were good. We were conscious of our looks, liked to hit the gym, cycle or run to keep fit. Swimming was a common passion in summer.

I never understood Pooja's thesis of neglecting fitness to make it into the IAS. Her burn factor – "I need to make it at any cost" – ran much deeper than mine. Lata too wanted to do well, but she did not try to determine my career. She believed I had already made some progress due to my plots. She was a more secure person due to the money her father earned and bequeathed. With time, I could sense that Lata, like Pooja, had made up her mind to take our relationship to the next level.

Unlike my situation with Pooja, I went with the flow to let life take its course despite the confusion, debates, apprehensions and misgivings in my muddled mind.

I was more settled in my career with my by-lines a common feature, though my income level was worrisome. I still used a two wheeler while my credit card was the lowest category. My assessment was Pooja loved me the way I was, while Lata loved me for the way I was, plus the high value plots.

"Your plots are zooming. Your net worth is high though you still ride a scooter. You could easily afford a SUV with plenty to spare," Lata would say.

"I am happy the way I am. I want to make money the real way, not via some speculative short cut," I said. Some of my father's character and genes were ingrained in me forever, surfacing at various junctions of my life.

Lata changed with thoughts of marriage. She was not too concerned about my diminishing desire for sex directly linked to our rising frequency of marriage discussions. Her focus turned to my commitment towards long-term health essential, in her view, to nurture and raise our to-be-born kids, considerations that never occurred to me at that stage of my life. She vehemently objected to my passion for food, especially the cheap street side steamed *momos*, chicken roll, *doner*, *tundai*, *galauti*, *kakori* kebabs and *biryani* cooked in high cholesterol trans-fat oil with potential to explode the heart like a Diwali cracker.

I gobbled the fat-infused delicacies at malls, restaurants, Sarojini Nagar, Lajpat Nagar, Chanakyapuri, Chandni Chowk and Kamla Nagar. I have never liked the vegetarian fare such as *tikki* and *chaat* that many prefer. Since healthy logic did not work, Lata used multiple stratagems reserved in a woman's arsenal to make me promise to her that I would stop consuming the street food that I loved forever.

To-be wives have a way of extracting promises out of future husbands that makes the entire exercise absurd as the pledges are bound to be regularly broken on the sly. "You know I am your friend for life. I have to think about your old age," she sobbed with tears running down her lovely pink cheeks.

"Don't worry I burn it off. The day I stop running I will stop eating," I tried to assuage her, wiping her tears with her handkerchief, as I never carried one. I wondered which scenario was worse -- Pooja urging me to become fat or Lata's teary blackmails that I stop eating what I liked.

Not one to give up easily, Lata plied me with articles that expounded the virtues of vegetarianism. She handed me literature about poultry caged, artificially fed in sub-human conditions and savagely killed with bare hands by twisting their neck.

She downloaded gory videos of lambs, chicken and pigs slaughtered in China in sub-animal conditions. She sniffed me closely to smell meat. She told me if I gave up my unhealthy food habits I would regain my libido as I would focus on sex instead of food. "Food and sex have the same effect on you. You become satiated. There is an unmistakable shine and satisfaction from both. If you give up non-veg you will want to have more sex that I don't mind. It is good for health."

"That is not good logic. Ideally, I should want both."

"I want you to turn vegetarian," she declared one day.

"Cows are fat and vegetarian. Tigers are muscular and carnivorous," I said.

"They put dog meat in the *momo*s. I got to know this from my family."

"If that was so, there would not be so many street dogs roaming around in Delhi," I shot her down. "They use cow meat," she said another time.

"Then there wouldn't be such a huge cattle presence on the road," I replied.

"The chicken roll has too much oil and cholesterol. The cooking is with sewage water. You are mistaking harmful stuff for good taste," she complained incessantly. She was really wearing me down. I wondered if such whining could get worse after marriage on subjects that I took for granted such as porn.

Lata's arguments did have merit, but, like it is with smokers, it was not easy to give up on a routine that had taken root, despite obvious harmful effects. Soon, I figured the cause of Lata's new food fads. It was linked to the way her family was, especially her *lauki* (bottle gourd) obsessed father involved in a life long struggle against gas that refused to empty out of his tummy despite rigorous efforts. Maybe he needed to turn non-veg (more about my future father-in-law later).

Still, like a devoted lover Lata accompanied me to many evenings spent gorging divine non-veg street food riding pillion on my scooter, Maruti 800, her father's Esteem, the high on status luxury car before the Honda, Ford and Hyundai versions were launched in India, followed by Audi and BMW.

The surroundings and ambience of roadside eateries and *dhaba*s were not much to write about given traffic fumes, dust, open and leaking gutters, muscular street dogs eyeing customers to quickly finish off and toss the leftovers.

Yet, the victuals on offer were a gastronomic delight. The chutney, gravy, onions, chicken *biryani*, mutton *korma* or *galauti* kebabs formed a mouth-watering epicurean concoction that gurgled gastric juices and aroused the palate the way no home cuisine could. The feeling approximated sexual ecstasy. I wrote this piece about my visit to the Rajinder Da Dhaba with Lata:

In India there are every kind of restaurants. McDonald's has taken root, so have hookah lounges and cafes, but none beats the dhaba experience, though there can be limits to taking a girl out to one.

For some years I lived at Chanakyapuri, which adjoins the diplomatic area of New Delhi and the residence of the Prime Minister at Race Course Road. Denizens of these localities cannot be blamed for thinking that Delhi is all about broad roads, beautiful landscaping, organized drainage, no power cuts, ample water supply and tall green well-protected and watered trees.

Daily existence is exactly the opposite in a locality such as West Delhi, with extremely high population densities. In Gurgaon, it is only the fortressed high rise complexes that can compare to the elite New Delhi way of life.

Anyway, tucked a couple of kilometres away from the high-security always on security alert Chanakyapuri area was a popular dhaba called the Rajinder Da Dhaba (RD from here on), the da in the dhaba a derivation from the local dialect Punjabi, meaning that the dhaba belongs to Rajinder.

The place was run by Rajinder's two ample sons, their dimensions by way of the enormous amounts of free chicken curry they consumed during their formative years, courtesy their father's line of business.

Dhabas such as these number several thousand across India, along highways, hill stations, in little crooks and crannies of big cities, towns and metros as they do not take up much space. They are usually located at illegally occupied public property, but provide very good returns given the minimal investment of bribing the lower level bureaucracy.

The beat cops and municipal authorities have to be kept oiled and happy by the owners, but they can come cheap. Sometimes, even a meal a day for the official and family suffices. Anything goes for dhaba chicken curry.

Traditionally, the dhabas are meant for tired truck drivers looking for a break from their long journeys, alongside highways. They offer value for money food, music and an open-air television played at full volume for everybody to hear over the buzz of the traffic and other sounds.

The customers can also rest on charpoys which are wooden structures that support knitted jute strings which is a tad uncomfortable bed, but the best ventilation with the high summer temperatures and erratic power.

Some of the popular Highway dhabas provide girls for a price who sing, dance and offer their bodies to pleasure the tired truck drivers. Prostitution is illegal in India, but still a flourishing trade. The authorities are not interested in rooting out the problem due to the extra money that can be made on the side. Making prostitution legal is a political hot potato.

Dhabas, however, have also defined themselves by the great food -- any Viagra talk pales in comparison to the ultimate turn on, a blob of chicken leg in a bowl of masala curry and mustard oil, tandoori rotis, a preparation of wheat resembling pancakes placed on a sheet of dated newspapers, onions sprinkled with pungent syrup and hot mint chutney -- most of the ingredients on offer fall in the category of recipe of disaster defined by new-age health gurus, causing innumerable lifestyle diseases that can range from heart failure to diabetes and hypertension.

But, if one is at a stage of life when taste scores over health, then dhaba food makes perfect sense. The government of Punjab, one of the wealthier states of India, lists Dhabas as an attraction worth a try by tourists with the warning that many a foreign visitor has gone away clutching his/her stomach, given the heavy dose of masala and mustard oil. So, one has to get used to it a little, before gorging on it.

The dhaba offering is, in my opinion, the true Indian curry. Also no social barriers matter here as, like cell phones, the menu here can be afforded by both the rich and poor.

The crowd at Chanakyapuri, where I lived, despite backgrounds where hygiene is an important consideration, was regular to RD for years. I don't form a general opinion based on a single episode, but the advice is that a dhaba is not the best place to date. At the very outset, Lata found the atmosphere a bit overwhelming.

She, if I may take the liberty to say so, belongs to the classes not the masses.

To begin with, a comment on the ambience of RD, like most others, include buzzing flies, grime, overgrown dogs and fumes as the place is located by the side of a very busy road. Most vehicles in Delhi are high on emission and exhaust though granted pollution under control certificates by authorized agents that tamper with their systems for a little extra cash.

The eating area is limited to a few wrought iron rusted tables, fixed to the ground to prevent people from hitting each other. The rest is open sky and the charred interiors of the tandoor, a huge clay stove filled with charcoal to roast the meat or prepare the rotis.

I loved to eat at dhabas, but Lata obviously had finer tastes.

When we arrived at RD, everybody stared at her, as they would an alien descended from a UFO. There were a couple of sari-clad women present, perhaps wives of labourers from a construction site in the vicinity, but it is a tradition in dhabas to stare at anything that arrives in a short-skirt. It is allowed.

A guy farted loud, just after finishing his meal.

I heard her say "Oh god" under her breath.

"Should we leave?" she asked.

"Just taste the food, taste the food and see for yourself, forget about anything else," I insisted.

RD, like any other evening, was bustling with customers, some old timers some new. So was the no-holds barred passion of gorging chicken.

Opel Astras and scooters, Cielos and motorcycles, truck drivers, bureaucrats and Indian diplomats, daily wage labourers and businessmen jostled for the limited space to wend their way for their piece of chicken leg or breast at Rs 25 a plate, delivered in steel saucers, the price the same for years, despite double digit inflation.

There are no etiquettes, it is an unlimited use of fingers and palms, no spoons, one is only expected to burp loud, an indication that draw the stray dogs who expect you to leave, depositing the remnants with them.

Sleeves rolled, noses running, heads bent, fingers dipped in gravy, well-heeled gentlemen stood alongside others wearing almost nothing. The burps formed a long spray of fog that hung in the air for a while as it was winter; some washed up at a running tap in a corner, others wiped their hands on their pants and left, to chauffeur driven Cielos or the bus stop.

We chose a relatively empty table. I could almost witness images of an up market, air-conditioned, liveried in white waiters' restaurant crossing Lata's brain, even as her expression changed from bad to worse.

I went off to fetch a plate of my favourite chicken curry as she reluctantly agreed to partake a couple of bites only and leaving immediately. From the short distance I watched a burly man built like a tank settle his plate next to her and proceed to devour feverishly.

The chicken was scoured to the minimum, lips gnarled in every direction, the bones cracked open and marrow licked clean. Even hungry hyenas in National Geographic in a drought situation couldn't be as intense as this guy.

To add to woes, the man was a sadist. He seemed a regular and guessed that my girl was in some discomfort. Observing her, he began a loud conversation, with nobody in particular but everybody around, who seemed to be familiar with his presence.

Laden with Hindi expletives which usually sound more obscene than their English counterparts, he talked of a fight a couple of days back that engulfed the dhaba. It started from the serving area when someone from one group spilled on someone from another group. Both the groups threw their curry at each other, scalding skins. The man pointed at the ground that still carried stains of the previous day -- blood and curry.

"One person lost his eye," he said adding that hangers-on and onlookers tried to intervene which led to both the groups pouncing on everyone, using their fists, plates and car accessories, such as tyre jacks, even as the food spluttered. The staff watched from the side-lines, waiting for the brouhaha, a common occurrence, to end, to carry on with their business.

The man had begun to speak in more graphic details about the brawl, when I returned with the chicken. Lata told me she was about to faint before she almost did, clutching my arm spilling curry on the ground and my pullover. "Water, water." I looked around to offer her a few sips.

Somebody brought a bucket of water and threatened to pour it on her. I managed to push him away. It was cold. Lata's eyes opened wide for an instant, emanating one final cry of desperation before she seemed to pass out for good. I held her while a crowd gathered, forming a circle around us, some holding pieces of tandoori chicken, as if they were watching a film shoot in progress.

"Make her smell a shoe, a shoe," one of the labourer women insisted. A man in rags and equally dirty shoes threatened to take them off.

In times of crisis, Indians response is usually exemplary. For example, following train crashes that are a common occurrence across the country, it is the local villagers that usually launch the rescue acts during the crucial initial period, while the authorities try to figure out their plan of action at some district headquarters.

In the case of the unclean shoe being offered to Lata, I, however, thought it prudent to refuse. "She will be fine." I stopped the well-meaning man who was willing to be bare feet in the cold.

"Let's get out of here," she murmured, her eyes still closed.

I was relieved that she spoke and tried to calm her by offering Walls choc-in-a-box ice cream that another kind soul handed me as I helped her to the car, like an injured player being taken off the field.

Inside, she opened her eyes in an instant, to launch into a blistering tirade at my hopeless judgment of hanging-around town.

She swore that she would never visit a roadside dhaba. I have never again been to a dhaba on a date, but rest assured I slip in time and again, however busy I might be, to grab hot and spicy chicken with rotis on a worn out newspaper rag.

It's divine.

ELEVEN

Sushmita in My Life

As emphasized earlier, my life was destined to be complicated. I was still seeing my future wife Lata when Sushmita invited me to her swanky apartment for dinner. It was a working day. Her husband was away on tour.

Sushmita lived in the Safdarjung Development Area, owner of the top floor. Her flat approximated the interiors of a luxury hotel, reflecting her husband's hard work --- wide-screen flat TVs in each room, jacuzzi fitted in the bathrooms, Bose speakers, designer furniture, sleek laptops that cost a bomb those days, remote controlled curtains, central air-conditioning. Two big cars with prominent 'Press' stickers that keep the cops at bay were parked outside.

The terrace was converted into a nicely manicured garden that created the effect of a small forest. There were fountains, a little pond and live fish under a netted covering to protect them from birds.

"So, you are the big cat here? This is where you bring all your prey, their final destination before you devour them," I joked.

"This is where I size them up," she laughed and showed me around her house.

Sushmita and her husband were high on disposable income DINK household that abound in India now. Expenditures by such cash rich no kids couples help pubs, restaurants, hospitality and travel sectors achieve revenue targets sustaining livelihoods of diploma-holding broken English-speaking sales boys and girls.

"Are you usually alone when your husband is away?" I asked her.

"I prefer not to," was her cryptic reply, though she quickly added, "my mother and sister stay sometimes. The maid is part-time; I let the driver go unless there is a late night party that I avoid if my husband is not there. I like people coming over."

I wanted to ask about special guests she invited when her hubby was away, but let it be. She would never tell me. I might have irritated her which would have dashed prospects of a pleasant evening ahead. We sat down on the sofa over strong Vodka, orange juice and lime that numbed the brain with the very first sip.

For some time we spoke about national politics. We re-filled our glasses. Sushmita looked extremely attractive, brimming with all that a man can dream about in a woman's body, face, lips and eyes. As happens with anyone in her vicinity, soon, every inch of my being screamed the extreme desire I felt for her.

Each body cell mutated into a producing unit of excessive male hormones that causes a man to lose control with a woman, grab her, pat her backside, kiss her, make a fool of himself, sometimes go to jail for criminal offense. I sensed the twirl of millions of sperms forming around the relevant portion of my body, dying for a release into the world that Sushmita closely belonged. I had to tell her. I needed to express myself or I would have exploded.

As explained earlier, I like to be upfront about my feelings with a girl. There is no point in beating around the bush. Drinking helps. I was unsure about Sushmita's reaction, but I said what I had to say. "I feel chemistry between us. If there was a litmus test like we had during science lab tests in school to ascertain attraction, the colour would be brightly positive, I am sure," I said.

She continued to sip the Vodka, swallowing bigger gulps, even as she eyed me closely. I looked back at her, feeling the tension under my pants the most.

I knew she could be aggressive if she wanted. Still, like earlier with Lata, I did not expect her to be rash, slap me, ask me to get out or call her disinterested husband who would probably advise her to dial 100 for the police while continuing to work on his get ahead in life presentation.

Most normal spouses would question their wives alone at home with a man at night. I was sure Sushmita handled proposals from men often even after marriage. A knee jerk or immature reaction was unlikely. She also knew I was gentlemanly enough to ask her, not jump her. Otherwise she would not have invited me over to her house to lead to the circumstance we were in.

"Positive or negative?" I persisted. I needed to know either way even as the over dose of alcohol and sperm was driving me completely mad.

"I think I feel the chemistry too. The litmus test is positive, nice and bright," she replied, following another big sip of her Vodka. We knew that our relationship was headed to the next level of intimacy. The many thoughts of her in my arms, eyes closed, mouth slightly open, while I made passionate love to her, flashed again and again and again in my subconscious self.

It was Sushmita who moved from her comfortable leather seat, without a squeak as is with expensive furniture. I closely observed every sinew of her lithe, strong and endowed body as she lifted herself and gently sat down on my lap.

Her *pallu* fell on her forearm revealing more of the cleavage than I had ever envisioned. I knew that the piece of cloth shifted position only if she wanted it that way. She controlled the *pallu* completely like a consummate artist.

"You took too long," she said. "You had passed the chemistry test some time back due to the catalysts, your dimples. I have wanted for so long to push you down on the floor and make love to you. If a woman could have it her way with a man, I would do that to you."

In the next instant, I was kissing the woman I thought would never consider me worthwhile, given her rich, famous and powerful suitors. Thankfully, they didn't seem to be any dimpled ones. She pressed and moved her full lips against mine, flipping her tongue in ways that I had never experienced before.

Her eyes were half open in pleasure, also gauging the immense reactions she was having on me. She could sense it for sure. If ever the Bruce Springsteen number 'I am On Fire' applied to anybody, it was me.

Our mouths were soon in perfect dance rhythm, with plenty of saliva exchanged. This may sound a little repulsive when talked or read about, but that's the way soon to copulate couples are, especially in the initial phase of a relationship. Later, I know of lovers who don't kiss but make out, preferring not to mix the two.

Kissing can be more intimate than sex. Bad breath from the sexiest mouths, pouts and lips, can be worse than an unwashed backside. Sex is a separate act involving a different set of stimulated body parts than can be cleaned before and after.

I quickly placed my hands on Sushmita's shapely bums to feel the part of her anatomy that I had fantasized about so often.

I was not sure how long we would continue this way and whether such an occasion would arise again ever. I wanted to maximize my pleasure moments with her as if it was a once in a lifetime opportunity.

Shortly, with one hand on her backside, I placed the other on her breasts, another of her tremendous assets that tortured my mind, body and soul so often. She shifted back a little and unbuttoned her blouse. I knew she was mentally prepared for us to go all the way. I relaxed seeking to soak in each micro second.

The act of a woman taking off her blouse in front of a man is one of the most erotic moments of love making. The few seconds of intense suspense when the bosoms and the silhouetted nipples press tight against the piece of garment that is being unhooked, is breath-taking. The next instant the cloth slides down uncovering and baring the woman's beauty in full for the first time.

Still, the process of disrobing in front of a lover can be matter-of-fact and natural. Yet, if the clothes have to stay on, that's the way they remain.

So many have spent a fortune, lifetime for the naked event to happen with a particular man or woman, but failed. When it does take place, one does not give it a thought moving onto the processes of physical pleasuring.

I disrobed without haste as my feet, pants, belt, underwear, shoes and socks tend to tangle especially if I am desperate to get on. I have yanked out buttons, torn bits of my clothing while undressing. I am mal-adroit at putting clothes back on too, a couple of times unknowingly wearing my partner's spotted underwear. Thankfully my mistake was noticed by my lover.

Sushmita has been my best paramour. She was perfect in bed. She could put any porn diva to shame due to skilful use of her body parts and vibrating tongue like the wings of a butterfly. Her expertise in bed included multiple permutations of her amazing breasts and my most private areas. I am sure the informed reader can guess what I mean. "Do you watch porn movies?" I asked.

"The inventions are mine, patented," she replied, as she moved her sensuous lips all over my body.

Later she said, "I am a *geisha* born to give love."

"You are simply the best in the universe," I told her.

"I have always been the best, though you are quite a stallion yourself," she said.

I don't know whether she used such pleasant terminology for her other lovers, that I am sure existed. She certainly was good for a man's ego and every fantasy.

Her husband should travel less or know he would be substituted, I thought. "What if your husband found out?" I asked her. "He cannot. I love him to death. There is no way I can hurt him or our marriage," she replied calmly, confident.

My private moments with Sushmita turned frequent that allowed me to massage and kiss her beautiful and bare back and breasts for long durations. She initiated our interludes as per her convenience. The intimate sessions were fixed when her husband was not around, which was quite often. As both of us were answerable to our respective partners the sex had to be scheduled.

"Are you free tonight?" she would ask. I never said 'no' except on important occasions such as my marriage day. There were instances she did not call me when her spouse was away. I guessed she invited others too or maybe went off on a luxurious rendezvous someplace out of town.

Sushmita knew how to pleasure a man probing areas that I never imagined could cause such ecstasy. I think I never shampooed and soaped myself as much as I did when I was seeing Sushmita. I even lathered my backside, for the first time in my life. I never had any woman pay so much attention to my nipples. I didn't know they could flare up like a woman's when worked upon. Two little breasts sprouted around the area briefly, which can be a little disconcerting.

Sushmita didn't need to be cajoled to a blow job, like it is with most high on hygiene Indian girls. She loved giving pleasure and acceded to plenty of play with her mouth. Once she had her fill, she let me take over. I was completely spent after I made lové to Sushmita. This never happened before or after.

With any other woman, I always sensed clusters of still semi-excited sperms circling about the torso area that made me want to make love again in a short time, maybe with somebody else. With Sushmita, the extreme lust and physical turbulence resulted in the super excited sperms spurting and spilling in the billions emptying out in big gusts. Perhaps, they quickly wanted to be one with her. She was simply irresistible.

I could never have enough of her. I behaved like a child being detached from his favourite toy, when it was time to leave her apartment. "One more time," I would insist till I was literally pushed out of the house. She told me she got along pretty well with a steel magnate and a senior politician known to be popular with women, which could only mean one thing. They too had a close feel of her bums and bust, I was sure. I was okay with that. Sushmita was a creation of God at his creative best.

She could not be revealed only to one. She needed to be appreciated by more. Thank God, she was married. Or else, I don't think I could have let even the Almighty, her creator, to get to see her again.

Sushmita's typical evening with me after work could be a few drinks at a South Extension pub, meat rolls at Defence Colony market and then to her house to make love. In public she wanted us to keep a respectable distance. That was understandable. She was on the invite list of a few five-star discos.

We also spent time at the gym or the pool, mixed cocktails, ordered food home and watched DVDs in bed at her house, next to pictures of the husband and her on exotic holidays all over the world, including Bali, Vevey and Goa.

I liked to watch the movies placing my head between her breasts, feeling her bums, sipping alcohol and feeding on some of the delectable kebabs that she prepared at home. Sushmita was a very good cook. I believe there is a connection between food and sex. Those who can feed others have the ability to give in bed too. These are the most fantastic traits that any man can want from his woman.

I usually went home late at night or the next morning back to work, empty of every speck of sperm formed inside my body. Although I never refused any of Sushmita's propositions (who would?), it did get difficult managing Lata as she liked to be in regular touch with me on the cell phone, like all good girlfriends in love with their boyfriends.

But, my situation with Sushmita was not the way it was with Pooja. When Lata called, Sushmita kept quiet. When Sushmita's husband called, I kept silent. We knew about the existence and importance of the other partner in our respective lives, though I often explored her body while she was on the phone. She too unzipped me when I was speaking to Lata. All of this was, of course, very erotic.

Lata was open to the idea of my spending a night at a friend's or cousin's pad in Delhi after a late night party, networking with important people of the city for stories. I used the usual journalistic excuse with wives or girlfriends of meeting an important source for an exclusive and messaged to say the same.

Sometimes, to incorporate a sudden change of schedule, I cooked up fantastic stories such as the office is on fire due to a short circuit or a colleague has met with an accident. Such excuses are tricky as they can spring up in conversations abruptly. For example, Lata asked about the recovery of the colleague a week later that I had forgotten about completely as the pretext of the day.

As Sushmita opened up more, she said that she did not believe in a monogamous relationship. "All talk about sticking to one sexual partner is hogwash. In most species in the animal kingdom, the male is never loyal to one female. It is no different for humans. Look at all the guys loyal to their wives. They take out their sexual energies on food and drinks to turn into fat hogs inviting diabetes, heart problems and lifestyle diseases. Later on they run into enlarged or inflamed prostrate issues due to disuse of the gland. Look at you. Why do you think you get the women? You keep yourself fit, you look good. You work hard. That attracts women. You will live long."

"I think I am just lucky. A woman such as you can have any man she wants. A man cannot unless he pays money to get a prostitute," I said.

"You will have women in your life always, let me assure you."

"Men are known to stray. What about females? Why would, for example, a woman such as you be in a relationship outside marriage?" I asked her.

"That is a totally wrong way to put it," Sushmita snapped back. "All my interactions with men or women cannot be defined in terms of existing within or without any other. Each is a universe of its own and demise or beginning of one association is not interlinked to another in any way."

For a moment, I wondered whether Sushmita had female lovers too. It was a possibility. She could attract any woman like any man.

"I understand about men straying as they stop thinking with their heads due to temptation, but, what about women and what about you? Can one relate this to the animal kingdom?" I queried further.

"Females can sense a good partner. That's their innate intelligence. A tigress, for example, will mate with the tiger that is able to protect its territory. She can instinctively read his good and powerful genes. At the same time she can also mate with any tiger on the sly who she considers good progeny material. But, unlike humans tigresses make love for procreation, while a woman can do it for pleasure. This is due to contraception, I guess. A tiger will never put on a condom."

"So, you make love to me because you like it?"

"Yes and I can get away with it, while a tigress cannot. I can choose not to procreate if that is the way I want it. I am more enabled," she answered.

"Then why marry?" I asked.

"Marriage is important for security, companionship and family. These are all long-term needs. Loyalty is incidental. The mind and body also need short-term fulfilments. As long as they don't turn into deeper emotional needs that a marriage should ideally offer, you are in safe zone."

"Why not get that short-term stuff also from the same person one is married to?" I asked.

"It is possible. But, sometimes it does not work out."

"Have you ever been in the unsafe zone?" I asked.

"It has happened but I realized I loved my husband more. One needs to be careful. It is important there is parity in a relationship. If one is married never be involved with a single girl. It will lead to complications. Although you are not married, you are involved with Lata and have had a past with other women. So, I kind of know that you would not lose it mentally when we got to know each other better. I like it that you are not obsessive and possessive. This can be trouble for a married woman like me who needs exclusive time with the husband."

"What are the chances of emotional attachments?" I asked.

"This is always a possibility. If it does happen, it can be dangerous. You will know on your own. That's the reason that a married person should ideally be involved with another in the same situation. The barrier to exit for both should be fair and equitable. Just as you gave up cigarettes as it did not suit you, relationships too die out if they are unsuitable."

I did not agree with all of Sushmita's opinions even though she liked to expound her theories to me as I have always been a good listener. Thoughts about dishonesty, morality, sex addiction occurred to me.

I think Sushmita was a lonely person whose husband fulfilled her money needs only and probably would be a good father sometime in the future.

She needed a little more romance, attention and probably sex to spice up her life that her spouse failed to provide. She sought such companionship in others and accordingly rationalized her situation to herself. I agreed with her on one count though. There was no point in revealing oneself completely to one's partner. It would only cause hurt and pain. I was beginning to understand my condition and situation in life better. It is called excessive libido. No amount of philosophy and theories could cover up for the same. I was being disloyal to Lata.

Yet my interludes with Sushmita were enjoyable. Even if I tried to reason with my mind against the relationship, I could not control myself, every time she called. My hormones went berserk. The sperm formations went on an overdrive.

I could hear a billion of them collectively scream for Sushmita like a stadium full of spectators urging their favourite cricketer to hit a six.

I had no choice. So, I decided to let matters sustain till she decided to call it off or moved on to other guys. I had to manage Lata till then without getting caught. Luckily or unluckily, I never recorded my good times with Lata. Making multimedia sex (MMS) videos with your partner was not the norm as it is now. I wrote the following about MMS scandals:

There has been another MMS sex scandal in India to add to numerous others involving usual suspects actors, actresses, models, school kids, god men and politicians, not necessarily in that order. This could be a sociological study of people in this country having some fun, a few on the side.

The one's I can recall include Swami Nityananda, who claimed he did not know what he was doing as he was in some kind of trance. Nobody, of course believed him. Another allegedly involved octogenarian N D Tiwari, proving that no Viagra is greater than being a politician in this country, given their enormous clout.

There was one involving actress Kareena Kapoor with her then beau Shahid Kapur that could have passed off as a tutorial on how couples should not kiss each other. The clip was vehemently denied.

Surprisingly, no cricketer has ever been caught in the act. At least I don't recall any, which highlights the excessive cricket being played by India. The poor rich boys have no time beyond wielding the willow. Or, maybe everybody idealizes too much Sachin Tendulkar who combines perfect professional and personal ethics.

Predictably, the latest sex video has gone viral online, again highlighting that scandalous porn by far elicits top rating in the virtual world beating hard work by PSY for Gangnam, Justin Bieber for Baby and Amitabh Bachchan Facebook updates, periodically endorsing his son Abhishek as a great actor.

The MMS sex clip involves an unfortunate actress called Mona Singh whose pictures have allegedly been morphed. I had not heard about Mona until news about her splashed on national news. Apparently she is a TV celebrity.

I have stopped watching Indian TV channels as they don't excite any of my faculties, including the dumb and unintelligent part. I have desperately tried to don an exponentially silly side, but have still failed to appreciate Indian TV programming. That's the reason I had no idea that a TV star called Mona existed, until the MMS scandal happened.

For a moment I did think, why Mona, why not anybody else? I feel cheated, it should have been me did I hear Poonam Pandey, the queen of self-generated scandalous MMS videos in India. Thankfully, there is no need to morph Sunny Leone, unless one seeks to make a clip in which she is not having sex. The creator of the Mona MMS clip probably loved Mona a lot to hate her so much now or may be just did not realize that the video would become such an online hit.

The cops I believe are trying to get to the bottom of the episode after Mona filed a complaint. The police are getting better at handling cybercrime. For long used to instant solutions by the wielding of the baton (lathi, danda in colloquial) the cops did not quite get it right, when cybercrime emerged.

They went about arresting anybody confused that downloading an illegal MMS clip is not the same thing as uploading or creating a MMS video. While the cops figured out such simple nuances owning a computer with a net connection almost became a security risk in India.

The policemen could probably arrest almost all rickshaw wallahs as the poor are the most creative users of cell phones in India, including MMS downloading. The poor may not have enough to eat, but do make sure there is enough balance on their pre-paid cards and constantly change ring tones. Such is the addiction.

All MMS scandals have not actually been for the bad. Please don't get me wrong here. But, if one were to apply Sociologist Ashis Nandy's argument that some corruption is good, all MMSs have not turned out as bad as initially envisaged.

As a matter of fact some suspect some MMS clips to be deliberate acts for publicity. Globally MMS sex queens have included Pamela Anderson, Paris Hilton and Kim Kardashian performing sexual acts with current or ex-boyfriends.

After being initially distraught, pretending or otherwise, these ladies have en-cashed their instant global e-fame into multi-million dollar businesses as fashion divas, brand ambassadors, singers, actresses, reality TV stars, intellectuals, animal rights activists and more. This does not mean that MMS scandals are for the good.

It is a gross invasion of privacy. But, as Nandy might put it, they may not be entirely for the bad for some. Mona, of course, should get justice. The perpetrator of the crime should be behind bars, even if Justice Katju wants him pardoned.

TWELVE

Finally Married

As I was beginning to expect, Lata called to say, "I have discussed with my family. There were many options, but I have decided to get married to you. Just say 'yes' and please don't complicate things."

After the Pooja experience I expected Lata to propose marriage. There was no reason for me to refuse, unless Sushmita was single and available.

"Okay," I said, feebly.

"Also, since I am the owner of four plots compared to two from your side, some compromises will have to be made by you," Lata said, firmly.

"What kind of compromises?" I asked.

"You will come to know," she said. I was informed about the adjustments after the grand wedding. And that was to shift to Lata's palatial house in Gurgaon where her parents resided. I was to become a *Ghar Jamai*.

I was okay with the idea to keep Lata happy, but others linked closely to me were very very unhappy. I will get to that later. "Marry her," Sushmita told me definitively, probably to ensure I did not fall in love with her due a sperm related effect that messed me up mentally.

"She is a straight forward, sober, hardworking, rich well-brought up girl. She will be good for you as you are destined to lead your life in multiple compartments," she said.

Sushmita believed I would stray into relationships the rest of my life, a possibility I did not rule out. Still, I did not agree or disagree with her.

I had arrived at no conclusion without knowing for sure how I would evolve post-marriage. According to Sushmita, it is impossible for any man or woman to be committed to one person after experiencing sexual excitement with multiple partners. Marriage is too boring for such fun elements, but essential, she told me launching into another of her tiger analogies, this time man-eating ones.

My family was somewhat taken aback when I announced my marriage plans, assuming I was joking while continuing with their normal routines.

My folks did not take me seriously in any case. Sid, earning exponential amounts more than me, had decided to wait few more years before "taking on" marriage as he felt additional responsibility would detract from his focus on work, progress, money making and CEO-hood

"He is finally being serious about something. He was never serious about the IAS. He is serious about marriage. It should have been the other way round," my father said before stepping out of the house for CCD espresso in the vicinity.

My mother, as usual busy with many household chores that revolved around making our life comfortable, said she would need some time to plan for the event, if I really wanted to go ahead. She advised I should not rush matters and like Sid take my time to commit to marriage.

"There is no going back once you decide. You must be sure you will be able to keep her happy. I do not want you to break her heart. Don't complain later that you are not able to handle the pressure." I heard out my mom solemnly.

Sid sniggered a few minutes when he heard about my intentions. "You mean you will have a mother-in-law and father-in-law?

Remember your wife's father will kill you if he finds out that you are two-timing his daughter, which I am sure you will," Sid expressed his blatant view.

I sometimes worried about Sid. I loved him. I wondered if his wife could turn into a personality like Sushmita with lovers on the side. I did not wish him such a happening though he pleasured in putting me down.

Long years of slogging had made him a trifle bitter about any little progress that I was making in my life, whether personal or professional. As I did not work as hard as him, in his assessment, I had no future but to fail. I was not a trail-blazer, but I believed I could be reasonably well off and happy with my life in general. Sid earned a lot, but hardly enjoyed the fruits of his labour.

He needed to expend his sexual energy, find himself a sexy babe to pamper and be pampered. He needed to visit a spa, massage parlour, holiday in Bangkok or Goa. I relayed back my family's views to Lata, who was certain we should get hitched.

I was confused about endorsing Lata's opinion that we should marry right away or my mother's that advised caution. Opinion of mother or wife is a dilemma that many men across the world have to face and especially in India where moms tend to be very attached and protective about their sons, who can do no wrong.

This is probably because social acceptance of a woman is enhanced considerably once she produces a boy. It is like clearing the IAS exam. I also know women obsessive about their daughters. I think in general mothers tend to lose it a bit with their kids. It is understandable, though I believe my mother has been always measured and reasonable. To impress the seriousness of her intentions Lata decided to speak to my family face-to-face. She arrived dressed in a sari, looking very elegant and sexy. I love the contours of a woman's body in a sari.

I felt like pulling her into my room, undressing her to instantly make love. I controlled myself given the seriousness of the situation, especially for Lata. Though my parents knew her as a kid, the changed circumstance of the visit was palpable. For some time everybody sat in the living room with nothing to say.

Sid was uncharacteristically silent though I could sense thoughts whizzing inside his overactive and hyper intelligent brain.

Perhaps, he was wondering he was the one who worked hard all his life, but I was walking away with the rich babe, which was unfair. Then my father began to talk, speaking about subjects quite unrelated to the purpose of Lata's visit, ranging from politics and cricket to his policing experiences.

After talking for a while about various global issues, my father turned his attention on my future wife – about how much he cared for her as he had seen her grow in front of his own eyes. He even mentioned buying high quality active baby diapers for her from abroad when she was born, on request by her parents. I think Lata was a trifle embarrassed.

It was quickly apparent to everyone present that my father was uncomfortable with developments in my personal life, just as he was not happy with progress in my professional sphere. I think both my parents believed I was not good enough to be married to a girl like Lata. They might have been positively inclined had she wanted to marry my high-earning elder brother. My parents were unsure about my value in the marriage mart. Rather, they thought I was valueless.

A married man is weighed by his ability to stand up for himself and his family, especially monetarily that reflected in a high credit card limit.

My father knew that my card was of the lowest student category, unlike Sid's unlimited usage with periodic offers of free aeroplane and movie tickets, access to luxury airport lounges and golf courses. Sid gifted an add-on facility to my father who never used the sleek black plastic card with his name embossed on it.

But, he showed it around as if it was an Olympic Gold Medal that Sid had won for the country. He might as well have worn it around his neck rather than carrying it in the wallet. "My son gave this to me," he said with immense pride and pleasure to friends, batch mates and relatives. People wondered why he reached for his purse when there was no need. Soon, everybody knew it was for the credit card. Shop keepers were confused when he showed them the card but paid by cash.

If I had been a pretty girl, my parents might have felt more confident about my wedding intentions. A guy's looks count for nothing without the IIT, IIM or IAS badge. My father maintained thick files of many marriage proposals for Sid that arrived at our house from the time he made it to IIT.

Families anxious about the right match for their daughters keep a keener eye on top competitive exam results than aspirants themselves. This is to snare the guy the moment he makes it and before anybody else.

The process is similar to Delhi nursery school admissions. Parents begin researching schools, networking and building contacts the moment the embryo heartbeat shows up on the ultrasound inside the expecting mother's womb. Admission forms are scoured to gauge various eligibilities including shifting to a local address to add reward points like it is with credit cards.

Unfortunately there was no need for my father to update or maintain any folder on me as there was not a single marriage offer to file, though pictures of me and my female friends adorned my room. Sid's corner was blank, a price he paid for making it big early in life. Finally, following many winks and hints by my mom, my father broached the issue foremost in everybody's mind.

"I hope you know he does not earn much, especially given the kind of lifestyle your parents have given you. He has been able to buy a second hand scooter on his own steam. His credit card limit is very very low," he told Lata.

"He is worth much more. He has the plots that no credit card can buy," Lata bluntly replied. "Plus, I love him." The declaration made me feel good. I think I completely fell in love with her that moment. The marriage was sealed despite my abysmal marriage mart value and credit rating.

"Now that you are getting married, don't divorce in a hurry," Sid warned me later. He hugged and congratulated me. Despite the sibling rivalry we knew we loved each other deeply. I could die for him.

My marriage was a grand affair courtesy our respective parents. My father pulled off a big show without spending too much money due to the power he wielded in Delhi. The guest list comprised the city's who's who. My father could have hosted the functions free of cost at several government-owned sprawling venues such as CRPF, ITBP or BSF mess lawns. He paid commercial rates, which were still a bit lower than hiring a private location.

My father used the occasion to reach out to the larger bureaucracy, batch mates, ministers and officials. They arrived safely cocooned inside big red beaconed cars escorted by armed guards in separate vehicles. The security men aggressively gesticulated with their fleshy arms and sophisticated guns.

Their torsos, fattened due to absence of any real work in their routines, protruded from lowered car windows to shoo and scare away traffic, pedestrians, three-wheelers, two-wheelers, buses, trucks, beggars, cows, rats and dogs on the road.

Two cabinet ministers turned up accompanied by their respective entourages, creating a buzz among guests. This contributed to the impact of importance my father was eager to portray though deep down I knew he was unhappy I had not lived up to his dreams and expectations. He was also uncertain whether Lata would be happy with me. Ideally, he wanted to marry me off as an IAS officer, preferably to Pooja who was still in touch with him, making it a point to post a birthday card every year. She had stopped wishing me.

Members of the opposite sex possess the uncanny ability to rattle off birthdays that could put Einstein's memory to shame. I can barely remember my own birthday while needing to put alerts on anybody else's that matters. Facebook and calendar features in smart phones are immense help nowadays.

Given his disappointment with me, my father showed off Sid to his guests, never failing to mention about his IIT, IIM credentials and the huge salary packages that he was sure to draw as his career progressed. To some he showed the credit card. A few guests thought Sid was the groom.

My father's important and status-conscious friends shook hands with me and Lata. Some had read my articles. They congratulated me on my writing skills conveying that I had a great future as a journalist. At least a couple of guests did mention, "They don't pay you much, do they? Unlike MNCs family-owned media firms are not good to their employees. Plus, there is no job security."

"I have no insecurities. I do what I have to do," I replied.

Lata intervened to say: "We also have the support of my parents. That counts. There is nothing for us to worry," she said with effect to impress her mom and dad who were always in the vicinity. My to-be mother-in-law in a few hours was making sure all gifts, cheques and cash were accounted.

"I don't want anything from your parents. We will manage on our own. I will sell my plots if that makes you happy," I whispered loudly to her.

"We will see," she replied, cryptically.

My father-in-law spent lavishly on multiple events such as *sangeet*, ring ceremony, cocktails and reception hosted at multiple five-star hotels in Delhi, Gurgaon and a farmhouse at Chhatarpur. The out of station invitees from Lata's side were sent air tickets, booked into top star hotel with free access to amenities such as pool, gym, spa, business centre, Wi-Fi and restaurants. Everybody was allotted full-time chauffeur driven air-conditioned taxi.

Though Lata and my near future mother-in-law decided the menu my father-in-law ensured many *lauki* (bottle gourd) concoctions, his favourite vegetable, were served. Thankfully, he ruled out Shahrukh Khan or Raveena Tandon live dance performances in tight fitting shiny leather outfits.

Many cousin sisters from Lata's side were SRK fans, insisting on his presence. The boys were smitten by '*mast mast* girl', Raveena. "We can have big LCD screens with their songs playing. That way they can be present without paying them anything," my father ruled.

For the main wedding, an array of neatly arranged eatables, live DJ, *lauki* corner, dance troupes occupied some space. A popular band comprising unshaven faces, barely visible due to long unkempt hair styles briefly played tunes of latest Bollywood hits for guests to dance and get drunk.

There were many gifts, including white goods from my wife's family, all neatly gift-wrapped in bright shiny paper, stacked around a large table, with price tags visible so that everyone knew the expenses incurred.

This was to emphasize the show-off factor my wife's family, with deep Punjabi roots, seemed keen about. The items included microwave, desktop computer that cost a bomb those days, music system, washing machine, TV, apparel, shoes, watches, gold coins, sofa sets, easy chairs, cutlery, crockery, cell phones. I was involved in selecting the electronic items, without paying for them as the expenditures were from my wife's side.

I did not have the money after buying the plots. My bank account was near empty. My salary did not make much of a difference to my economic status or purchasing power. Although I did not request for any gifts, I considered it foolish to refuse them as Lata would use them too. She was accustomed to comforts I could not afford unless I sold my plots that I did not intend.

My father-in-law gifted us a spanking new Honda City that was parked at the porch of the South Delhi five-star hotel, the wedding venue. The vehicle was bedecked with freshly plucked flowers for me and Lata to drive away after the marriage was solemnized.

The roses were arranged to spell my name on the bonnet and Lata's on the windscreen. The car was decorated with many heart-shaped garlands. I was happy to be the owner of the car. I still commuted to work in my scooter, bus and occasionally my father's Maruti 800. A Honda City was a big jump.

I wouldn't have minded driving it around waving to guests, the way Indian cricketers do after a victory, delighting the makers of the vehicle due to free publicity on TV. Unfortunately, that was not possible inside the hall of the hotel.

Arriving guests admired the top-line Honda City for some time, a few sitting behind the wheel to check out latest features. A live camera beamed pictures of the car onto a screen inside. The invitees from Lata's side included property dealers, agents, middlemen and real estate developers. They were dressed similarly in traditional attire of property agents, big and small, across India -- in all white.

The shoes and socks were the same hue. In Nehru style, a red or maroon coloured hanky peeped from many breast pockets. The trousers and loose half or long sleeved shirts was no cover for big paunches courtesy extra large quantities of lager beer fat consumed over plenty of chicken *tikka* and *seekh* kebabs.

As property matters are settled over long-winded discussions and negotiations, food and drinks are an essential add on. The wives of property dealers dripped diamonds probably worth an apartment each. The male guests could have easily passed off as an assembly of extremely unfit white flannelled test match cricketers that regularly lose matches. Many reminded me of the portly Sri Lankan cricketers, Arjuna Ranatunga and earlier Duleep Mendis.

Yet, the spotless white camouflage hid nothing as property matters in India involve black money, coercion, evasion and cheating, in re-sale, pre-launch and original bookings. "Your crowd is weird. I feel as if I am surrounded by unfit traffic policemen on duty," I told Lata between guests.

"Shut up," she said between smiles, "Do you know the net worth of these guys in terms of properties they own? It's billions of rupees. My father says at least a couple of them are likely to be ministers in the Haryana government or centre."

The guests in white attires lined up to congratulate me and Lata. "We know about the plots. Very wise and intelligent decision for such a young couple," a few winked in admiration.

Nobody from Lata's side mentioned about my job profile. It did not matter as long as we were owners of the prime land.

Of particular interest to me was the arrival of Sushmita and my village girl for the ceremonies. I invited Pooja, but there was no response to the wedding card. My father gave me her latest phone numbers. I called her but her mobile went unanswered. She probably had mine saved in her contacts and chose to ignore.

Yet, I was in the vicinity of three women I had known intimately. I visualized, in a rather filmy way, each one of them naked lying next to me after we made love. There are particular private moments with each lover that remains etched in the mind – an expression of climax, the oral sex, moments of extreme fondness, admiration, care, stroking the hair, sometimes anger.

I recalled each one of them blissfully asleep after making love, eyes fully or half closed, with a sheet or quilt partially covering their bodies. With the village girl, it was the charpoy on the terrace of her house; with Sushmita, on her soft mattress bed wrapped in imported sheets; with Pooja it was my house, in my room, in Chhapra, in the tub, car.

My village girl was not aware of my situation with Sushmita who in turn knew my past. Lata was too caught up in proceedings to suspect anything. She did not know about my antecedents with Sushmita or my village girl.

Sushmita was observed closely by everybody due to her extraordinary beauty and perfectly voluptuous body that I strongly felt like caressing all over again.

She was simply irresistible. A week prior to my marriage I spent a few immensely pleasurable hours at Sushmita's house, enjoying her and her hospitality that included spicy Thai food and drinks. I had gone to hand her my marriage card, but the evening turned out much more eventful.

At the wedding, Sushmita's primary attention was on her husband, making sure to be by his side, fussing over his snacks, comfort and drinks. She involved him in all conversations with the many people who wanted to speak to her, to mentally tick mark having spoken to such an attractive woman in their life.

Women and men who stray in marriages tend to make a public display of being extra attentive and caring about their spouses. It is due to guilt. Normal married couples can comfortably ignore each other for most of an evening together.

It is a sign of stability. Soaking up a bit of her attention, Sushmita's hubby did not have a hint about the multiple compartments that existed inside his wife's brain.

He was disinterested in the proceedings of my wedding. He seemed distracted, in a hurry to get back home, probably wanting to work on a presentation. He looked fit due to time spent at the gym that I also frequented when he was not around. His sharp physical attributes was part of the overall package to portray his own self better than the rest of the world, competitors, clients and everybody else.

Ideally, he needed to give his wife more attention and make love to her more often, given her male admirers, though it is never easy to balance family, work and sex. He was too caught up in the rat race while his wife and often her lovers enjoyed the material benefits of the slogging.

My village girl had shifted to Noida, another high growing Delhi suburb, from Kanpur as her husband was looking to expand his business to export that needed access to an airport. I got her address from a cousin who was in touch with her.

She looked happily prosperous accompanied by her two bonny kids who looked a bit like her. They thoroughly enjoyed the evening consuming copious amounts of Pepsi and ice cream. "She is the perfect girl for you," my village girl told me in Hindi, as we hugged warmly on the podium.

She had put on weight due to her kids but seemed completely at peace with the extra pounds. I guess she was too contented to worry about such mundane matters. It was good of her to turn up for my wedding with her family.

My village girl had moved on in life. Sushmita was destined to be part of my life journey, as must have been the fate of a few more lucky men. For how long, I did not know, though my sperm producing body parts would have wanted her forever given the tumult she caused, even during my nuptials.

****

There was an unexciting footnote to my first wedded night. A strange feeling engulfed me that had nothing to do with liberal quantities of Whiskey downed over days. My urge to make love to Lata had evaporated.

When she was my girlfriend I could not disengage my hands from her body. On our first night as a married couple I just didn't feel up to the sex, while she was desperate to have it. She thought it was auspicious to make out.

The perfume she was wearing was exotic, expensive lipstick tasted sweet, the tinkling of fluorescent bangles sounded surreal in the bedroom of our new rented accommodation in Gurgaon. The lights were dim while I could smell the fresh new linen, rose petals strewn on the brand new soft mattress and bed cover.

Each element, the occasion, beautiful bride could only combine to create a heady aphrodisiac that could drive any man wild.

The room had been done up by Lata and her mother, now officially my mother-in-law. Yet, I felt like a footballer at the end of a-90 minute gruel. I was completely out of wind. Lata whispered into my ears that she wanted me to ejaculate inside her instead of my tummy or hers. "You can feel free now. No need to stop yourself," she said biting my ears and licking my face I would have found extremely erotic anytime of the day or night.

Though I believed it was a bit early to start trying for a family, I did not want to initiate a debate on my first night as a married man. The thoughts of kids, however, contributed to reducing my sexual appetite further. I tried every mental stratagem to make it happen. I thought about porn sequences, MMS videos, making love to Sushmita, Pooja and the village girl by turn. I thought about Bollywood and Hollywood actresses in various erotic situations. They were of no help.

"You don't want it as the chase is over. As long as you were unsure about me you wanted sex all the time. Now that I am your wife you are no longer interested," Lata told me even as the sun rose and my life as a married man commenced.

"I think I am just a little tired with all the social activity," I lied.

"You have never been tired for sex. You should give up non veg," she retorted.

"Maybe age is catching up," I said, to pre-empt another lecture on my food intake.

"How can someone age overnight?" she said.

"I think it is called marriage. Maybe, I need to get used to the whole new atmospherics of family and all," I said as I struggled to make excuses.

I managed before breakfast, but it was no fun. I probably squirted a few thousand sperms. I had read somewhere that one out of millions of released sperms makes it to the woman's egg to fertilize into a child.

We were certainly not making any baby on our wedding night. Later I elicited Sushmita's views which were different, just as she was. According to her, my marriage would definitely turn more exciting in the days to come.

"You are going through too many changes in your life -- marriage, shifting out from your parents' house, exit of Pooja and now me."

She claimed my daily living would soon slide into a steady state which would enable my body to discover its' primal self once more, courtesy her.

"Marriage can be boring but in my company your male hormones are going to be in a hyperactive state. Your condition will be a state of perpetual horniness and erections will happen without use of any supplements. Since I am not available to you all the time, some energies will be diverted to your wife, who is the only other female available to you as I presume. So, she will benefit."

"Does your being with me, for example, make it more interesting with your husband?" I asked.

"It surely does. The whole principle applies vice versa. For now, though, don't clutter your mind. When you are with me, think of me only. When you are with your wife, focus on her. She is an attractive woman. If you do not give her what she wants, she will easily find it elsewhere."

Sushmita's views had an impact. The thought of Lata with another man did not settle down well with me. Soon, I resumed my love making with some vigour.

"Tiger, what has got into you again? Are you back to being a teenager?"

"I am entering the steady state of marriage," I told Lata.

I think I again began to cross the million sperm mark. One of them was surely going to make me a father. And, it did.

I wrote this piece about being a father of a daughter:

It is a disadvantage being a father as the mother will always know and do better.

I don't argue the assertion – she creates the child from her body; she bears it for nine months, the bond develops before birth. Is it my fault?

I am prepared to be pregnant, if only to save my wife the anxiety that can be mentally, if not physically, as difficult for the father, apart from the adjustments to routine, sleep, work and entertainment.

But, say as much as I may, the wife says I am saying it, as it is not possible for me to do what I have offered myself for. Call it the absence of pre-natal bonding, I found that coming to terms with my baby took me more time than it did my wife.

She seemed to trapeze with practiced ease the rounds of nappy changing, potty washing, bathing and more. I haven't managed bathing without fearing that her tiny body would slip off my palms though she is a year and a half old now.

She senses the strength of my grip and wails every time I try and wash her. I call my gawkiness a genetic aberration; my wife calls it a lack of commitment.

She is working, so am I, so we spend as much time with the baby, which can never be enough; thus there can be no alibi that one partner has the unfair advantage of spending more quality time with her, except before birth when my wife claimed she communed with the being inside. I have tried to think up as many explanations to my incompetence vis-à-vis my wife, try as much as I may.

There is one more reason, apart from the pre-natal one. Don't mistake me as chauvinistic, but I think I could be a better dad if my baby were a boy.

I know as I was a boy once, what a boy wants, see the world through his eyes, a world defined by me in a way that a guy sees -- playing sports, watching porn, proposing to girls, cycling, swimming and climbing hills.

I have never seen the world through the eyes of a girl, although there were several girls I loved, but never loved enough to see things the way they saw it, until my baby came. I wonder, will she play golf, read Ludlum and listen to hard rock?

My wife never does, but could I or should I teach my daughter to do the things I like to do? I admire my role models, but do I need to study female role models, who may be different? Who would I like my daughter to emulate? Tiger Woods… I am sure she will go her own way and define her own rules; I want to do what my father did, though I never followed what he preached.

It is my duty now to see from my baby's eyes and define and study closely the world of women leaders -- of Thatcher, Rowling, Sarandon and the standards they set. My wife drowned the arguments.

"Philosophy is okay, but cannot take away from the immediate reality of changing nappies, feeding from the bottle and doing it well," she said, and was right.

I tried hard and without being immodest must say was reasonably okay by my standards only. She hears the baby cry in the middle of the night before I did, and do. She is up and away from bed much before I do, or to make matters worse I am frequently even slower than my mom-in-law who resides in the next room.

I am good at several things, playing golf for one, but cannot figure out why my wife is better at this, though looking after a baby is no sport. Yet I compare with golf which is languorous while parenting is not. I went through another period of introspection and arrived at another answer.

I like to delegate, provided the work is done well. I want the best for my daughter, and there is no better nappy changer or potty washer in the world better than my wife. So I have delegated and am happy about it.

I discovered this when my wife was away on a business tour. I was fast, faster than ever, never gentler.

I think my mother-in-law sensed it, but has kept it to herself as in her eyes only her daughter is number one, which is fair enough, as long as the mother-in-law is not number two, I reasoned. Sadly, my wife will never know my real prowess, as whenever she is around I subconsciously delegate. This could be genetic or I wish I had not read too many management books, but I have decided I will never beat my wife, but should at least better my mom-in-law.

She is fast, I am faster, but my wife is the fastest. And that's the way it stays.

THIRTEEN

The Ghar Jamai

Lata and I tried to manage our rented accommodation for some time then gave up. We moved into my in-laws house. It is never very comfortable to live in somebody else's house as a *Ghar Jamai* as opposed to one's parents' home. It is not a rosy situation for the parents-in-law as well.

There are occasions of discomfort -- the kind that a young adolescent girl can sense in an extra short skirt at a party, with all eyes on her exposed thighs. There is privacy in one's own house. Till class ten I would run around naked at home when in a good mood, unconcerned about my flapping penis. "He has gone mad again," my mother would say, sipping her tea or knitting a sweater for me or my brother.

Now I dressed appropriately even in my bedroom lest my mother-in-law walked in. Actually, I did not care if she saw me naked. I think my wife would not have liked it and I was concerned about that.

For some time I believed there were people eavesdropping on me and my wife making love. I am a horny kind of guy and prefer actual action to regular shagging the semen out in the shower or under the quilt.

Though I tend to believe I am good in bed without the aid of any Viagra versions, domestic or overseas, spurious or real, it was disconcerting that our voices in passion could be heard elsewhere in the house occupied by my new relatives. Lata believed in being noisy when we made out. I read somewhere that women could be faking the decibels to turn the man on and progress towards climax.

I think my wife might have read the same article on chain mail. But, she need not have bothered with the sound effects. It does not take much to get me going, apart from the brief period, post and pre-marriage that I have spoken about earlier.

Though I am not the kind of guy who delves too much into family or office politics, I quickly figured that being a *ghar jamai* is not the most comfortable situation in this country. People perceive you in a funny way.

This is politically incorrect. They should not. But they do. As if you are a eunuch or a homosexual who are as human as any one of us, though, to be frank I would never advise my kids or anybody else's to turn out that way.

I mean I would never ask my son or daughter to marry somebody else's son or daughter, in that order. I will like the pairs to be in reverse.

The same-sex practitioners do not help their cause by organizing parades in absolutely unfashionable clothing and horrible make up that approximates unpleasant tattoos on the face. It only deepens prejudices some espouse about such sexual inclinations.

I think it will take a while for mind-sets to change even if gays and lesbians are recognized and accepted sexual behaviour in any society. But, life has its little surprises, so one never knows what one may have to face up to.

My wife's parents stayed in a palatial house in Gurgaon. The lavish bungalow was courtesy my father-in-law's buying cheap and selling dear property expertise. One brother of Lata studied abroad, obviously sponsored by his father, with no intentions of returning in a hurry. He apparently was creatively inclined and did not find any inspiration in speculative property dealing matters.

Lata told me she feared her very sensitive brother might be gay, though she kept her suspicions to herself as she did not want to shock her parents, who probably did not understand such relationships.

There was a small glass lift to the basement and three floors, at Lata's independent dwelling. There were guards from Bihar posted in blue uniform outside, many maids for cleaning, two cooks, masters in vegetarian cooking laced with *lauki*, the favourite vegetable of my father-in-law. Families prefer multiple food items that are usually liberally consumed by everybody -- tandoori chicken, Baskin Robbins ice cream, Haldiram food. In my in-laws' household, it was *lauki*.

The day staff included two drivers and part-time gardeners. A professional agency had been hired to supply on-call carpenters, electricians, plumbers, polishers and other manpower when needed. A supervisor stationed at a corner room in the basement was responsible for overall coordination of the servants, their routine, hygiene, cleanliness, clipped nails and uniforms.

All the factotums were provided cell phones so they could be reached instantly. Intercom facility provided room-to-room connectivity. Despite their high living standards, my in-laws were lonely. There was the added issue of security in such a large residence. There were too many incidents of servants looting and killing aged employers in Delhi.

"Is this a hotel or a household? Are you royalty, a *Maharani*? Have I missed something?" I asked Lata when I visited her house for the first time.

"Welcome to Gurgaon. There are many like us, better, we don't have a personal lap pool. They are all over. Daddy says we may have one," she replied.

"Half of India has no access to any form of drinking water and there are those who need swimming pools," I wanted to say but did not. There is no point criticizing the rich when one is linked to one.

****

Lata did try to manage our rented apartment initially. But, she had not been brought up to run a home. She fancied herself as a businesswoman taking after the many successful, smart and eloquent lady professionals played up by the media and pink papers. They included leaders of banking, software, rising corporate India and Ekta Kapoor. Lata joined her father's business, perhaps also to assuage his disappointment about her brother's indifference to the profession.

My father-in-law was another father unhappy about his son's choice of vocation and career, like mine. Either the fathers don't get it right or the sons.

While at work Lata possessively used the same chair on which we used to make love while her old man brought himself new seating. I could not resist thinking about using the furniture of my father-in-law's office again.

It had to be someone else or nobody. It was not possible to try out the porn positions with Lata anymore. I don't think my wife would have been amenable to the acrobatic sex. Women give into men's aberrant sexual fantasies when there are uncertainties in the relationship that engenders insecurities and possessiveness.

Not when one has settled into the monotony of matrimony. The sex is also more mechanical and business-like than passionate that can be pleasurable but not exotic for the guy. I don't know about the woman.

Lata worked hard. She had ambitions to take the business to new levels of income, including floating of a new property and infrastructure development company. The DLF people, owners of massive land banks around the country, were her idols.

Initially, she used the Internet to tap overseas customers managing to attract a large number of investors from America and Europe that kept their emotional connection to India alive via Karan Johan movies. Besides love for the motherland, these moneybag investors did not want to miss out on the astronomical returns investing in

India's real estate sector offered. Lata earned big commissions from developers that contributed to my transition towards spending more time at golf and exotic holidays. I knew the back up money was there in her accounts that I managed.

"We will do an IPO one day," she would constantly say. "Raising Rs 250 crores is my aim." "You can do it,"' I egged her on, thinking about ways to spend that kind of money. There was a limit to eating out, buying new clothes and holidaying.

I thought of taking up an expensive hobby such as photography. I bought an expensive Nikon camera that could be fitted with powerful lens that extended like an elephant's trunk in front. Like Lata, I too was disinclined towards household management and wanted to focus on my career, like my peers, cousins and Sid who were doing quite well for themselves now.

Prior to my marriage, all household concerns were quietly handled by my parents. I assumed them sorted while occupying my time chasing girls, playing sports, attending birthday parties of friends, occasionally studying.

Courtesy my father, there was always the battery of over eager batmen and lower constabulary to do the odd jobs around the house. At our spacious South Delhi government neighbourhood where I grew up, there was plenty of room for everybody, like foreigners, to be polite to each other.

As I realized, rented homes are never easy to manage on one's own, despite romanticism linked to setting up house as a newly married couple and doing things together. There are ceaseless problems such as electrical and plumbing issues, flush not working, dead telephone, no water supply, quarrels with neighbours over parking, car servicing, washing clothes and cooking as there is a limit to ordering home delivery given the usual extra-spicy, extra-oily trans-fat menus on offer.

At our new address in Gurgaon, space was a constraint. Premium high rise buildings with well-demarcated areas for each household were yet to take off. Parking was the most debated subject at resident welfare meetings.

It was a highly emotive issue on which neighbours fought and occasionally assaulted each other, with men hitting men and women hitting women. Parking spots were delineated like an India-Pakistan Line of Control, with no room for any infringement or buffer zones.

There is reason foreigners tend to be well-behaved and polite. The populations in Europe or America are puny compared to the sprawling hospitals, roads, restaurants, malls, airports, rail stations, anywhere, with ample parking spaces.

In India, there are always a million car tyres or bums vying for any spot – a seat in the train, educational institutions or doctor appointment. One cannot get by without being boorish. Living on our own in Gurgaon, there were also the disinterested, nonchalant and inefficient maids to be managed. I was used to orderlies, obsequious and very scared of my father, take care of household chores.

I never knew unpredictable maids could become such a big factor in my life. Domestic helps in Gurgaon lead cushy lifestyles and are spoilt for choice due to the many high-income earning households desperate to hire them.

Schools and maids can never be out of work here. They call the shots. There should be a domestic violence law protecting employers rather than employees. For the maids, employment is readily available whenever they feel the need to earn (not work, mind you), given the rising young upwardly mobile population working in MNCs endowed with high fertility rates and resultant kids.

Given double income families, kids are raised by maids while both parents are busy earning the big MNC moolah requiring frequent business class overseas travel and conference calls at odd hours to keep Chicago, London or Singapore timings. Due to the kid factor, the maids are treated like goddesses, sometimes paid more than school teachers despite being uneducated. There are households where the help lives in a bigger room than grandparents, fitted with LCD TVs, music system, air-conditioner and tub in the bathroom.

The children are strictly told to address the maids as "*didis*" to continually impress the domestic about her premium spot in the family hierarchy. The maids, themselves, arrive in two categories, the good and bad looking ones. The unattractive lot is desensitized by their harsh lives, living conditions and upbringings. They do not care about anything, especially work.

Their bags are forever packed ready to relinquish their current employment any moment over issues quite irrelevant to anybody normal and sane -- simply bored or irritated with employer, not enough TV time, monotonous gossip involving neighbourhood servant community or being disallowed cell phone talk hours. Only the spare time is for work. The comely maids, meanwhile, are prima donnas with looks that could approximate a Nandita Das, sexy and alluring.

They constantly chat over cell phones with sundry boyfriends referred to as *bhai*s or brothers that could be drivers, gardeners or cooks. The drivers are the big studs sought by maids due to better salaries and access to a car to move about on the sly.

The multiple maid-*bhai* love affairs cannot be just over airwaves. Depending on benefits of hanging out with a particular *bhai* the maids ask for leave which not granted can mean overnight resignation, submitted face-to-face or over the phone or via some proxy *bhai*-boyfriend.

Some maids boast of private sector executives, businessmen and lonely working expatriates as suitors. Not to marry, but for a good time, expensive gifts and direct money exchanges for sexual favours. I have spotted several maid-expat couples at movie halls, food courts, fast food restaurants and coffee outlets around Gurgaon.

Given the linguistic barriers, they don't have much to say to each other, but the poor guys starved of company, sex and female proximity, desperately need to hold onto any available woman. While at work, the pretty maids amble about the house with heads tilted, phone nestled between ear and long glistening shampooed, conditioned hair loosely spread over their slender shoulders.

They talk in whispers. Only a trained eye can figure they are speaking on the phone alongside the sweeping, cooking and cleaning jobs. Of course, these girls are in no hurry to marry.

They value their independence, income and several lucrative relationships. With laptop, netbook, tablet prices dipping, the day is not too far away when maids could tot computers, loaded with multi-lingual software, like cell phones.

They could demand Internet surfing and online chatting time using local dialect software, alongside TV watching hours and cell phone conversation, as part of their employment deal. The double income families would have no choice but to accede to maids' demands. The *bhais* would have to spend more as cell phones can be much cheaper than computers.

I remember one pretty maid at Lata's house who boasted five expensive cell phones. "They have been presented by my *bhais*," she told me. "Why do all the *bhais* give you cell phones only? Why not other gifts?" I asked her.

"Cell phones are the easiest to sell to anybody, like potatoes. I can pass them on to anybody in my family including aunts and uncles when I go to my village. The poor in India are desperate for two things only – food and cell phones," she replied in Hindi, that I have translated. Smart girl, I mused.

Most maids in Gurgaon are from Jharkhand, a state where the tribal population has been exploited, ravaged and impoverished by the rapacious mining mafia.

I believe the money earned by domestics has done a bit to revive economies back home, just as Middle East bound nurses from Kerala have transformed lives, built houses and educated their younger siblings or kids by remitting incomes. This has also gone some way in helping cell phone companies meet their sales targets, I am sure. So, every time I paid maid wages, I assuaged my seething about their lack of professional ethics and competence, as my bit for charity to douse the rising Maoist problems in eastern India due to exploitation of the tribal population.

I penned the following about maids after my daughter Alaynah was born:

Don't read me wrong, but for as long as my memory goes maids have been a subject of hot discussion of my grandmother, mother and now my wife and her mother. "She takes leave too often, steals, drinks milk from the fridge, dirty, ill-behaved…," have been the common complaints.

Maids have been spoken about by women of my household with the same passion as I may talk about cricket, golf or shares. Frankly, I have considered them a nuisance and maid issues very silly woman talk, until I have had to take part-responsibility of babysitting Alaynah. These girls know that they have you by the b…ls (pardon the language) when it comes to the kid.

A couple of bad experiences I can recall are when I had to multi-task between Alaynah and a stiff deadline, which I thought I could manage with the maid. I made the mistake of snapping at her on some issue I don't remember.

She promptly told me "Saab, chakkar aa raha hai (Sir, I have a headache)." When a young girl speaks about such a problem, it only means one thing and one has to let her go to her room and rest.

During my early days of handling Alaynah with a maid, I lost my temper at one and she promptly packed her belongings and left. Then began a mad scramble for a new maid and soon I realized getting one is an organized racket involving agencies that charge a hefty service amount without any guarantees.

The agencies, as a matter of fact, encourage maids to leave employers so they make more money by re-cycling them elsewhere. Further, given the pace at which the Indian population is procreating, the maid sector is a monopoly.

Now I look at handling maids as a very serious matter and have had discussions with my mother on the issues involved. "Be gentle and diplomatic," is her advice.

Our current maid has negotiated TV time for her favourite soap operas and spends quite a bit of her day talking on the cell phone (call this emancipation due to technology and cheap call rates) to sundry drivers and gardeners, spread all over the country. I good naturedly pretend all of this is very funny.

****

It was around the time that my father retired that I decided to shift to Lata's. Superannuation can be difficult for government servants with power, security and perks wiped out in a second. Some take it to heart and suffer coronary failure. Others have been known to brood and watch TV for the rest of their lives.

When my father retired, I did the newspaper job and drove to Delhi from our post-marriage rented apartment in Gurgaon. As Lata worked with her father, we decided to take up accommodation there, as I have talked about earlier.

As I was rightly presumed to be hardier I was expected to make the journey from Gurgaon to Delhi rather than the other way round. I did not mind as I often drove the Honda City over FM music and effective air-conditioning.

My relations with my parents had not soured yet, though my father continued to be deeply unhappy about my failure to crack the IAS.

On his final day in office, my father refused to believe that soon he would not be part of a powerful network that he belonged over three decades. He could not accept his services were no longer required by the nation as he believed the system needed him more than other way round.

My father was close witness to many of his seniors retiring and taking it quite badly. Yet, he was convinced of an "extension" that a privileged few considered close to political masters were offered on attaining official retirement age. My father had any number of astrologers that cultivated him for favours such as new passport foretell, in the name of planetary surety, that he would achieve his ultimate dream of being appointed governor of a state. This was not to be.

Like many before him, my father expected a fax from the Prime Minister's Office approving his extension, until the last minute of his career in government. The PM had other pressing matters to attend and the order never arrived.

On his last day of service, I sat with my father from 4:00 to 6:00 pm at his office, inside the plush wall-to-wall carpeted room fitted with sofa, TV, coffee maker, latest widescreen desktop, printer, fax machine and the works.

The room could have passed off as a suite of a five-star hotel. It was a reflection of government being impacted by private sector office decor. The state machinery is always quick to copy stuff that benefits them. At the same time, there is huge resistance to easing delivery of services to citizens as this reduces discretionary element and chances of making money on the side.

My father and I did not speak much on his last day in office. We did not talk much to each other in any case. The last serious one-to-one serious conversation we had was when I was appearing for the IAS exam, first attempt. He briefly told me the government would be a mess unless he was around to take care of important matters of national relevance such as internal security and threat of overseas terror.

I worked on my laptop while he browsed some files marked 'urgent'. All files in government offices are marked 'urgent'. That is why most are not treated with any sense of urgency. For my father's sake, I really wished for the fax machine to buzz with the Prime Minister authorizing his extension.

There were many communications that arrived, but none from the head of government whom I cursed repeatedly in my mind. At 6:00 pm when my father stepped out of office for the last time, the staff, already in a hurry to catch their chartered buses back home, quickly garlanded him, wished him a happy retired life and departed. The same underlings would have hung around till eternity had my father got an extension due to need to cultivate him further.

A golf set was hurriedly presented to my father though he never played the sport. This was one of the sanctioned expensive gifts that could be handed to retiring senior officials. So, it was procured for my father as it was the least bothersome to obtain, with an inventory maintained by some department that handled the issuance.

They checked the records that my father was truly retiring and endorsed the set. My father was a little bewildered by the unexpected attention of his staff and appeared like a person who has suffered a slight knock on his head to lose his bearings. Government functioning can be pretty insensitive at times. Noticing my father's disturbed state of mind I went home with him, informing Lata accordingly.

Next morning my father woke up as usual, tried unsuccessfully to wake me up for a few minutes, went for his morning walk, tea, newspapers, bath and breakfast, changed into his uniform, but had nowhere to go.

His official car did not arrive to ferry him to office. He called his former office to be told by his former secretary that the vehicle had been allotted to another officer. My father finally realized he was well and truly out of the government, though his pension would still be out of tax payer's money which he fully deserved.

My mother was uncomfortable seeing him roam around the house in Khaki with nothing to do. Nobody was happy.

My parents soon shifted to a DDA flat in West Delhi from the spacious South Delhi lodging boasting well-maintained green lawns in the front and back, maintained by an army of under employed government gardeners.

It was a matter of prestige for my father to be allotted C-1 housing grade compared to the lower D-1 and D-11 category. The highest levels are ministerial bungalows, residences of defence heads and very senior IAS officials.

Many retiring officials try to hang on to their official accommodation beyond their time and eligibility, making excuses such as wife's terminal sickness while desperately seeking an extension or important post such as governor, member UPSC or vice chancellor of a central university. Some are evicted via legal action and others physically removed with unpacked belongings strewn about. Quite a few still manage to hang on using their clout and networks.

One piece of good news was that Sid landed a big ticket consultancy job in London. He called to tell my parents not to worry. He declared he was planning to buy a bungalow in Vasant Vihar in the near future where all of us could live together in good comfort and status befitting my father's position and rank.

My father was very happy to hear the apple of his eyes make the offer, though it never materialized. Sid married in London and bought properties there as per wishes of his wife, who now dominated his thinking. He belonged to the ilk of guys deprived of girls in the early part of their lives.

Such an existence meant once they did get hitched, they accommodate every whim and fancy of the woman and her mother, due to the bedazzling presence of the opposite sex, for the first time, in their vicinity.

My parents visited Sid during summer months to soak in his success. My brother looked after them well. They went for long walks in the leafy parks, visited Starbucks and watched Wimbledon tennis or cricket at Lords and Oval.

But, they preferred to come back to India after a while to the comfort and independence of their own house. Even though my father was trying to come to terms with his superannuation and my IAS failure he could not digest his second son turning into a *"ghar jamai."*

"He is dead, my son is dead for me," he declared to my mother. His deep-seated angst of my not making it to the IAS made it even more difficult for him to accept my new situation. He refused to meet me and expressed his views over phone that he could not accept that I had become a "*ghar jamai.*"

Another relative echoed my father's views and told me he thought I was a parasite. Though the relations wanted to keep my father happy, given the regular favours in dealings with the government, such as getting a FIR lodged due to a stolen car, I realized that passions about dealing with a *ghar jamai* were quite strong.

So, I chose to keep shut, though it required enormous amounts of self-control to keep quiet to taunts every time. An aunt said she equated *ghar jamai*s to dogs.

"Who cares about your views?" I retorted, calling her a "bitch" in my mind several times. I never liked the lady due to her inconsistent behaviour, especially towards me. When her kids were little she hissed warnings against my "bad habits" that included girlfriends, going to discos, pubs and restaurants, smoking and drinking.

"I don't want you both to be like him when you grow up," she told her children, pointing a wildly shaking finger towards me. If she was not related to my mom or was not a lady, I probably would have twisted the finger till the bone snapped.

When her kids grew up and turned out like me in many aspects, which I think is pretty normal, she defended them, "Times have changed. Who doesn't go to restaurants and discos? All young people do nowadays. Who does not have a boyfriend or girlfriend nowadays?"

"Screw you bitch," I abused her several times in my mind, in the presence of my parents. She was lucky to be a relative or I would not have kept shut.

****

Like before, Lata wanted to change my food habits, post our marriage too. The big influence was her father who was a teetotaller, vegetarian, frugal and strictly believed in eating right. This was due to a history of tummy ache, excessive gas and acidity dating back to his childhood.

He was at constant war with constipation incorporating extreme forms of discipline to ensure his morning motions were uneventful and smooth. In terms of professional achievement, he was a hero, the kind that are written and spoken about -- a poor village bumpkin who cracked every exam that came his way due to sheer hard work and uncommon focus to make it big.

I believe there are more like him occupying the highest leagues of achievement -- Lal Bahadur Shastri earlier, Manmohan Singh, my father among others. However, due to his medical situation, my father-in-law applied some of his immense focus and dedication towards dissipating extra air that refused to exit his body.

He had his stomach and intestine scans done in Singapore and was planning another in America. He possessed a huge collection of books on the subject of tummy care and another big shelf brimmed with medications that ranged from homeopathy, allopathic and Ayurveda to Yunani.

He was on a constant look out for any emerging schools of medicine or new therapies. Depending upon his condition and mental inclination he would ingest and experiment with any one or multiple forms of medicines, water treatments, yoga, long walks, sleeping on his stomach, Baba Ramdev, Vipassana, meditation, Deepak Chopra, Art of Living and more.

He said he was close to achieving nirvana, not of the spiritual kind that results in the mind, soul and body being one, but the ability to eject and reject anything that agreed or disagreed with his tummy via an inner physical force. The whole process did not appeal to me much.

But, being a powerful personality my father-in-law had a big influence on his family that included his daughter Lata, her mother, cousins, aunts and uncles. One of his self-evolved theories from personal experience was the efficacy of *"lauki"* in ridding the body of toxins quickly.

Thus, *lauki* was served during every meal of the Lata household. Boiled *lauki* chunks were mixed in steamed rice; the vegetable was grated into the *dal* apart from being a main course item; omelettes had *lauki* fillings.

Lauki juice was served as a substitute for wine during family occasions. *Lauki kheer* or *halwa* was the most relished homemade sweet dish. The damned vegetable was grown in the backyard of Lata's house. Her father maintained a farm to specially grow *lauki* to pre-empt any back end supply problems. He had figured out various horticulture and greenhouse techniques to grow *lauki* round the year.

Any person with a sane palate living in Lata's household would have despised *lauki* in no time. I never had any issues with *lauki* preparations, until after my marriage. Over time I even stopped liking *bhindi* (lady's finger), the second most popular vegetable at my in-laws due to frequency of consumption.

My guess was too much *lauki* was the cause of my father-in-law's problems. He needed to rid the vegetable from his system and focus on partaking tasty butter chicken and prawn curry to set his digestive juices right.

I, however, chose to keep my views to myself as indigestion was a sensitive subject in Lata's family. I did not want to appear frivolous. There were two matters that my wife's father chased with some zeal – property and potty.

Despite the efforts, he would fart about loudly in the house that nobody, except me of course, would notice and sense. I admit my father too farted in high decibels around our home. I think it is a head of the family thing, probably an innate dominant male behaviour similar to lions or dogs urinating on bushes, shrubs, grass, car tyres to mark their territories, females and kids.

Lata, however, pointedly told me I was being very rude if I happened to blow wind in her of her family's presence. There is something about fathers and daughters that I have never figured out. The father can do no wrong, including farting loudly. The husband, on the other hand, does not get anything right.

Guys while courting a girl present a picture of perfect etiquettes, fart-free demeanours, non-stinky breath, even shaved armpits. This cannot carry on for too long. Once in the comfort zone of marriage, inhibitions disappear, though I believe wives still prefer to keep private matters personal unless absolutely necessary.

Like an excessively horny spouse wanting to have it every night which is not possible for a woman biologically. Husbands, generally lose restraint in some time. Most prefer to return to normal existence of infrequent bathing, unclean toilets, messed up clothes and farting with abandon.

Lata did not allow me liberties, especially in the presence of her parents. I think she construed it as an insult to her entire family. "You should step out of the room," she told me, a few times when I blew with some force in public with everybody around and about, including the servants.

The household staff physically continued with the motions of doing whatever they were doing, but every ear was trained to the conversation that was to follow. "What about your father? He could pass of as a bio-gas plant. His contributions should be added in India's renewable energy installed capacity," I said.

"Don't joke about an old and sick man," Lata retorted sharply. I gauged that this was an issue she would definitely fight about. It was better to let it be

"Okay I am sorry. Next time I will hold back and suffer a tummy ache. Then I will be forced to eat only *lauki* and everybody will be happy," I replied.

My father-in-law was not very old. He was 60. In the West rich new fathers at this age is common occurrence. The second or third wives of such men happen to be in their good looking 20s or 30s who stand to gain wealth either way -- divorce or death of husband. With increasing riches, there is some talk about the growing number of sugar daddies, seeking to marry young trophy wives in India as well.

A rising number of Indians are living to late 80s given access to good medical care during later stages of life. This is due to mushrooming of private hospitals catering to western patients looking for cheaper but quality treatments here.

Medical outsourcing to India means upper middle-classes and rich Indians have ready access to state-of-the-art health care, locally. Hospital staff is trained about equal importance of good communication skills and behaviour to deal with global clients. Most, however, are like travel guides, who can answer only a given set of questions. Responses that need a little intelligence usually border on the stupid.

As close-knit Indian families accumulate in large numbers during any medical occasion of a relative, the new age hospitals like international airports and malls offer services of large food courts, elaborate menus serving delectable *biryani*, sleeping lounges, shopping arcades, movie screens and spas.

While the immediate kin of the patient fret about latest medical reports, the rest socialize, mingle, network, exchange gossip .and jokes. It is like a family visit to a nearby mall, a weekend break, a marriage, movies or birthday party.

In keeping with such wholesome resort experience, hospitals could soon boast putting greens, swimming pools, ping pong and pool tables and tennis courts.

Apart from hospitals, large Indian families are also very happy when they are out to a pure vegetarian Haldiram or a Bikanervala, India's local answer to McDonalds. The food is spicy, tasty, fattening and cheap. The place is noisy and crowded with crawling kids high on French fries, noodles and cola.

As these joints are relatively clean, air-conditioned and occupy large spaces, the parents don't mind children running about, slipping and falling over each other adding to the cacophony of giggling, laughter and cheer. People scream, guffaw, talk loudly and generally feel happy without being drunk.

There are large well-maintained loos so that the ladies feel comfortable, can exchange girlie notes in private and don't feel the need to go home in a hurry. There is no problem in handling kiddies *susu* and potty as well.

This aspect doesn't matter to the men folk too much. They can unzip almost anywhere to relieve themselves. The poor of India, however, continue to be at the mercy of over-stretched, dirty and uncouth government staff and state hospitals. They cannot afford to eat out even at the cheap Indian eateries.

They die untreated young and in large numbers of diseases that can be easily pre-empted or prevented by basic medication.

Government hospitals resemble filthy Indian railway stations with people scattered about, lounging, sleeping anywhere, among beggars, spit, street dogs, pigs and shit, waiting for perennially late trains.

The only difference is that in hospitals, the wait could be forever, in the absence of on-time treatment. Given such a sorry macro scenario, food habits and my pop-in-law's gas problems were minor occurrences. Yet, I was also not thinking much about the conditions of Indian hospitals, rail platforms and the big picture, at that time. I was thinking about my own progress. I wanted to be selfish.

****

My mother-in-law was a slight woman with a brain honed and sharpened over the years to one instinct -- protect and provide for

194 *An Offbeat Story*

her daughter. She defined herself as Lata's personal and emotional bodyguard.

It was not easy for me to decipher within the diminutive and harmless looking middle-aged housewife, my mother-in-law's mind was frenetically ticking away as the singular self-appointed defender of her daughter's interests and rights.

As I was physically bigger than her own offspring and weakened by indigestion husband, my mother-in-law was convinced they needed her care and safeguarding.

It took me some time to be accustomed to the not so subtly hostile post-marriage environment at my in-laws residence. Indian culture and upbringing is such that children are told to respect elders as a universal principle.

This sometimes defangs the young against the older lot that maybe crooked, like an aging Colonel Gaddafi who allowed his many children to loot Libya, until the citizens got even. Even though my God-given physical built can be a little intimidating, I am mostly a very docile person, unless severely provoked.

I sometimes scream, shout and make caustic remarks. I rarely hit anybody, stronger or weaker than me. Lata and her mother were natural allies. They were quick as *jujutsu* fighters to defend each other which did not make me feel very happy. Still I refused to bottle up any irritation as I had read a *Reader's Digest* article that advised against internalizing stress which is not good for health. I needed to give it back in the same spirit, though this was not easy.

Like it is for any healthy letting out steam husband-wife argument, I did smash a couple of cell phones, in a state of animation. My mother-in-law instantly jumped into the fray aggressively siding with her daughter, hissing out warnings that I stay away. "He turns into a mad man when angry. He is mad, mad, mad."

Somehow, I never took offense when my mother called me deranged when she was not happy with me. I did not take it too lightly addressed the same way by my mother-in-law. "You are the one who is mad. This whole family is mad. It is because your brains have turned into *lauki*s," I screamed back.

Many prejudices awaited me after I shifted into my wife's house, the kind that Indian guys spoilt by their mothers' food and fussing are not accustomed. I was used to being pampered by my mother, who had trained herself to high levels of culinary skills just to satisfy my palate directly and ego indirectly.

She stopped preparing cheese and corn based baked items, among my favourite dishes, when I shifted to Gurgaon. But, by the time I was facing the world on my own my mother had fanned my male ego needing to be pampered by a woman to the size of an overgrown pumpkin.

I expected every woman in my life to indulge and make me feel very important. Pooja too played a part in fuelling this view. My mother-in-law believed in the opposite. She wanted my ego to be deflated and squashed to the size of a ping pong ball with my only mission in life to keep her daughter happy.

In the beginning of our interactions, I incorrectly imagined my mother-in-law in the image of my mother – caring, giving, sensitive, sacrificing and loving, with her focus of life the welfare of her family. In some way, she was all of that, but only to her own kin. I was always the outsider.

When I met my to-be *saas* for the first time, she fussed over me, my personal comfort and the quality of snacks on offer, the sugar and salt balance in the lemonade. She knew I was an important person in her daughter's life. She worried that I drove a scooter. "Why don't you buy yourself a car?" she said. Perhaps Lata had confided about her long-term intentions with me.

I was touched by her concern, though later I realized she could only have thought about her daughter Lata having to ride pillion. Otherwise, I could have crashed into the next dumper, for all she cared.

While Lata was vocal about supporting her father, her relationship with her mother functioned on a totally different plane. It was via subtle signals, a complex secret unwritten Da Vinci code, that the two could instantly read and decipher each other.

Thus, without uttering a word, Lata knew her mother was upset, tired, angry, hungry, sick and perhaps, by extension, wanting to visit the loo. The communication worked both ways. Soon, another facet was added to the mother-daughter invisible and obscure vocabulary -- not happy with her son-in-law or husband, as applicable. This particular signal was used most frequently with time.

The messages my mother-in-law conveyed to Lata via her facial expressions could put any *saas* in real life or even in an Ekta Kapoor serial to shame. She should have auditioned for TV. Over time, I think I figured a few.

For example, if she grinded her teeth like a baby refusing to eat more, it meant that she was very upset. A baby, of course, looks cute anytime, while my mother-in-law only looked like an older version of my wife, with eyeballs alert and scheming.

If she walked past Lata in a quick gait without making eye contact or small conversation, she was again not happy. If she lay down in bed for no particular reason, while her health was fine, it meant she was very very disturbed.

Over time my guess was all silent mostly undecipherable indicators conveyed only one meaning to Lata -- that her mother was angry with me. Post-marriage my mother-in-law saw me as the greatest threat to her darling child's peace and happiness for no special reason. I have still not figured out the cause of her angst.

There were instances that Lata would enter her mother's room in a happy mood and exit cross with me. "Your mother puts ideas into your head about me which would have otherwise not occurred to you. She is not good for our marriage," I told her. "You imagine too much. Focus on your work," Lata said.

My mother-in-law believed in sharing minimum information with me as a natural corollary to her feelings towards me. "I am going out," she told me one time when my daughter was a little baby. "Where?" I asked with some alarm, as I would have to babysit as Lata was away.

"I don't know. Somewhere," she said.

"How long will you be away?" I asked, not very happy to be saddled with the domestic household responsibility, even if I was otherwise free.

"An hour," she said.

"If you know how much time you will take, then you should know where you are going," I remarked.

"I don't know where I am going. I am going somewhere," she said. I rest my case.

As I realized, it was not easy for Lata to accept criticism about her darling mother who spent two hours every morning preparing tiffin for her husband and daughter. If my father was passionate about being honest, my father-in-law property, my mother-in-law was focused on right food for her kindred blood family only.

My mother-in-law wanted to make sure the best ingredients settled in the tummies of her delicate daughter and forever constipated husband. She personally cut the fruit, supervised the sautéed vegetables, *raita* and sweet dish.

All the eatables were sprinkled or mixed with boiled and grated *lauki* like it was done with cheese in normal households. The victuals were carefully wrapped in silver foil and packed with care in special imported lunch boxes that maintained the heat and moisture. Such dedication of time meant Lata and my father-in-law were extremely sensitive about any criticism of my mother-in-law.

For my day long work trips, my tiffin was prepared by the servants who made it a point to pack either *bhindi* or *lauki*. The domestic staff is always quick to read the political undercurrents of any family.

In mine, I was the lowest in the hierarchy of importance while my mother-in-law was the highest.

A couple of times I lost my temper at a particularly loyal underling to register my superior status. I was immediately told by my wife's family to keep away from handling of servant matters.

"If you have any problem with the servants you need to discuss with us first," my father-in-law said sternly, farting loudly as he spoke. He needed to blow wind to emit forceful words, like some propulsion machine. It was okay for him to fart whenever he wanted, but if I did my wife thought it to be very rude.

"I will talk to anybody I wish to speak to. I don't need anybody's permission," I replied. "You should not talk to my father like this," Lata intervened.

"I am not talking to him. Why should I want to talk to him? He is talking to me," I said, even as Lata pulled me away to our room.

Although the matter rested there, I stopped saying anything to the servants. They were too peripheral to my existence and thoughts.

My mother-in-law also made sure that expensive, seasonal and unseasonal eatables, especially fruits, were stored away at locations that could not be accessed easily by the ready to steal servants and later me.

Her bedroom doubled up as storage for the foodstuff that was reserved for her better half, Lata and close relatives including her sisters' family who were frequent visitors. The cupboards were brimming with expensive strawberries, grapes, custard apple, plums, cashew nuts, almonds, pistachios and walnuts. Imported packets containing prunes and dried apricots were neatly lined in shelves. Imported peanut butter bottles and expensive pickle completed the picture.

"Your mother's bed room is a *mandi*. She should put price tags on the items on display. The government could arrest her for hoarding. No wonder prices are rising and the poor are suffering in our country," I told Lata.

"Everybody has their own style. You should learn to respect it," my wife immediately responded. Still, purely to neutralize my mother-in-laws intentions, if I happened to enter her room, which occurred only if Alaynah or Lata were also around, I helped myself to handfuls of whatever came my way, including exotic fruit such as Kiwi that cost a bomb, even if I was not hungry.

She was quick as a professional boxer to react. She promptly called in the carpenter to install new wooden shelves and cupboards in her room. The locks were repaired and the keys probably hidden in her bathroom that I never visited.

I have never been one to walk into a ladies' toilet. The fruits and cashew nuts promptly disappeared from view. In order to keep matters politically correct my mother-in-law told Lata the new space was needed to keep ants and termites out. In the recess of her mind I was the big black ant that she wanted to keep away.

To me she was no less than Mohammed Ali, ready to sting and wear down any opponent. But, I was no less than Joe Frazier who kept coming back.

I tried coaxing her to share her hidden booty. "Can I have some pistachios?" I once asked her, when my wife was around.

"They are finished," she lied, I am sure. On another occasion I asked for custard apple not in season and quoting a price that one could buy a cell phone or I-Pod. They too happened to be over.

Another bone of contention was cheese that I savoured a bit. My mother spent quite a bit of her time discovering various varieties of cheese stocked in South Delhi markets patronized by diplomats. She prepared concoctions with corn, broccoli, mushroom that tasted divine.

The situation at my wife's house was different. I could not figure out where the cubes or tin would disappear when I spotted some cheese in the fridge. There were many refrigerators in Lata's house – two in the pantry and two more really big ones, the size of cupboards, in my mother-in-law's room.

There was one each in the kitchen, laundry and basement. My guess is that she had one in her toilet where the cheese was finally hidden. I helped myself to liberal chunks of cheese, whenever I could as part of my strategy to meet aggression with aggression. Invariably, the next time I looked at the same place, the cheese would have disappeared for good.

I noticed them tucked away at corners in any one of the fridges where one would least expect cheese to be stored – in the vegetable section, ice cabin, inside empty ice cream containers or behind water bottles. It was a deliberate act to cut me out. I reciprocated by devouring big portions anytime I chanced upon any cheese.

The overeating and gorging did affect my tummy a few times. There was also the deleterious effect of accumulated fat that could only be burned via long and regular visits to the gym or running or plenty of sex. Despite the stomach trouble and risk of extra weight, I was always on the hunt for cheese at my wife's house that I hoped would be a temporary abode for me and her.

****

I soon realized a *ghar jamai* has to accept obtuse treatment as routine. My situation popped up in conversations more often than I envisaged. Indian society has only progressed in pockets of liberal behaviour. The majority espouse thoughts and actions that are conservative. In order to fend off barbs, I had to constantly innovate and improvise like a cricketer faced with a bad pitch, good bowling and excellent fielding side. I tried.

I must admit I am no natural at it, like a silken-touch wristy cricketer who waits for the ball till the last minute to turn it to fine leg for four despite a fielder patrolling the area, like VVS Laxman or Mohammed Azharuddin earlier.

I don't like Sachin Tendulkar too much despite his achievements. I think he psyches out when the team is under pressure. He is a joy to watch when he gets going, plays freely, especially in the first innings. There is no better sight in world cricket. For me a Dhoni or a Yuvraj are cool in tough situations for one-day internationals and Rahul Dravid for Test cricket.

Cricketers have it very good in terms of fame and money. As a *ghar jamai* the census people who calculate India's rapidly reproducing population did not know where to fit me in their count.

They did not have an entry in the form that defined my status with the father-in-law as head of family. The categories included father, mother, wife, son, daughter, daughter-in-law and grandchildren. They did not know where to slot me.

The census lady, an assiduous primary school teacher, was flummoxed. To add to more time wasting, she belonged to the tough genre that wants to set an example of uprightness to her kids and those around her by doing a good job.

Government servants are either too honest or too corrupt. Both are equally inefficient and irritating due to inflexibilities of absolutely following the rule book rather than the spirit or not following any norms at all.

The serious census teacher wanted to make sure I was counted as one more in the humongous Indian population of uncultured literates and mostly semi-literates and illiterates. I was of no help. "You live with your parents?" she asked.

"No, I live with my in-laws," I answered. The lady should have seen the name plate outside – it had my father-in-law's name in big bold letters that a half-blind person could spot from a distance. I sensed this conversation would really waste my time.

"This is your house. Your wife lives with you and her parents live with you too?" she asked.

"No this is my father-in-law's house. I live with them," I said. "You can go and check the name plate outside."

"What about your parents?" she asked.

"What about my parents? They are alive and well, unless you know something that I don't as it is your job to keep track of the population of the country," I told her.

"Where do your parents live?" she asked, patiently. I think for a government official she was doing quite well. Anybody else might have walked out of the house or maybe asked for a bribe to include me in the population count of the country that I was beginning to really not care about anymore.

"They live in their own house in Delhi. That is the last I heard," I answered.

"Your wife lives with your parents?" she asked.

"Why would my wife live with my parents? She is not married to them. She lives with me," I answered.

"Where do you live?" she asked.

"I live here. Why do you think I am moving around the house in shorts?" I answered, pointing at my hairy legs. She looked at them and then looked away.

"But, this is the house of your father-in-law. How can you live here and your father's house at the same time?" she said, probably to avoid a double count.

"I don't live in my father's house. It is better to stay in one location unless one is in love with shifting luggage all the time," I said.

"Why don't you live in your father's house?" she asked.

The queries were taking us nowhere and I was a little tight for time.

It is not as if government officials in this country take an appointment to arrive at your house. They just drop in and expect everybody else to be free to attend to them. To cut a long story short, I realized I had to explain matters to her in a language that she understood or ask her to leave which could have led to an ugly confrontation.

"I am a *Ghar Jamai*," I declared to her. She instantly studied the form closely.

"I don't know where to enter you in the form. If you were staying with your father, that would be simple as father son combination with the former as head of family is defined, but son-in-law with father-in-law as head of family has not been categorized," she said, "There are not too many like you."

"In case it is causing you problems, don't include me in the census," I said. "It does not matter to me."

"It matters to me," she replied. "I want to do my job properly."

I complimented the lady for being a diligent worker. I asked a servant to fetch some tea and biscuits. Too many state employees today do not care about their jobs. They perform efficiently only for those who corrupt them for illegal electricity connections or land usage or some such matter.

The census lady scribbled some notes on the blank spaces in the form that I could not read from a distance. Till date I am not sure whether I am accounted in the population count of my motherland.

Subtract one from over billion of us, I think. Does it matter despite repeated reminders about sacrifices made by our forefathers to win us our freedom and be counted in a democracy? God bless their souls.

****

I faced a similar set of queries at the police station for passport renewal. "You are a *ghar jamai*," the inspector quickly caught on following usual queries that instantly turned from indifferent to guarded to tense.

"Any criminal record?" he asked curtly, smelling of strong tobacco and bad breath to add to odour of urine that unfailingly pervades police stations in particular and government offices in general.

The slothful personnel here, I am sure, just pee on any available wall rather than make the effort to walk to a loo that in any case are badly maintained with pieces of shit or splashes of urine all over.

"No. My parents are straight forward people. They will be very unhappy if they found their son is into illegal activities," I replied.

I thought of the official as useless and corrupt, living off the tax payers' money, doing a rotten job that describes the personnel of his ilk in general.

"Any court cases?" he asked.

"No. In any case how does it matter if there is a court case or not? I could be innocent and involved in some judicial wrangle."

The inspector either ignored or did not understand my views. It probably did not make a difference what I was saying. Opinions of private citizens in this country do not matter, especially to authorities.

"If you are a *ghar jamai* you must be unemployed. We keep a record of such youth in our database as potential first time criminals," the repulsive inspector said.

"I am a journalist. Out salaries are next to nothing in any case. So, you can mark me as unemployed," I said. Again, the silly man pretended he did not hear me.

"Why have you become a *ghar jamai*?" he asked, as if I was a castrated human being sitting opposite him. He had no business asking me the question, but he did.

In India everybody feels the right to comment on anybody's personal life. One does not need to be celebrity with a frenzied paparazzi following to suffer such intrusions. I was not quizzing him about his private choices or hygiene.

"Why does your breath smell worse than a rhino or maybe a camel that in any case are animals that cannot brush their teeth without access to toothpaste?" I felt like asking him. "And, how do you sit here all day in this dingy pee perfumed office?" I wanted to tell him.

"My wife wanted me to," I actually said.

"What about your father? Is he okay with this?" he asked.

"No. But, I listened to my wife."

"If you wife asks you to jump into a well, will you?" he asked.

"No. Actually, it is more comfortable to stay in the wife's house. I am lazy. Things are taken care of and I can do my own things," I replied.

"Like what?" he asked.

"Like writing a book," I said.

"So you want to become a writer?"

"Maybe a film director also."

"I think you will become nothing," the officer said, with a puff of extremely bad breath and attitude. Our interactions were going nowhere. There was no way the damned official was going to recommend renewal of my passport. Thankfully, he had not asked for a bribe. I would have refused and the quality of our interactions would have turned from pits to worse.

There was an awkward silence between us. I would not have been surprised if the foul smelling inspector asked me to leave with my work undone. But, his curiosity about my status in life was not satiated yet.

"I have still not completely understood why you became a *ghar jamai*. It does not reflect well on your personality," he remarked

I realized I had to be diplomatic as passport clearance depended on the inquisitive inspector keen on judging my personal choices negatively. The answer needed to fit the officer's limited social and cultural purview of the world.

Or he could hold up the passport for eternity. I was not sure that my father would have helped in procuring the document given my post-marital shift to my wife's house. He had problems with that.

Otherwise, a phone call would have been enough to ensure the passport was delivered home, with the same inspector donning an absolute obsequious smile, reserved exclusively for seniors, politicians and crooks that pay them bribes.

Since this was not likely to happen, I had to deal with the second-rate police inspector, whose father probably bribed somebody to get him this job. He could easily report to higher ups he needed to investigate my "shady" antecedents.

My case could be converted into another file opened, never closed, forever forgotten, like millions others. That's the reason the lower bureaucracy or *babus* resist computers so vehemently. Paper files endow them with power to make documents disappear into cabinets and dingy rooms that nobody can trace.

Even if somebody tries, the smell of urine would put them off. There must be personnel assigned to pee on old files so nobody tries to retrieve them. Urinating on files is one official responsibility performed efficiently and diligently. Online database, on the other hand, cannot be tampered easily, though I believe there are more and more hackers that regularly damage saved files and folders that are suspected to be an insider job to escape responsibility.

"I have not told you the real reason I became a *ghar jamai*," I finally said. The officer was all ears. He wanted to hear this one for sure.

"It is to help my wife look after her father as he is a terminal case," I lied.

"What is his problem?" the inspector asked, concerned.

"He has cancer of the lower intestine caused by accumulation of too much gas and may die any day. So, we are looking after him till the end."

"Are you interested in inheriting your father-in-law's property after he dies?" This was another one of those questions that should not have been asked, but I had no choice but to answer delicately.

"No. I will live with my parents and look after them in their old age," I instantly invented an answer, sounding like a faux saint.

The mood changed. The greying official looked suitably pleased. "You should have told me this earlier. This is how the younger generation should be. Looking after the older generation," he said, making some notes in his diary. I wished when he was dying there would be nobody to look after him.

I had fitted into the idealistic worldview of the funny man. He asked no further questions. "When will you send the all clear report?"

"No worry. I will send it tomorrow. You should have your passport within the next two weeks." The document arrived within the stipulated time. Thankfully it did not smell of piss.

FOURTEEN

Standing on My Feet

I was well into my marriage by the time I managed to be financially independent, excluding value of my plots, without support from my wife or her family. I managed to earn a bit, own more properties of value, without a *Bharat Ratna*.

The urge to upgrade my economic situation was building inside me. Journalism did not pay since I valued professional integrity and guarded it zealously. A hack can be vulnerable to appeasements.

I respect those who refuse to buckle under pressure. I was still lucky, being better off than many other journos that struggled to pay even the depressed East Delhi rent, school fees and grocery bills, all rising at a pace higher than non-existent salary hikes. Many newspaper organizations handed a box of chocolates as annual bonus. That does not go very far.

I had the buffer of the plots. My wife was working and my in-laws were rich. A healthy pension and free medical expenses extended by the government ensured my parents were well taken care in case needed. My brother was close to becoming a dollar millionaire. With everything else in place, my only problem was me and my low salary.

I got a career break that earned me income comparable to successful corporate salaries earned by my MBA peers. With rising focus on India matters, especially business, I was contracted as an India analyst by an overseas consultancy. I felt important.

"We can offer $450 dollars for a 1,200 word project on issues that you write about such as elections, politics, defence, international affairs and energy. We would like to present your exclusive opinions to our clients," Caroline Harbinson said to me, sitting across the table at the coffee shop that overlooks the large swimming pool at the Ashok Hotel, in the diplomatic area of New Delhi.

Caroline headed the South Asia division of the global consultancy with offices in New York, London and Singapore that specialized in country specific market intelligence, risk assessments and analysis.

She was carrying with her a file of my pieces that ranged from terror issues, Indo-Pak relations, state and national politics, strategic affairs, Kashmir, real estate, auto, software and more. I never thought my essays, many of which I wrote under differing moods and under pressure of multiple deadlines, were so seriously scrutinized by people completely disconnected to my immediate existence.

I was happy somebody was maintaining a folder on me too, like my father did for Sid's innumerable marriage offers. "I am a big fan of your writing and read your stories online in London often. Your views are always balanced and never slanted or biased," Caroline continued, reminding me of Sushmita's views about my work.

Internet was surely a boon. An online presence enabled individuals to turn into minor global entities, automatically marketing work anywhere for free.

It is similar logic that allows an Amazon to take on Wal-Mart and succeed. And, unlike the dot com era that went bust along with such high-sounding coinages as "content is king" that made journalists feel like revenue generators for a change, knowledge outsourcing is stable business model.

Many hacks bitten by the dot com bug had quit their jobs, only to find themselves jobless in no time as the bubble burst. Some, realizing their little worth in the employment mart, went on to do MBAs from any available second rung institute to land jobs in the fast growing services sector (read hotels, airlines, travel agencies). Others picked up NIIT diplomas to make it abroad as software engineers.

In some ways the dot com shakeout was a blessing in disguise to escape the drudgery of a low on cash high on city bus travel journalistic life.

Caroline's offer translated into Rs 20,000 per submission. 'The foreigners have lost it,' I told myself. Perhaps, they did not know about Indian journalist salaries. I was no networker either who could offer them ready access to politicians or bureaucrats, for a price. Conversely, may be they needed me.

An emerging Indian economy had transformed into a big market riding on robust sectors such as software, auto, outsourcing, telecom, hospitality, tourism. It was possible my views were a worthwhile investment for informed corporate decisions and strategies that relied on multiple sources of information. I had already sensed a change in coverage of India in foreign newspapers and TV, a reflection of transforming readership and deeper investor mind-set.

The India stories were evolving beyond terrorism, possible Indo-Pak war, Kashmir, nuclear holocaust, naked fakirs, kite flying and snake charmers.

Hard news ranged from domestic politics, retail, insurance, energy, renewable power, defence deals, oil and gas exploration. Features focused on knowing the Indian way of life more, culture, cuisine, Bollywood and cricket.

India was a market where big money could be made given the large high on aspiration middle-class with growing purchasing power. More and more people were interested in the inner dynamics of the country and its people. Given prospects of profits, the interest was turning beyond war mongering and writing about Indian caricatures that unfortunately included Mahatma Gandhi.

"Do you think the money is less? I could push it to US$500," Caroline interrupted my thoughts looking at me earnestly with her big blue eyes. She could have been sexy if one ignored her slightly crooked nose and thin lips. She was wearing formal trousers and shirt. Her body was taut and fit.

Such size zero physiques can only be achieved via a strict diet, hours at a gym or aggressively pursuing a sport like skiing or skating. I had to be careful not to convey sexual vibes, in conversation or expression, to Caroline.

There was no need. I tried not to smile, lest my dimples confused or muddled her thoughts. "$450 is fine. More would better. Then, I can devote more time to a project. But, this is enough for me to take up the offer," I told Caroline, allowing her flexibility to decide the final price already beyond my expectations.

I did not want to lose out on the work. At the same time I did not want to sound too excited as I did not want my client to suspect they were over paying me.

Given the money involved, it was safer to call my articles "projects". It was apparent Caroline already had approvals to sign me on. Unlike Indians, who vacillate and negotiate endlessly, when overseas employers make up their minds, they stick to their decisions. This works the other way too.

If white bosses or clients decide to terminate services, there is no second chance. One can beg Indian employers, who can be quite considerate once medical emergency, family expenses, little kids school fees, caste kinships and old parents who need looking after are brought to forefront of negotiations.

Global honchos, married to individualist utilitarian philosophies, multiple wives and litters of kids, some similar aged than the new wife, do not understand such emotional equations and needs.

"How many projects would you need?" I asked, Caroline. I had my pen and worn out reporter's notebook on the table to appear as serious as possible. No smiling, no dimples, I was trying very hard to ensure.

"Four to five at the minimum every month," she answered. "Our clients want to invest in India and want to know more about how the country functions. Bigger projects may involve travel and intensive fieldwork."

I immediately calculated the money to be a minimum Rs 100,000 per month. Caroline's offer was not a bad deal for somebody like me just six years into journalism. It translated into a top MNC salary at the time and I was neither employed in the corporate sector nor a MBA graduate.

'I should do the best while the going is good,' I thought to myself as Caroline prepared the contract papers that I was to sign. Foreign clients are methodical about legal documents. Indian customers don't care as they have little faith in long drawn out, never ending judicial processes. It is word of mouth and trust that counts. I am not sure which system is better. Given the rising instances of chit fund scams in India, it may be better to opt for proper paper work.

Caroline's offer to me seemed solid, though the money appeared bit out of proportion to the effort, I felt. There were journalists with more experience, knowledge, bigger and hungrier families to feed, who would be willing to do the job at a much lower price to provide for non-working wives, kids and aging parents, always depicted as coughing and TB-stricken in Hindi movies.

All of this was not for me to worry about. I needed to encash the opportunity as long as the going was good, work on new professional relationships, establish trust and equity with new clients. I was not the only person in the country blessed with such a windfall. There were many more in vocations that ranged from finance, e-education, software, animation, graphic design, law and more who benefited due to the big cost arbitrage of getting the work done in a developing country.

Caroline handed me the confidential contract papers. I duly signed them. After she left, I watched the clear blue chlorinated waters of the Ashok pool a floor below for some time. I never like to swim in a crowed pool with children and foreigners drifting about. The kids must pee freely while it is not exciting to share the pool with overseas folks who use toilet paper to wipe clean their soiled back sides.

At the pool, a couple of swimmers, probably from Japan, seemed hung in mid-air as they slowly back stroked their way across the length of the pool, their bodies arched, arms moving in perfect rhythm as taught in coaching manuals. The Japanese are assiduous about everything, even swimming for pleasure.

Atomic bombs and tsunamis have turned them into a different breed of people, unlike Indians who consider nirvana as having to do nothing for an earning.

Why else would government jobs continue to be the main attraction for the youth of our country? The Chanakyapuri area where I grew up was just a couple of kilometres away from Ashok. A colony friend's civil servant father had been offered complimentary family membership of the Ashok pool courtesy his important post in the tourism ministry.

I and a few colony pals often used the facility, including steam, sauna and Jacuzzi. The club rules barred any guests unless their charges were paid separately. We never paid. The hotel management could not refuse us as long as our friend's father held the powerful post in Delhi.

We jumped into the pool flouting more rules, wearing shorts instead of swimming trunks, drinking beer, annoying the ladies, creating a racket and indulging in plenty of boisterous talk. I think the hotel must have lost a few membership renewals.

We did not believe in tipping the expectant staff that soon stopped smiling or acknowledging us. There was no money in our pockets as our fathers were powerful, but not rich. When my friend's father was transferred, the news spread rapidly, the freebie was withdrawn instantly and we were not allowed to swim any more. The management derived some satisfaction in barring our entry.

They had waited for this moment for some time. But, it was good while it lasted. One of us said "fuck you" to the duty manager the last time we used the pool.

It wiped the sneer off his face. He probably would have called in bouncers to bash us up but saner counsel prevailed as we were still the spoilt kids of government officials with connections. "I can afford the Ashok membership. And, I will again want to abuse the manager though he was only doing his job," I told myself the day I was contracted by Caroline.

****

I quit my newspaper job. I filed my tax return as an independent journalist and consultant. More clients followed as I learnt about the business of risk analysis.

The money I earned was more than anything I estimated a year or so earlier. Most of my investment plans centred around my wife's income as she was earning much more. I debated renting an office space, but chose not to.

Gurgaon commercial rents are very high. While saving on regular overhead expenditures, I wanted to create an e-work office environment. My employees or retainers worked from home, like me, on their computers with deadlines and parameters clearly defined. I employed fresh graduates, experienced specialists, full-time or on project basis.

I set up a website working a couple of days and nights figuring out the HTML process, instead of spending money due to my in-built frugal middle-class upbringing. In order to deliver projects, I sought inputs from former defence chiefs, chief secretaries of states, heads of security agencies, former foreign secretaries and more. Like my father, most had been cruelly cast aside by the same official machinery they lorded over while in service.

Shielded by the vast government machinery, most did not give a damn about the multiple hardships faced by private citizens in India, until they retired. I felt sorry about their existence in congested apartments set amidst the smog, sewage and stink of East or West Delhi colonies, which were a far cry from spacious bungalows that some of them occupied earlier in South Delhi.

Grotesque plaques presented during official events adorned shelves of their tiny living rooms. The retirees did not mind the extra income I paid them to add to pensions. I got access to their vast knowledge gained by years of experience in powerful posts. I signed them on by doing the India International Centre and the India Habitat Centre circuit for a few weeks, where such individuals are permanent invitees to speak their mind on various subjects.

Soon, I could afford a better lifestyle on my own steam. For my professional travels I chose to incur basic expenses unlike some of my friends who flew business or first class, checking into super luxury resorts on company account.

As an independent professional, my budgets were included in the fees. So, I bought low cost economy air tickets and stayed in clean and safe lower star hotels patronized by chunky, freckled and muscular foreign nationals, often accompanied by pretty young partners, who perhaps felt secure with them.

I put up at a *Haveli* turned into a 5-room home stay operated by a friendly local family in Jodhpur and moved about in an auto or bus. I splurged when I travelled with family. I patronized the Taj Group and usually hired a full day air-conditioned big car for local sightseeing and shopping. There is a big gap in luxury between a guest house at old city Jodhpur and the Umaid Palace, run by the Taj people.

I was comfortable in both. I can be flexible. After driving a scooter in Delhi and commuting in jam-packed city buses, rudimentary facilities such as air-conditioner work quite fine. I do not think my wife and daughters would be so accommodating.

As payments accrued and more zeroes added to my bank balance, my profile details were picked up by quick business sensing and often irritating credit card companies, insurance agents, relationship managers belonging to HDFC Bank, Citigroup, American Express and ICICI all doing well in a booming Indian market.

Some persistent callers turned out to be difficult to refuse, smart English talking female executives ready to meet at a coffee shop, home or club. For a change, I was being sought for my money rather than my cuteness or dimples, though, like others, I too could have done without the pesky calls for sure.

I wrote the following essay centred round evolving India:

An indication of a changing India is the phasing out of two lifestyle products that defined Indian middle-class existence and aspiration in the 70s and 80s. The decision (by respective firms) to stop production of the Bajaj Scooters, my trusted travel companion for years, and entry level Maruti 800 cars, the private space that I have used most with the opposite sex, from metros to begin with, is purely business related -- sales have sagged.

But, it also reflects a different mind-set, another India and a new era that fancies faster motor cycles, bigger and better cars.

In the 70s Bajaj Scooters symbolized middle-class stability, although the engine fitted on one side, made the machine unstable. And in the current situation of rashly driven powerful vehicles and 24-hour call centre cabs, two-wheelers are very unsafe.

Yet, back then, father on the wheel, mother on the pillion, younger child standing in front with head bobbing out, older sibling squeezed between mother and father, everybody with their arms around each other for balance and protection, epitomized the complete Indian family, "hum do hamare do". (We two and our two)

It was idyllic. Needless to say, the famous ad tag line "Hamara Bajaj" (Our Bajaj) translated into brisk sales.

The strict father, seeped in the idealistic hangover of Mahatma Gandhi or Jawaharlal Nehru, could have typically worked in a government department, university professor or even a trader; the mother, a housewife, dedicated her life to the family, spending hours in the kitchen preparing perfect healthy meals, cleaning the house and praying for the welfare of her husband and kids at the mandatory puja corner in the house

The unified aim of the husband-wife duo was to ensure their children a good education to turn them into engineers (via cracking the coveted IIT exam) or doctor (via the equally difficult MBBS entrance exam) or make it to the IAS, the top government job (via the even more difficult UPSC exam).

With such focus on study, a big sprinkling of the Bajaj kids did make it and many of them went to America, the land of opportunity, to become software czars, top cardiologists, reproducing kids who today call shots in political stakes as campaign managers, fund givers, Bobby Jindal, driving big BMWs or Mercedes Benz and collecting bikes for passion that probably cost more than their parents whole life income, many times over.

Some of the kids called their parents over from India, selling off the Bajaj scooters as junk, while others forgot about the elders, providing endless sob story themes for Hindi movies described as meaningful art cinema due to all the crying.

Meanwhile, the Maruti 800 was launched in pre-liberalized India in the 80s when the License Raj prevailed to shackle any enterprise. Access to state authorities or grease money was needed for anything -- owning a telephone, a passport, a driver's license or a gas connection and a house.

In keeping with authoritative behaviour, most marriages were arranged. Gandhi and Nehru were forgotten entities, their pictures framed in every government office, ideals obliterated.

The Babu (read lower government official) was King. Cordless phones a luxury item, compared to over 500 million cell phone users today. The bulk of youth (everybody could not make it to IIT or IAS or MBBS) aspired to be part of this Kingdom and wield the power to dole out telephone connections or hand out nationalized bank loans and progress in life -- from Bajaj Scooters to Maruti 800s.

In a way the spiffy, quick pick up, not very expensive Maruti 800s that took on the ambling Ambassadors and Fiat cars that dominated Indian roads was the first challenge to the Raj, though there were car quotas still and one needed to bribe a Babu to procure one, maybe by offering foreign made liquor bottles.

The Maruti 800, fast, flexible and individualistic, though a tin pot compared to the safety features of cars today, indicated the 90s and new millennium that would usher a new India.

Today a typical middle-class Indian family travels in a snazzier Maruti Swift or a Hyundai I-20, financed out of quick processing private bank, visits choc-a-bloc malls during the weekend, watch high-priced multiplex movies, while the kids feed on pizza and burgers, probably from McDonald's, home delivery or take away, resulting in new age problems such as obesity.

The parents' lead jet-setting corporate lives, grapple deadlines, keep global times; some fight lifestyle related heart problems and hyper tension, while others spend time at the gym or spa to de-stress and detoxify. There is no space for the Puja room with every corner taken over by big Plasma screen TV sets, state-of-the-art music systems or a personal gym.

Telephone connections are not a problem, bank loans available online, cars can be brought off the shelf like a pair of jeans. There is freedom to choose. Love marriages are on the rise, so are openly gay relationships and divorce rates.

Discussions centre on Nehru's affairs with foreign women, rather than his beliefs and vision. Gandhi is remembered in context of Bollywood masala flicks such as Munnabhai MBBS.

The ones who have made it bigger via the stock market or real estate windfalls, commute in bigger Honda cars or even a BMW, travel abroad for holidays and spend evenings at expensive clubs, discussing art investments.

Mobile phone-toting maids connected to roaming parents look after kids who spend time on computer games and TV.

The children imbibe good social skills in private schools followed by an expensive MBA (in India or abroad) and find ready employment in domestic service sector jobs that need more smooth talking and less thinking -- hospitality, banking, insurance tourism, outsourcing or at MNCs such as Coca Cola, Pepsi or Nestle, offering perks and foreign postings.

A lot needs to be improved in India, such as regular electricity supply and roads without potholes. A well-behaved Babu is still a rarity.

Though there are masses poor in India still, there are masses of the upwardly mobile too. India has changed -- for better and worse.

The era of Bajaj Scooters and Maruti 800s is history.

I wrote the following piece about a low cost retreat in India;

It is height of summer in north India. With schools shutting for annual vacations, everybody is headed to the hills. Traffic jams for Shimla begin at Delhi; one has to walk from Dehradun for any reasonable chance to make it to Mussoorie

Meanwhile auto air conditioners are being re-checked and replaced to prepare for the likely event of converting vehicles into mobile bedrooms for the family, given the inevitable long power cuts.

Like every year, power ministry officials have said there will be no outrages this time. Unlike weather forecasts, electricity supply projections have been incorrect since many years before I was born and I am not that young any more. Last year the power grid collapsed in whole of India.

Given such contexts, over the years, during summer I prefer to briefly move into top-end five star resorts that have proliferated around Delhi and Gurgaon where I live. These cater to the rich, overseas tourists and corporate clients.

The idea of the break is to beat the heat, dust, pollution, fumes, power cuts, traffic, no water supply, monotony and routine at Trident, Taj, Leela, Marriott and Westin among others to enjoy the facilities by paying minimum, staying maximum duration, while availing all discounts assuming that the reader, like me, seeks to make each spent penny count.

It can be rejuvenating pool, spa, gym, sauna, food, drinks, movies, tennis, ping pong, badminton, reading or working on the laptop, all located within a full power backed up centrally air conditioned ambience, lounge, in house library, butlers, smiling hostesses and more. It is best to check travel portals, credit card offers and hotel websites before booking. This is non-tourist season, (in the plains that is)

There can be healthy cash backs, if one is alert. Check in early, check out late. Put in the request up front to the reservation desk when your negotiating position is strong. If the room is not ready, deposit the luggage at the locker and hit the pool.

I prefer to opt for packages that exclude food and drinks that can cut costs by half. Buffets are psychologically debilitating. If one has paid for it, one is obliged to gorge. My idea of a holiday is not to over eat, rest between meals, listening to the tummy gurgle instead of music while popping antacids. Most resorts, in any case, have on-going corporate conferences due to which restaurants resemble packed metro coaches during meal times.

If at all go for breakfast buffet but make sure to load the bigger plates with items you may like to consume when hungry again later in the day. I, for example, assemble two big platters of uncut fruit and bakery items cover them with napkins while heading back to the room after a hearty breakfast.

Unlike booze, most hotels don't mind resident guests carting out the buffet fare. There could be an odd overzealous manager who may object. The solution is to appear irritated, pretend to be on the verge of screaming, while walking away.

The matter is too minor for the hotel staff to risk a scene or raised voices in the presence of other guests. Too much food is wasted at star hotels for the management to bother about a few extra apples or muffins consumed.

I prefer to carry my own groceries for other meals, while asking for as many free fruit platters, tea and coffee bags. The mini bar and electric kettle can serve as an effective kitchen.

Request housekeeping to empty out the mini bar containing Rs 20 chocolate bars priced at Rs 200 or Rs 50 beer pint bottles at Rs 400. The fridge can be used to store milk, bread, butter, ham, juice, cheese, curd, mangoes, booze and more. Use the kettle to boil eggs, Maggie or pasta. I have made rice too. Check out the pastry shop late in the evening. They usually offer half price happy hours.

Some hotels can be squeamish about bottled water for no particular reason. They can charge Rs 100 for a bottle that costs Rs 15 a step outside. Water can easily be boiled in the kettle and stored in the mini bar. Gyms usually have little bottles for patrons. I carry away 3-4 at a time. You could also keep a look out for trolleys parked along corridors, while the staff is inside the room, cleaning.

Pick up a couple of sealed bottles. In case somebody happens to notice, ask very politely whether you can take one. If they spot you on CCTV cameras, they will not bother you for picking a couple of bottles of water.

I was reading recently that Indians are big filchers of hotel items. Steal, but smartly, without going overboard or getting caught or embarrassing yourself.

Those who have moral concerns about such behaviour are requested not to read beyond here. Most big hotels in India today are owned directly or indirectly by those connected to power, government, politics and bureaucracy. These folks have made their money by embezzling hard earned tax payers' money.

So, there are many who don't mind secretly screwing those who are already unlawful. Breakable items such as crockery, soap dishes, coffee mugs, wine glasses, breakfast buffet plates are easy pickings.

Most hotels allow for handling losses due to breakage and don't bother about such missing articles. Hangers, bottle openers, bathing gowns, hand towels are never tracked. Be careful about the bigger linen, though.

This is unsafe zone. They are carefully counted. I know a few who walked away with curtains, bed sheets, bed covers and pillows. The hotel called to clarify the missing items. This is unnecessary. A weekend at a resort during summer is not a bad deal, if one can get it right, along with a few wrongs.

FIFTEEN

The Steady State

"Is it mine?" I asked Sushmita, when she told me that she is pregnant.

"It could have been, but I cannot cheat my husband on this. It would be unfair that he should raise somebody else's kid," she replied. She probably used the same explanation for her other lovers too.

"Is it your husband's?"

"Yes."

"You didn't say you were trying," I said.

"I think it just happened. Maybe the condom burst," she replied. She used protection with her spouse. We never did.

"It could not have unless you wanted it to. You must have snipped it," I said.

"I wanted it," she said. "Don't worry; I will be back in shape quickly."

"Enjoy this period," I told her, "There is no rush."

It could not have been my sperms that knocked up Sushmita. I was careful. It was her husband's or somebody else's. Expectedly, Sushmita's calls became infrequent. She intermittently missed her beat briefings, probably dealing with morning sickness and other prenatal issues. We met a few times but mostly went our ways in the evening. She still looked beautiful, not as a sex kitten, but as an embodiment of impending motherhood.

Lata was happier as my late night outs and secret meetings with sources diminished though the appearance of Seema soon after quickly destroyed the harmony. As with drugs or alcohol, the sudden exit of a beautiful woman such as Sushmita from one's routine and life can engender withdrawal symptoms.

The adrenalin and hormonal rush caused by such presence cannot be approximated or substituted easily. Although I had managed to give up smoking, I had failed to be loyal to my wife. I did not want to betray her again.

I immersed myself in work and family routines, including attending birthdays and anniversaries of relatives that I usually avoided completely. The extra sensory highs caused due to the proximity of an enormously attractive Sushmita were difficult to get over. As a single guy, I had willed myself into a relationship with Pooja to forget my village girl. But, as a married man I was determined to be loyal to Lata. I did not want a repeat of a dual woman situation post-Sushmita.

****

I took up golf with vengeance, honing my skills at the driving range during weekdays and spending time at the course during the weekends. I heard the game was addictive. I needed a new fix that was not another woman.

I could afford to play the sport now. I made sure to use the golf set my father was presented when he retired. It was lying unused at my parents' house. I wanted to remind myself and my father that life was better post-retirement. The baton had passed onto my brother and me too.

Since I was fairly good at racquet games such as table tennis, lawn tennis and badminton, I knew a bit about arm, shoulder and wrist coordination that extended to the irons and drivers. I began to enjoy the sport and long walks around the many new greens that had sprung up in Gurgaon and older ones in Delhi. Time at the fairway was soothing. I felt less horny about Sushmita.

I also occupied my spare time assessing my plots and scouting for new real estate. I read up on financial matters. I wanted to build a diversified investment portfolio comprising rent giving commercial and residential properties, stocks, mutual funds, and commodities such as gold. The strategy was to build an income stream irrespective whether I worked or not. That would make life easy.

I sought to know a bit about running a property business in Gurgaon, including shady dealings that one invariably hears about. There were inquiries from my overseas clients about investing in real estate in India as well. Property dealer Mukesh Yadav had been calling me for months as value of my plots spiralled. Initially he phoned a few times, then more often.

Real estate agents have a way of knowing about land titles. Yadav was no different. I met him a few times. He picked me up from my house in a newly acquired black Ford Endeavour that cost over Rs 2 million.

"I don't like his looks," Lata told me.

"Neither do I. And unless we are considering him for marriage to somebody in the family, it does not matter," I said.

I understood Lata's concern. It is best not to be on the wrong side of a business deal with people such as Yadav. It is not safe even on the right side. Property agents can be dangerous and unscrupulous, killing, kidnapping, maiming for money, whether owed or not. This is because realty business in India involves dirty money, illegalities and greed.

To be successful in this vocation, one has to know how to play the game unfairly and wrongly. In Haryana, particularly around Gurgaon, the local population aspires to be property agents only, unlike young boys or girls from rural, urban, semi-urban India who look to be IIM managers, IIT engineers, IAS or IPS officers, lawyers, doctors, or seek BPO, multinational and software jobs.

Many kids in Haryana are brought up to be real estate agents and taught early to physically fight for their rights. Their parents don't mind them picking up skirmishes with cops, brandish guns at pubs and earlier in school, drive rashly, tease girls. They are encouraged to beat up pedestrians and bouncers in hotels and also get bashed up at times.

It is part of the growing up process, to be rough and tough. Some exceptionally bad characters forcibly pull girls from streets into their vehicles to molest and even rape. These guys need mandatory military training to set them right psychologically to fruitfully channel their energies and respect women. If they persist with their debauched behaviour they should be neutered like animals.

For the regular Haryanvi, success is flaunting a SUV -- a Scorpio or a Tata Safari -- the two vehicles, usually driven rashly on Gurgaon roads. They are symbols of ultimate property agent power, the way it has been with red beacon light Ambassadors for ministers and bureaucrats.

Lately, high powered BMWs and Audis, involved in horrible crashes, are also being patronized by big money makers to portray faux class.

Any conversation, whether with taxi drivers, waiters or rich property agents in Gurgaon veers to land that brought riches to somebody or the other known personally in the village or extended caste kinship. It is an addiction.

All talk centres round windfalls due to rising price of plots, apartments and regularizing builder flats. For some time I connected people who made money in India to those who spoke good English, except traders and shopkeepers who only understand the language of money making.

My hypothesis was those who knew English were educated in expensive private schools, belonged to families with good liberal values and healthy aspirations. Thus, they landed top jobs and professions.

Their adolescent years did not comprise beating up people for a bright future. Maybe they did recreational drugs and listened to

Pink Floyd. Most managed to grow out of it, though one can listen to Floyd for a lifetime without any side effects. One prototype is the Doon School, St. Stephen's, US degree variety. The rapid growth and urbanization of areas such as Gurgaon has meant more tickets to economic emancipation than education.

Big money today co-exists with archaic social and cultural practises in sections of the unread and unlettered population. The local Gurgaon society can be regressive despite the instant upward economic mobility. A girl from a particular Yadav or Jat community marrying outside her caste could be burnt alive along with her paramour, even though both families could be very well off.

As per traditional rules boys and girls in the vicinity of demarcated villages they originally belong cannot marry. If they do, they are hunted down and mercilessly killed by their own brethren. Such "honour killing" has the backing of village elders and local *Panchayats*. The police dares not to interfere.

Before leaving to meet Yadav, I assured Lata that no decision about my plots would be taken without consensus in the family. Lata was keen I discuss realty matters with her father or somebody nominated by him. I did not agree.

I had no intentions of selling the plots. I wanted to occupy my free time with activities that took my mind away from Sushmita. There was no point in wasting effort of someone known who could put pressure on me to sell the plots via my wife's family. I knew I was no final decision maker on property matters.

This was rightly reserved for my father-in-law, the in-house expert on eliminating gas from the body. I also had my mother to consult who would have been more than happy to help. I wanted to understand realty business a bit due to my growing investments in the sector and some professional interest.

Mukesh's Ford Endeavour sported black tinted glass, the kind that cops and courts have banned, to block out happenings inside. These could range from drinking, threats to competitors in business, assaulting defaulters, large cash transactions, to making out with prostitutes. A murder or two can easily be added to the list. The cops never pulled up Yadav's vehicle.

They knew he was not the kind of guy to be meddled with. Rather, he was one of them. Big sections of constabulary are usually in cahoots with the nefarious in India. Otherwise, crime would not be such a booming industry, the way it is.

The Chulbul Pandey character essayed inimitably by Salman Khan in the *Dabangg* series is pure imagination. Even if Yadav was caught for any misdemeanour there would be phone calls from higher ups in the police department, who would have been castigated by political bosses that have a vested interest in shielding Mukesh and his ilk. Anybody who has some clout and black money in India feels the need to keep close tabs on the property market given fantastic returns.

People such as Mukesh are good conduits for latest ground level realty movements, potential land grabbing opportunities and distress sales.

Sitting across the table at a five-star hotel Yadav attended to ceaseless calls on his latest Nokia Lumia phone munching chicken kebabs and sipping the Red Label Whisky soda. He was paying for the Scotch and snacks.

If I had to foot the bill, I would have opted for a coffee shop. 99% of Yadav's clients did not work out; such is the nature of realty business. But, the 1% was good enough to sustain a lifestyle few could match, including a second wife.

Mukesh was approaching 40, fat, fleshy with uncharacteristically dark and perfectly cropped hair on his head. Probably they were artificial, woven.

Constant drinking had turned his face chubby with a prominent double chin that enveloped most of his neck. Had he been fair, his face would probably be ruddy due to excess alcohol circulating inside him. I had read that a man's performance in bed diminishes after 35, unless he keeps himself fit.   .

I was sure Mukesh popped Viagra, the imported international version and other illegally smuggled and poached local concoctions of tiger nails or rhino horns, to get it going with his young and sexy second wife. Or, maybe he just focused on oral. I was already drinking Red Bull and Gatorade to keep up energy levels, though I was much fitter and younger. Yadav leaned over the table at the dimly lit pub, to whisper in rough Haryanvi Hindi dialect, which never sounds comforting to the ears even if one is used to hearing the language often.

He did not want to take any risk despite the loud music. He did not want anybody to know he was meeting me. He never met me at the same venue twice, though they were all very expensive locations. His trade was plied with utmost secrecy, hush money and cash. He did not trust his own brother with a deal.

"Boss, the plots are quoting over Rs 4 crores each as the new Gurgaon master plan and metro routes have been announced by the government. I could negotiate to Rs 4.5 crores. The party is rich, NRIs. They can pay dollar cash," Mukesh hissed, his thick gold chain clinking against the sparkling glass containing yellow Whisky.

He wore two gold armbands too, with '*Om*' emblazoned on them, though it would be foolish to surmise that Yadav was a religious person in any way. He probably prayed after he cheated or killed somebody.

His offer was better than the last time. I pretended to be excited. "Arrange a meeting when you can. That will be good," I told Mukesh. I wanted to play along to see how the deal could progress including meeting the NRI buyer, discussions about cash payments. It would be good learning experience.

If Mukesh managed to broker the sale he could earn almost Rs 20 lakh as his cut from buyer and seller put together. Yadav's thick flesh-coloured lips contorted as he spoke. I thought about his young and beautiful second wife.

It could not be a palatable experience to have him close, unless she thought hard about his money and being driven in tinted Ford Endeavour. Mukesh did not look the type to chew gum or pop 'Polo' prior to any intimate act with the opposite sex.

If he ate kebabs he smelt chicken, if he drank Whisky he smelt alcohol, when he smoked the odour was tobacco. Probably, there were days he did not brush his teeth, or maybe he did not clean them at all as they were yellow, black and red like a smudged rainbow. He would probably replace them with golden ones once they rotted, which could be soon. Though his breath was foul, his clothes always emanated the fragrance of the best duty free perfumes.

"Speak to uncle*ji* (referring to my father or father-in-law), auntie*ji* (my mother-in-law). If you want I will speak to them, *bhabiji* also (Lata). Think about this seriously," said Mukesh.

"I will. Let me be satisfied with the buyer first, then I will involve them."

Courtesy my father-in-law, Mukesh knew about my family. I had no intentions to talk to them. There was no need to sell the land as there was no requirement for money. I was making more than enough to sustain wife, family and more.

Rather, I was earning beyond what I thought I ever would due to converted dollars, pounds and Euros. It is good to be an exporter of anything in India due to a weak rupee, depreciating more due to ever growing oil and gold imports. Hail market pricing.

"We are thinking of selling (the plots) as there may be unexpected medical expenses. My parents and in-laws are old now and I may need the money to look after them should the need arise. I want them to die with dignity," I told Mukesh, lest he suspect I was wasting his time and money at the pub.

Mukesh's eyes lit up. He quickly sensed a business opportunity due to talk of illness and death. Health issues are always a welcome twist to property dealers due to sellers need for quick cash to pay off exorbitant medical bills.

Mukesh knew families played an important role in property decisions. No house or plot could be sold without clearance by the lady of the house and, in my case, my father-in-law. But, a medical emergency always worked best as the transaction was executed in haste. Mukesh went for the kill.

"Bring family one day, *bhabiji*, uncle*ji* and auntie*ji*. We can go to Rohini Adventure Park with children. Everybody will enjoy. Ladies will be happy not to cook at home. We will drink," said Mukesh, raising his glass, re-filled four times already, large, in mock celebration.

There was no way Mukesh could be part of my social life. 'That would be the pits,' I told myself. No part of his being, personal, intellectual, linguistic, professional, excited me in any way.

"I can reduce my cut. We will negotiate hard with the buyer for a good price. The market will stagnate now, right time to sell," Mukesh rambled, until his cell phone buzzed again. I checked for messages and mails on my handset. There was nothing requiring immediate attention.

My clients were spread all over the world, but I expected Singapore and Hong Kong to be shut by now. It would soon be office time in America. Europe was busy, but would wind down without fail by early evening. Unlike Asians and Americans, Europeans were laidback professionals.

Their lives revolved around planning the next holiday while working in the intervening period. Nobody functioned during weekends, beyond office hours and Friday afternoons. This could not last long. With business and growth moving to India, China and Southeast Asia, the recession was bound to shake Europeans out of their semi-sedated work profile.

I checked my messenger. A couple of friends were online, but I was not in the mood for chat. Technology had changed my existence, personally and professionally. That evening at the five-star hotel, Mukesh spoke animatedly about the immediate need to sell my plots to make a killing.

Intermittently, he spoke *sotto voce* on the phone chasing other deals. I knew a bit about Yadav's personal life. He maintained two big households to prevent the wives and resulting kids from fighting.

He took them by turns for holidays to Goa, Kerala, Himachal and Southeast Asia, Malaysia, Singapore and Hong Kong. Bangkok and Phuket he went alone with similarly placed property dealer/s for obvious reasons.

Mukesh's second wife was old enough to be his daughter. She married him for money. A few years back he was just a part-time property agent and full-time PCO operator. His office was a telephone booth located in the front room of his house while his business vision extended to converting the same space into a grocery or stationery shop. His parents were proud that he was managing a PCO booth.

Mukesh impregnated his first wife on the first night of their arranged marriage. She bore him kids from the age of 16. A few cows, goats and buffaloes that lived off a cordoned barren area completed the household.

Then acquisitive private developers comprising target-bonus driven executives, decided to build a mall, hotel-cum-high rise residential complex that overlapped the tract of land Yadav owned. It was a jackpot that catapulted Mukesh and few more like him into a league that his ancestors could never ever imagine.

His first wife, who spent most of the day sweeping, cleaning and cooking, turned irrelevant with the first whiff of her husband's success. She stood no chance. The new wife spoke rudimentary English, the knowledge much more than the first wife could ever muster. It sufficed to bowl over Mukesh for whom an English-speaking spouse was as much a prized possession as an expensive plot.

I bumped into the second wife, accompanied by Yadav, at the Ambience Mall that boasts several expensive lifestyle and jewellery stores. Her attire, including bag, perfume, cosmetics, spanned more brand names than MS Dhoni and Sachin Tendulkar could endorse together.

"I looking for diamond set. He (like all good Indian wives, she did not address her husband by name) agree to pay Rs 4 lakhs," she said, using English words beyond what her husband could ever manage.

"That is too little for Yadav*ji*. He should agree to twice the amount," I replied.

"Given the way it has been in the past, I am sure she will spend much more," Yadav said, in Hindi.

"I join gym too," she said, mentioning an expensive fitness centre that had been advertising for clients.

"You should take Yadav*ji* with you. He could do with some exercise," I said.

She reminded me of Mallika Sherawat or maybe Rakhi Sawant, sexy and strong headed. Her body was taut and sinewy, despite being mother of two children. Her small perfectly rounded buttocks fitted nicely into tight figure hugging jeans; her skin was earthy deep brown due to time probably spent cultivating fields under the harsh sun or shepherding goats and buffaloes during her youth.

Her cheek bones were distinct while a strong jaw line indicated an aggressive woman, probably in bed too. Yadav reciprocated by keeping her happy with diamonds, club and gym membership.

Like Yadav, she too belonged to a family that eked out a living from an ancestral wasteland part of the New Gurgaon sprawl today. Her father's smart move was to ensure she attended English-speaking classes. Yadav fell for it big time.

To continue family tradition, she enrolled her elder son at an expensive International School that dot Gurgaon to accommodate kids of foreign nationals, expats and NRI's employed in large number of multinationals in the area.

Yadav boasted about it, like normal parents do about their wards in the IAS or IIT. I was not sure what Yadav's kids would grow up to become. English-speaking sophisticated property agents did not sound right.

No doubt, Yadav was zealous about his second wife as land and money. He could easily torture and kill any paramour on suspicion. For those so inclined, it is best not to screw around with local Haryanvi women and stick to chasing outsiders from North, South or East India.

When Yadav dropped me back, both of us were quite drunk. "How are the *bhabiji*s doing?" I asked him. "Very well. I take care of both of them. I am the perfect husband to both my wives," he said.

I wrote about my golf experience:

The rich and famous are in one league. Golf is happening everywhere, sights that one would not have encountered a few years ago -- the time is 7:30 pm, the floodlights are on and the golf range at Siri Fort, located at the up market south Delhi, resonates with the sound of clashing club heads and ball.

The pace is feverish as scores of Delhiites with wrists cocked, knees bent, heads straight, tees firmly in place, are lined up in the quest for the ever-elusive perfect golf swing. I categorize golfers as following:

Career Golfers: *They are the hardest hit by the images beamed into our drawing rooms by satellite TV. The icons are Tiger Woods, Ernie Els, Jeev Milkha Singh, Jyoti Randhawa. Suraj, a picture of intense concentration is practicing hard as he desperately wants to make the cut for the Indian tournaments.*

"In India, team sports have always been on the forefront, whether it is cricket, hockey, kabaddi, kho kho," he says, "we have never done well in individual sport. In golf when I win, I get all the credit. Nothing is

shared." This is true-blue individualism in a country that started out being Socialist at the time of independence in 1947.

Not too far away from Suraj, is Zia-ul-Haq, a government officer who presides over the training of his young son. He narrates the strong influence that parents have had on the careers of the top stars of today, from the William sisters in tennis to Sachin Tendulkar in cricket. Zia, though, is cross with his ward.

"He was disqualified in the first round of an amateur tournament at Delhi Golf Club, recently," said Zia, "I am very disappointed. If this is the way things are going to turn out, I am sorry to say, Saif's future is bleak."

I was not allowed to speak further with Saif as his father felt media exposure at this stage would not be good for Saif's career. Maybe, he was putting too much pressure on his young son.

Business Golfers: They cart the most expensive golf sets, rattle off quotes from Ian Woosnam's video series and can explain the most intricate nuances of the game. Yet, if they had it their way they would not mind kicking the ball to beat the course. For them it is striking the right banter, not a birdie that is at stake.

"I have paired up with the Army Chief, union ministers, police commissioners, cabinet secretaries, cricketers," said N. K. Vohra, a businessman, who had driven all the way from his farmhouse a good 30 kilometres away. Vohra's game belied his theoretical knowledge, but courtesy economic progress, this category has burgeoned learning all the tricks golf can offer.

S Singh, who works for a MNC, was there with his wife and young daughter, sweating profusely with a contingent of coaches around him.

Singh struggled to rectify a basic hurrying flaw that had crept into his swing. "He is keen to pick up the game as fast as possible," says his wife, "his new German MD is an avid golfer."

Tortured Golfers: They have been at the game for eons and are the brooders and strugglers. Many of them can be seen with scowls on their tired faces and it is anybody's guess that they have had a bad day at the green.

Of course, golf is like a game of snakes and ladders and it is equally likely that one would see them up and about the next time round. Ajay Mehra, an Indian Police Service officer, seemed to have got everything right. Spikes, golf hat, deep blue Greg Norman T-shirt, well-balanced stance. Yet, his misdirected divots dug a veritable crater around his playing area. "I have been playing the game for 20 years," says Mehra, "and I have learnt to enjoy it within my limitations. There are days when one just keeps on hitting clean. The satisfaction is immense."

True Golfers: They scurry about the range, picking golf balls hit in all directions, hidden behind umbrellas as shields. There is an army of them at Siri Fort.

In the evenings one does not get to see their faces but it is in the heat of the afternoon sun that they brandish their irons to catapult the ball beyond any of the Big Berthas that converge during the regular timings.

For them, golf is bread, butter and life.

There are certainly a few Feroz Alis and Ali Shers, former caddies who have gone on to greater golfing glory, lurking among them.

Which brings me to the last category to make the account complete. I am left with myself, the struggling-golfer-journalist. I do not think there were any around, poking their noses into everybody's life rather than letting them be and focusing on their golf.

SIXTEEN

The Mistake

I got involved with a single, but very pretty girl Seema. Within six months of knowing her, she wanted me to divorce and marry again, a suggestion that was unacceptable to me. I was already a father.

Although, the fun element existed, Seema was an absolute error of judgment. Sushmita had warned me about her. I surmised Seema had a past with men and, like Sushmita, would keep deeper emotional attachments at bay. But, that was not the case. I happened to be her first boyfriend, unfortunately married.

I haven't fully figured why she chose to be with me and fall madly in love. It could be my dimples, it could be my destiny. I too liked her a bit, simply because nobody had irrationally loved and adored me as intensely as Seema.

While I was sure my sperm count crossed a billion with Sushmita, Seema pumped up my ego to levels I never experienced before. She found my jokes perfect, thought I was the complete man, professionally competent, financially stable, physically perfect, without any faults in personality or character.

This was unlike the position of many personalities in my life such as my father, Sid, mother-in-law, father-in-law and probably my wife under the influence of her mother. Seema told me she continually experienced "little orgasms" in my presence or due to my touch. The O's turned bigger and better in more intimate situations. I Google searched the matter. She was not fibbing.

I read a piece that said any woman could really feel the heat if the man she truly loved and not his money held her hand or kissed her or was close to her. Seema seemed to fit such descriptions quite well.

Seema told me the only hitch between us was my marriage that could be sorted with a divorce. It was a very tricky scenario. Although American fast food concepts have proliferated in India spawning generations of obese kids fattened on Pepsi, Coca Cola and McDonald's French Fries, quickie divorces have not really caught on here. Any breakdown of marriage is a deep emotional event that involves both families and long drawn out legal procedures. Children also don't have it easy with other kids poking fun in school.

It is possible I might have chosen Seema over all the girls I was with earlier. But, her arrival into my existence happened late. I was still rooted in middle-class values when it came to walking out of a marriage even though an extra-marital affair isn't really the morally upright thing to do.

I did not have the guts to step out. There were no divorced prototypes to follow in my family. Everybody, my parents, aunts, uncles, grandparents, stayed wedded all their lives. I attended a few 50th marriage anniversaries in my extended family, with couples re-committing to be happily together for life or whatever remained of it. I think the longevity and sticking with each other genes ran deep with my ancestors and by extension me.

I also surmised my father-in-law would set goons of the Mukesh Yadav variety from the property sector after my life if I tried anything rash with his daughter. As I was the father of his granddaughter he would probably instruct them to pluck off my nails and not kill me. That is still very painful.

I feared I could be pulled into a moving car and bashed up for good. Maybe, the attackers would puncture my balls so they would be of no use in future. Then there was the guilt factor of hurting Lata.

I loved my wife. The equations were settled between us. There were common areas to interest -- kids, present and future, property, parents, work, finances, health, food and more. Being with Lata was like playing golf -- languorous and relaxed for most periods with moments of high intensity like it can happen at the fairway or putting green. The passionate moments could be a quarrel or sex. The bedroom action could follow a good fight. The two are related.

Sex can substitute anger in letting off steam. Arguments could be triggered by small matters of placing shoes or bathroom towel at the right place. Women are particular about such aspects men tend to ignore.

Despite rational arguments against straying as a married man, I did miss the rush of blood, hormonal churns, hyperactive sperms and adrenalin triggered by proximity of a very pretty unknown and undiscovered woman. Sushmita and Seema fitted the genre. Being with them was like watching a T-20 match live. Their presence created an impact of heightened sensitivities, attraction, non-stop action that can only be intoxicating and promote sexual promiscuity.

But, it is never a good idea to be addicted to good looking women. I began to live life dangerously. My involvement with Seema was unnaturally natural.

It happened within a very short span of knowing her as with my other relationships -- lucky or unlucky me. As I worked from home, I took Alaynah, who was almost 2-years old, to the local park in the evenings where Seema exercised regularly.

There were many old fogies about who descended there at dusk, some chased out of their homes by rude daughters-in-law, but mostly to stare at brisk walking tight-bottomed women in shorts or track pants. This was the closest they could get to making out before they passed away from the world for good.

Comely women can be more amenable to converse with a man and progeny together that could follow attention to the offspring. For a guy on his own, chances of such friendly interactions with the opposite sex are remote, in a similar park scenario, unless he looks like Tom Cruise or drives an open sports car that sounds like a powerful motorbike. This is due to application of the universal principle that girls generally like good looking and slightly spoilt rich brats.

There have been instances I have said hello or smiled at a pretty face, usually young, passing by, flashing the supposedly deadly dimples. Mostly, I have been ignored, which can be disconcerting.

To escape being noticed by others in the vicinity, I continued to smile pretending to acknowledge a lovely colourful bird in the sky, or quickly donned a serious look as if nothing has happened. Seema was tall, fair, pretty, strong and slim. Any man could caress, love and hug her long shapely legs for a lifetime.

Her expressive full and red lips oozed innocence, attributes that can turn any guy protective and violently possessive. Girls such as Seema, like most very pretty girls, can be quite crafty about their survival and don't need much male support though they could pretend that they do. This is an in-born god-gifted good looking girl survival mechanism.

My eyes invariably followed Seema's pear-shaped taut bottoms as she took her rounds at the park, though I had to be careful to keep an eye on Alaynah getting into a tangle. At two kids walk, run, fall a bit, throw about balls, swing a plastic bat and are very conscious of their environment. They can pick up fights over toys with fellow tiny tots. They need to be entertained and watched by the minute.

The ideal situation would have been one eye on my daughter and the other on Seema's butt which is not possible, though I tried. Seema was sexy, not the smouldering, dusky full-bodied appeal of Sushmita that could weak-knee any man. She was virginal, untouched, yet fun-loving genre that smile and laugh in ways that can equally besot a man in an obsessive way.

I mean I could shoot anybody acting weird with Seema, although I did not know her at all. I tried to fit Seema in the pantheon of women I surfed, searching for their leaked MMS sex videos, movie adult scenes and bikini shots.

There were shades of Cindy Crawford, Claudia Schiffer and Penelope Cruz in her. Within India, she approximated Aishwarya Rai or lately flawless skinned Anushka Sharma who dances on-screen with the abandon of Madhuri Dixit or Madhubala in the past. It was sometime since I was in the vicinity of a beautiful woman who set my pulse racing. I could sense the hormonal build up that heightens sensations around the loins. Though I interacted with Sushmita, our relationship was history.

She was busy with her family, I with mine. While Lata regained her fitness and figure after Alaynah was born, Sushmita glowed happily in fattened motherhood, tossing aside some of her tigress philosophies for some time.

Seema's attention to Alaynah got us speaking. It happened quite simply. Alaynah passed her by. Naturally, Seema could not ignore. She picked her in her lap and we got talking. Once she spoke she jabbered non-stop, a bit like Kareena Kapoor in the movie *Jab We Met*. Within five minutes of knowing her, I lost track of her multiple family connections, relatives, friends, strangely no boyfriends.

I tried to mentally retain some of the unfamiliar names uttered in quick succession by Seema, but gave up. Girls are like that. And then they expect the guy to recall all the associations. Men are inclined to retain details about an ex-boyfriend, but most girls, in India at least, are averse to speak about the subject.

This is unlike guys who can claim half the world to be ex-girlfriends. Still, anybody seriously trying to woo a girl should covertly switch cell phones on record mode, for reference before subsequent interactions. Girls don't repeat. They expect the guy to remember. It can happen with the wife too.

"So, you did not ask me how the crucial presentation went," Lata has often asked.

"How did your presentation go?" I replied, trying to recall the existence of such an event, probably mentioned by her many times earlier in the week.

"What's the use of asking after I have reminded you? You should have remembered on your own. I told you this one was important. This shows you do not care. You are too selfish," Lata said.

"How does it matter whether I asked? As long as the presentation went off well, it is okay. And, I am sure it must have gone off well or else you would be complaining about it," I would say, trying not to be incited.

"That is not the point. The point is you did not ask. My mother asked the moment I stepped into the house. You did not," she would say.

"Don't compare me to your parents. You should have married them if they are so perfect," I would say. This could be the beginning of a long night.

I have read somewhere that limited memory of men is because their brains are cluttered with big-sized images linked to porn and sports action sequences.

This leaves little space like it is with a hard disk, to store other data. Women, on the other hand think differently with very little smut and games in their mental radar. This permits retention of quality facts and figures, like birthdays and anniversaries. Later in life men also learn the hard way that wives when psyched about an issue speak about it endlessly, while the husband has to patiently listen and offer solutions that are usually shot down.

Ultimately, she will listen to her father or mother. When husbands are stressed they have to keep quiet and figure out a way, lest it alarms the wife, her mother, and there is more to handle. Plus, the hubby will be blamed for not managing his matters efficiently. I had no problems listening to Seema as long as I could watch her pretty face and lovely full red lips.

In no time she told me a bit about herself and her family's life history. She had graduated in History from St. Stephen's college a year back. It required high marks to qualify for the course in the prestigious institution whose alma mater prides itself as superior to everybody else in India and rest of the world.

She told me about her PG life at DU campus, including inevitable attention from many guys, which made me falsely believe she must have been intimate with at least one. Seema's father, God bless him for playing a little part in creating such a beautiful girl, was a-civil engineer who had shifted to Gurgaon given opportunities in construction.

Earlier he was involved in setting up big power projects around the country due to which Seema was fluent in Bengali, Punjabi and a bit of Marathi. Her younger brother was in school and an older one was studying engineering in the South. Her parents must have been disappointed he did not make it to an IIT.

Seema spoke highly about an unmarried rich and caring maternal uncle who sponsored her entire family, except her father with whom he did not get along, for holidays all over India. I could relate to such sentiments. Courtesy her uncle, she had travelled to America once.

Seema was an ordinary girl, with extraordinary looks, who belonged to the usual hard working, straight forward honest middle-class family, like mine, with parents slogging their butts off to make lives of their kids comfortable and secure.

They saved aggressively, lived frugally to be able to enrol their kids in expensive coaching classes to attain middle class nirvana – picking up one or more *Bharat Ratna* -- IIT, MBBS, IIM or IAS. After passing out of St. Stephens's, Seema worked in a BPO for some months. The money was good but she quit her job as she did not like night shifts to keep American customer timings and accent.

"There is so much coffee and junk food one can tolerate to keep awake the whole night. I turned into a zombie. It affected my skin.

Plus the put on accent had a very bad effect on my throat. I became laryngitis prone," she said.

"Call centres make the body cycle go for a six. They turn you into bats, hanging upside down for a living. It cannot go on," I said.

Seema laughed. "That is a good way of looking at the profession. I will tell my friends," she said. There was no FB at that point of human existence for a single wall update to reach all friends, known and unknown. Seema told me she was still figuring out what next to do with her life.

"It could be MBA, GRE, I don't know. I may work for some time," she said.

"As long as it is not the IAS, any career is fine. That would be another body hanging upside down move for a city girl like you," I said.

"The IAS is so non-happening. Who wants to spend years trying to sort out a backward rural district or town with lecherous corrupt politicians and their cronies for company? For me, it has to be a metro, New York or California."

I think I began to like Seema as a person too. I liked anybody who did not like the IAS. I met Seema frequently at the park. Soon we timed our visits.

Given expenses on education, her family had leased a low-rent builder flat close by that was part of an independent house. In India there is the illegal and legal route to doing things. One illegitimate example is builder flats.

Plots are meant for standalone houses, statutorily. But, a sly builder with connections and profits riding on very poor construction standards, like it is with roads in the country, offers an alternative to the owner of a plot who may not have time or money to build a house.

The seedy builder takes on responsibility of construction while ensuring clearances such as electricity and water supply by bribing petty officials. The owner of the plot retains rights to one apartment for free. The other two floors are sold to recoup the initial investment and profit.

Several such lodgings abound in Gurgaon area. The residents of such quarters have turned into a pressure group on the government to recognize their property titles. Too many wrongs create a constituency to turn it right.

Seema's house was visible from the terrace of my in-laws' lavish abode. My mother-in-law was instantly suspicious when she noticed me hanging about the top floor fitted with an open air jacuzzi that was never used as nobody in the family had any time for such indulgence.

My mother-in-law hovered in the vicinity, pretending to supervise cleaning, to try to figure out my sudden appearance in the area, probably suspecting I may use the jacuzzi, which she obviously did not want me to.

I stretched my limbs and told her fresh air, long distance vision, greenery and exercise is good for health and eyes. She did not believe me. "You can do that in your room also. Open the windows and there will be plenty of fresh air and a good view. Why come to the terrace? You could fall off."

"I did not think about the window. I will do that next time," I told her.

God created my mother-in-law to be wary of me whether I was on the roof or basement. I did not mind her stressing herself thinking I was about to commit suicide. She did not want that for the sake of her daughter and granddaughter. I was their biggest Man Friday. My dying would cause them discomfort.

I kept going to the top floor, with a skipping rope I could not use in the room. I may not have re-visited the terrace so many times, but I wanted to make a point of not listening to my mother-in-law. I tried the taps of the jacuzzi. As I expected, there was no water. The supply had been deliberately cut off. Anyway, I did not want my mother-in-law to dominate my thoughts when there was Seema.

"I keep getting offers for modelling. I have done a couple of assignments. I may take it up more seriously now that I have more time in hand," Seema told me.

"You should give it a shot. It can be good money though you need to be careful about fakes who make false promises to pretty girls," I warned her, recalling an incident of an ambitious, good-looking college friend who posed in underwear for young boys who pretended to be fashion photographers. The boys had a lot of fun, I would assume.

I wanted to caution her about the hyenas in the field, the photographers and model coordinators who extract their pound of flesh from the swarm of young girls with dreams of making it big in the glamour industry as models, Miss Indias and Bollywood stars. Though the body cycle remains intact here unlike BPOs, girls need to go down on their knees to progress. I decided not to be negative and let the matter be. "I know it is not an easy field. One has to compromise on values and sleep around a bit to make it. There is no other way," she said.

"I am sure it is. Are you okay about doing such stuff?" I asked.

"Depends, how serious I am and the money I am making. Then one has to do what needs to be done. That's competition for you."

Clearly, Seema was an ambitious girl who wanted to get ahead in life. Given such views, I surmised she could not be a virgin. "She must have been through a phase of wanting to know about sex. And must have," I wrongly figured.

Following a few more conversations at the park, I asked her out. "Let's meet up and chat sometime," I told her. I presumed Seema would not agree, but she did

I told her to call if she was interested in getting out in the evening after park time. I did not expect her to ring. I did not want to phone her.

It does not behove a married man with a kid to be over eager to date a girl a decade younger, though the urge was very strong. She called.

We drove to Haldiram on the Gurgaon-Jaipur Highway where we ordered lots of sweets, south Indian dishes, grilled tomato cheese sandwich, *Raj Kachori*, pasta, coffee, cold drinks over hours of conversation about our past and present.

Such outings were a relief from the sterilized menu peppered with *lauki* regularly served at my wife's residence. It was nice to cruise the Highway in the gifted Honda City with a girl as pretty as Seema. Lata insisted on driving her older small car that she found more convenient to park and manoeuvre around.

I preferred the smooth Honda engine fitted with a powerful music system, effective air-conditioning, power steering and ample leg space, essential for a tall guy like me. One needed to be a scooter user and bullied by every vehicle, including a Maruti 800, at a Delhi roundabout to value the big car.

With Alaynah at home, I was able to focus more on Seema. She was uncommonly beautiful. Despite being slim, she was a big eater like me and burnt the calories with vigorous exercise. Her evenings at the park followed time at the gym in the morning. "Walking is not enough. One has to run to be really fit. I do that on the treadmill," she said. "I totally agree," I replied.

Though she chattered a lot, I spoke about my personal life too. There were times I felt the need to share my offbeat story with somebody. As I could not speak to anybody connected to my family, friends or work, Seema was a safe bet. She was detached from a further set of common people known to both of us.

I presumed she would be off to wherever her career or marriage took her. She could only be a temporary neighbour. I told her about Sushmita, our relationship, how I missed her and the theory of compartments.

"The gist is we had some good times together and went our way. We continue to be good friends." She listened with interest.

"It was easy to part ways as both of you had commitments elsewhere. I don't think it can always be so simple," she observed. Later, Seema told me that she found it awkward that I spoke about my extra-marital affair.

"It was kind of kinky. How can two married people justify their time together to the rest of the world? It is best the matter stays between them, if they do end up cheating their respective spouses," she said.

"You must be right," I said.

I also advised Seema it is best not to live with in-laws as it creates frictions between husband and wife that are unnecessary. "Some negativity is bound to exist between any couple. Standalone a man or woman may not notice or ignore such aspects. But, they are observed and overblown by naturally over protective parents of either spouse. This can create issues."

"I will try to work it out with my mom-in-law. I will give it a chance. If things still don't gel, then we will see," she said. I never thought about such dynamics when I was her age, but I guess girls tend to mature quicker thinking about marriage, in-laws and related matters that boys usually never bother about.

I told her I did not think much about the media created rift between St. Stephen's, across the road Hindu college where I studied and others such as Hans Raj, Kirori Mal or Ramjas.

"Life it too complex and long for a label to be such a big determining factor. Shahrukh Khan is from Hans Raj and Amitabh Bachchan from Kirori Mal. It is the same reason I don't believe qualifying for one exam such as the IAS or IIT should be such a big differentiator. There are many others who could do a job equally well. The barriers are artificial."

"I agree, but there is no harm it one picks up a good degree for a good career start and be part of an effective network. Then it is about ability and hard work. This is what my father says," she said.

There is something about the hold that fathers have on their daughters that I have never figured out. I wondered whether it would be the same between me and my daughter. As our interactions increased Seema's behaviour towards Alaynah turned friendlier at the park. I could sense jealous eyes of old fogies who mentally disapproved a married man speaking to a single girl and expressed it to each other, I am sure. Their bodies might have degenerated, not minds.

Of course, the same nearly dead men would think nothing of absorbing every attention of a young woman should such an occasion arise. I wished some of the oldies that visited the park regularly died soon. Seema spent a bit of her time playing with Alaynah that relieved some effort I had to put in.

I asked her out for a movie. She agreed. Our hands intermittently grazed as we shared a large popcorn box at the multiplex. Several couples at the last row were more involved with each other than the cinema. There were no cops to trouble them. Seema ordered Pepsi while I sipped hot coffee without sugar as my body metabolism was slowing with age. More sugar translated to more body fat, even if I was more active than earlier.

"Your hands are cold," I told her.

"My body loses heat with air-conditioning," she replied, cupping her hands around the warm disposable coffee glass.

"You drink coffee, I can have Pepsi," I told her, ignoring the sugar.

It is best not to be overtly sexual in interactions with a pretty girl that may be a little more intimate than earlier meetings. Girls know and deeply suspect that guys only want one thing, which is the correct assessment. I am sure Seema's parents, friends, cousins and most importantly father advised her same.

At the same time, girls don't take time to judge the guy, his intentions and attractive index that could be calculated by aspects such as achievement, money, looks, smell and more. They figure out in a couple of meetings.

I wanted Seema to be comfortable, relaxed and have fun with me. After the movie we went to *Sagar Ratna*. Then I dropped her home. Shortly, I suggested dinner. She agreed. Post the repast at a mid-range restaurant that served good Indian Mughlai and before dropping her back, inside the car, I asked whether she had ever kissed a guy before. "No," she said.

I did not believe her. I presumed her assertion to be the natural reluctance of girls, unlike boys, to boast about their love life. When we were a little away from her house on a quiet stretch of road that was not illuminated, I slowed down on the side. "Do you want to know how it is to kiss?" I asked.

"Are you sure?" she said. "Let me show you." I gently placed my lips on hers. She let me kiss her for a few seconds and then moved away.

I rubbed my hand on her breasts, below the pink *chunni* but over the similar coloured cotton *kameez*. The thin film of cloth was hardly any protection against the warm soft skin of her small but rounded bosoms very different from Sushmita's that were ripe and big. Seema was still as she closely observed my hands on her breasts. "Don't worry, this is enjoyable," I told her.

I did not pursue her further physically. I dropped her home to let her mull over happenings of the evening. I was unsure about Seema's past. She was insecure about the kiss. Maybe, my assessment about her sexual antecedents was wrong.

Maybe, she was not lying that she never had a boyfriend before. Matters could have gone either way between us from here -- she could have refused to talk to me, stopped coming to the park or gone with the flow.

It was unlikely she would have asked us to be "best friends" the usual ruse of girls who want to hang out with a guy without physical intimacy.

It allows them activities they would probably not be able to carry off with their girl pals or family. This could include attending a late night party with the "best friend" assigned the drop and pick up job or sometimes hang out in the evening when there is nothing much to do.

I could not be her platonic "best friend" as I did not believe in the concept. I was not her college or school study mate as I was too old for that.

Plus, I had already kissed her, a favour not usually granted to the "friend" despite his logistical support. I ruled out Seema storming my house and accusing me of molesting her. Firstly, I had been careful not to force anything.

Secondly, such an allegation would certainly shut out her freedom and outings for good. Her family would not allow it anymore. They would not stand for a scandal in the neighbourhood involving their daughter. She knew that.

Instinctively, I felt she did not mind our little sexual episode. My hunch was she wanted to discover the feelings, her sexuality more. Though the final call was hers, it was difficult for me to stop myself now. My hormones had gone viral again for the first time since I was with Sushmita.

The next day she called early. "What time are we meeting?" she asked. She was dressed smartly in tight blue jeans and a white shirt tucked inside, when I picked her up her up late in the evening from outside her house.

I carried a couple of beer pint bottles and keys of a new apartment I had purchased in Gurgaon. It was unoccupied. I had semi-furnished it for my parents to shift should the need arise as they were getting on in age.

"Let me take you to a place where we can be on our own," I told her.

"Let's go," she said confidently.

She seemed to have made up her mind to go with the flow. At that stage, I was still not inclined to believe I was the first guy she was being physically intimate. Still, I had to take it slowly and pace my advances in a way she was comfortable. It was important not to rush her.

I was the big cat on Discovery Channel waiting for the right moment to charge the prey and make the kill. The cover had to be good, the wind direction right. One mistake and the deer would be off for good.

I also did not want a scenario wherein I lost control due to a hormonal or sperm overflow begging her to make out with me. I don't think this is a very pretty sight and a situation any guy, especially married and with a kid, wants to find himself. I showed her about the apartment, including a photo corner with smiling framed pictures of me, Lata, Alaynah and other family members.

"Your daughter looks just like you," she said, even as she observed my wife closely. I took her in my arms and kissed her gently. She hugged me tight. I sensed a faint shiver. I kissed her face, neck while my hands probed her slim body under the shirt that I pulled from under the belt. I asked her to take off her clothes.

"Are you sure?" she asked.

"Yes. Don't worry it will be good. You will like it," I said.

Her body was lean, fairer than the exposed skin, slim at the hips, with taut flat buttocks and small breasts indicating her recent transformations as a girl.

Her physical form was different from Sushmita's or my wife's. She giggled when I caressed the really private areas. "You really know how to touch a woman," she said. "Thank Sushmita," I replied.

"I want to meet her one day," she said. "We will," I told her.

"Are we having sex?" she asked me later.

"Yes. Is this the first time for you," I asked, a trifle concerned.

"Yes."

"How does it feel?"

"Nothing great; it is as if I am washing myself there with soap."

"Haven't you had boyfriends before?"

"No."

"I think this is quite the wrong moment for me to find out," I said.

"What do you mean?" she said.

"Nothing important; Just enjoy."

By the time I finished, she was in tears. "You were very rough."

"Only, towards the end; that's the way it is."

I held her for some time, gulping the strong beer, till her silent sobs, deep breathing subsided and tears dried up. From the supple feelings within her, she too had some fun. "I will not be able to tell my mother about this," she said.

"There is no need. This is between you and me. Once you learn how to orgasm, you will like it a bit," I told her.

"I did, many times over," she said.

"You know about such things?"

"Girls too watch porn on the Internet," she said.

I checked my phone. There were five missed calls from Lata. I messaged saying I was with a source for a story for an overseas magazine and would be back a little late. There is no profession like journalism for making excuses to the wife. I took Seema for dinner at TGIF in Vasant Vihar. She was uncharacteristically quiet and ate her food slowly.

"Do you love your wife?" she asked.

"Yes, I do," I replied.

"You will have to stop loving her and start loving me," she said.

"Ok," I replied.

"I am serious," she said.

"Ok," I said. I wondered whether I should have held myself back due to her sexual status before she met me. The next morning Seema called.

"My underwear and sheet are stained red due to blood," she said.

"Have your periods started," I asked.

"No," she said.

"Are you a virgin," I asked.

"I was till yesterday," she said.

"Are you in pain," I asked.

"A little," she said.

****

Unlike with Sushmita, Seema phoned often. I spoke to her from the corner of the basement of Lata's house that was converted to my work area.

I had the space enclosed to remain out of sight and hearing of the army of domestics that hovered about, including the supervisor's corner at the other end.

I had to guard against the Christian maids who understood English. I needed to watch porn undisturbed whenever I wanted. My mother-in-law arrived a few times in the day to keep tabs, while pretending to talk to the supervisor.

Seema wanted to hang out with me every day, which was not easy to manage. I had to deal with my wife's phone calls to inquire about my whereabouts and scheduled time of arrival home, with little margin for error. Seema called 24/7, when I was with Lata or elsewhere. Sometimes I messaged her with an excuse or put the phone on silent mode. She called relentlessly.

Often, I woke up to over 50 missed calls in the morning. She rang the land line, though she hung up if somebody took the call. It prompted my mother-in-law to say -- "Someone calls and does not talk," she said. "Can't blame the person for not wanting to talk to you," I felt like telling her, but chose not to, in order to preserve the peace of the house. I was already handling more than I could and was in no mood to fight with Lata by being rude to her mom.

There were occasions I stayed away from home in the evenings when Lata returned from work to avoid potential volatile situations arising due to excessive calling by Seema. I preferred a coffee shop, fending off both my wife and Seema's calls. I read the papers or a book, worked on the laptop over a hot cappuccino or Frappe, depending on the season of the year. That was relaxing and peaceful.

Lata, caught up with Alaynah's bath-play-dinner-sleep routine, let me be, but Seema rang up several times to make sure I was working. "If I find out you are out with another woman, I will kill you," she said more than a few times.

"I am already a dead man," I told her.

As Seema needed only few hours study for the GRE exams, I involved her in some of my projects to keep her busy, mentally occupied, earn some money and most importantly be in happy mode. This also diminished time on the phone during the day so I could work undisturbed.

As I expected, she did a good job with her assignments. She had a good future as a professional, provided she controlled her emotions. I hoped her obsession with me was just a passing phase. It was still fun to hang out with Seema with intermittent nocturnal visits to my empty apartment. The sex was fulfilling.

Seema was passive compared to Sushmita, but I did not mind the change. With time, I experimented, including the chair. I tried to re-live some of my exciting moments with Lata, Pooja and Sushmita.

Yet, her bouts of irrationality and outbursts were sometimes difficult to handle. I bought a new Hyundai Santro for Lata, so she could rid her old Zen afflicted with teething axle, alternator and suspension issues.

The Zen had served the years and it was time to pass her on. Lata was elated. She received many gifts from her father, but a car from me, her husband, felt different. I think she was proud of me. I was happy that I could buy her the Santro.

Keeping the Zen in running condition required regular visits to an authorized service station that cost a bomb. These outlets believe in replacement, not repair, unlike roadside mechanics who patch up any part.

The intelligence here has been passed on by "*ustads*" (masters) trained on erstwhile Ambassadors and Fiat cars that were always knocked and screwed back to working condition. There were readily available duplicate and cheaper spare parts for any damaged or non-working portion dissected to the last nut and bolt.

Today, the age of "*ustads*" who believed in an honest hammering job and hung pictures of Nehru and Gandhi on the walls of their little shops is over. The newer car brands running on advanced computerized machinery and injector systems are difficult to beat into place.

The Gen X mechanics are also greedy, like everyone else impacted by the all-round consumerism, including gadgets, bikes and girlfriends among the mass of maids and nannies subsisting in cities. Handing over any vehicle for street side repair work is risky, unless one keeps a personal eye on the automobile.

Otherwise, the coolant can be diluted with water, a few litres of expensive oil drained off and machine parts replaced by fakes. The boys are no different from evils doctor one hears about, that make off with the kidney of a patient given a chance. It is best to rid an old car and procure a new one as maintenance cost begins to overshoot the EMIs in some years.

Anyhow, I happened to be with Seema in the new Santro. I was proud of the purchase with my own down payment money, as I do not believe in loans and EMIs, like my father. Seema was in a good mood initially as I drove her around in the brand new car, but soon lost it.

"How could you buy your wife a car? If you are going to spend all your money now, nothing will be left for us when we are together."

"The more you spend, the more you earn," I said, remembering the concept that was a best seller book, in order to side-track her charged mind. It did not work.

She insisted I pulled over. The traffic was heavy. She abruptly got off the car, found a brick and smashed it against the shiny new silver grey bonnet. The stone could have ricocheted anywhere hitting the windscreen or striking a passer-by or another vehicle. It was a violent act that attracted some attention.

In India, there is always an over-inquisitive population hanging about anywhere with nothing to do. They are most excited by any action in their midst that is an escape from their wretched, sad, impoverished and bored existence.

I continued sitting not knowing how to react. Seema stepped back in coolly. I drove off even as the quickly accumulating crowd that would have naturally sided with the girl watched. "*Laundiya* (girl) *tej hai* (is fast)," somebody remarked.

The same set of lechers would not have thought twice about eve-teasing or groping if there was an occasion, late evening when any girl is alone road side or inside a crowded bus.

I observed the rear view mirror with roadside loafers intently watching us. If the brick had hit someone, a few bystanders would have definitely given chase on a bike or scooter. I could have been assaulted with the same passion that rebel forces decimated Colonel Gaddafi and his sons in Libya. Idleness and underemployment can make people do funny things in this country.

There are too many mad dogs on the roadside hanging about doing nothing. With true justice delayed, twisted and manipulated by authorities and rich, mobs are known to take the law in their own hands and inflict instant judgment in the form of a good beating. Often, innocents can get caught.

Since I was with the girl I was guilty. It is assumed any guy with a girl deserves a thrashing, just as a car driver is squarely blamed when a rash biker is knocked down. No one is wrong. It is the corrupt politician-contractor nexus responsible for absolutely unsafe roads with no isolated thoroughfares for pedestrians, slow moving cycle rickshaws and two-wheelers that abound.

The authorities should be publicly flogged or handed over to the Taliban for their failure to provide basic education and livelihoods to millions that festers innumerable irrationalities. Chaotic traffic and illiterate minds engender a dangerous mix. Even as I worried about my momentary life and limb threatening situation, Seema said, "Never bring me anything that belongs to your wife. Since you have bought this car for her, do not use it with me."

"What about the Honda City? It was gifted by her father. You don't have any problems with that?" I asked.

"That happened before I was in your life."

"Should I label things in the house, post-Seema, pre-Seema?" I could have said, but desisted, lest she jumped off the car to throw a bigger stone at me.

I later told my family I hit a cow that appeared on the road suddenly, the horns squarely hitting the bonnet. My father-in-law expressed unhappiness about failure of Gurgaon administration to manage city roads, security and inadequate civic amenities affecting property prices.

Lata advised me to drive carefully. "You sometimes act like a kid, especially when it is to do with a new car or gadget. You should behave in a more mature manner. You are a father," she said.

My mother-in-law did not believe me. The next morning I saw her closely inspect the car. I did not care what she deduced.

"Was it a cow?" she remarked, "I noticed some red brick marks."

"If you don't believe me get a DNA test done, of the red mark and your distorted brain," I felt like saying, but kept quiet to pre-empt domestic strife to my already difficult situation. "Must have been blood," I replied.

Luckily, the insurance guys bought the accident story. The car was fitted with a new bonnet without any extra cost. I needed to be careful with Seema.

She flared up again when she chanced upon a-Rs 1000 dinner bill (the same meal would cost Rs 4000 today) inside my wallet that I spent on Lata's birthday.

"How could you do this? If you spend on your wife, how will you manage things with me? In any case, how dare you go out with that slut?" she said fiercely, tearing the bill the way angry protestors sometimes destroy an official document, flag or effigy in front of TV cameras or Parliament.

It is never palatable to hear the wife being abused, but I kept quiet. For the first time in my life, I mentally thanked my difficult mother-in-law for instilling in me qualities of patience and forbearance, by default.

I sincerely wished God had not endowed me with high libido and girl addiction. I was glad I was not gay though. "What is the connection between a dinner with Lata and you and me? We are doing fine. You do your work, I do mine and we have some good fun together," I said.

"What about marriage, divorce? You will have to buy a new house. More kids. Your financial burdens will increase a lot. Do you realize that?" I kept quiet and thought of the good times when life was simple, I was single and happily married, with only a mother-in-law to contend as my father had stopped speaking to me.

****

When Seema uttered the word "divorce" it always stayed with me for a while. Earlier in my life, Pooja pressured me to "get married". Now I was required to "get divorced" and then "get married". I believed the current scenario was much more sensitive and volatile.

I could sense big trouble coming my way unless I was smart and sensitive. I could not risk the situation spiralling out of control, which basically meant Seema told my family about us in a fit of irrationalism, my father-in-law had my nails plucked, my wife had a nervous breakdown, my father had another reason to be disillusioned with me and my mother-in-law tried to poison my food. Even my mother would not have sided with me on this one.

"Give me some time, I will take care of things," I told Seema as I held her close to me in my apartment, one night. The best way to settle differences with a woman one is close to is to hug and hold her for a while.

Words don't matter. It is the two audible heartbeats in the silence that can do all the talking. It works. Seema had confused her first physical intimacy with a guy with love and extreme attachment that can happen to anybody.

She had to get over me, but I needed to give her time. I again read material on the Internet about extra-marital relationships going awry. I had made a similar inquiry when I was seeing Pooja and Lata. Unlike earlier, there was more relevant information easily accessible now, courtesy Google. Not surprisingly, substantial matter was readily available for search words such as "married man, lover, kill, suicide, divorce, ugly, violence, jail, alimony, murder."

The pieces did not look good. They were gory. Married men accused of rape by lovers happened frequently. There was one tragic tale of a young man caught between two women. He committed suicide by drinking poison. His wife was pregnant with his child. She miscarried. I had no intention of killing myself.

I watched clips of movies starring Smita Patil, Shabana Azmi and Michael Douglas themed on straying, marriages gone awry and obsessive love. There was literature about psychosomatic link between body and mind in a state of flux, animation and stress. Studies suggested married men in affairs were more vulnerable to heart attacks and strokes.

Could Bill Clinton's bypass be linked to Monica Lewinsky? At the same time I assessed every extra-marital relationship could not end in tragedy. Otherwise, fewer men would exist in this world. It is only the ones that end tragically, that are talked about. Movies exaggerate, I concluded.

I visualized my father who fought the odds in his life and stood by his principles. I needed to deal with the situation that I had created. As the older and more experienced partner, it was important to be controlled and responsible, given Seema's state of mindlessness.

I had to manage her in such a way that she regularly met single guys her age and succeeded in finding herself a boyfriend or husband. The process had to be gradual. It was important to keep her happy. This was not easy. Her exit from my life would definitely cause me angst. I would miss her. But, I was in no mood for a divorce. I never considered that. I liked to be with Seema, but there was no long-term rational basis to our relationship.

I gave her more work to do to channel her mind to constructive thoughts. I encouraged her to systematically apply for a further degree abroad. I promised her part payment of expenses if she did not manage a full scholarship.

"Then I will come back and haunt you for marriage," she joked.

"It is important for you to be settled in your career first. Marriage comes after that," I told her earnestly, holding her hands at a coffee shop to pre-empt her from throwing the cup and saucer at me.

I planned a trip with Seema to Goa. She was excited. I told Lata an important client was hosting a conference at a beach resort. That is usual. My wife was happy I was making headway as an independent professional entity which in her view was never easy. My father-in-law patted me on my back.

My mother-in-law was silent. I was too pre-occupied to figure out her distorted juvenile thoughts. It could not have been anything positive. "You should take Lata along also," she finally remarked.

"I would love to. But I will be under pressure as there will be important clients around. I want to be on full alert in trying to make a good impression. I don't want to be distracted," I replied.

Lata looked at me proudly even as my father-in-law nodded in agreement. "Yes, it is important to focus on work. I think you should go alone. There will be many other occasions to travel together."

I do not think my mother-in-law liked I was being sweet to her. She strongly suspected something amiss. I had a great time with Seema in Goa, doing all the stuff couples in love are supposed to do – walked for hours along the beach holding hands, tried delectable seafood options, spent time at the pool, consumed plenty of beer, vodka, Bacardi rum and cocktails, watched movies and visited the spa.

We massaged each other's bodies inside our room, shared a perfumed tub bath, showered together and partied late into the night with a whole bunch of jovial foreign and high-spirited Indian tourists. Such relaxations meant our bodies were ready for long love making sessions in no time. Seema did not mind it at all.

It was much easier to manage Lata long distance when I was with Seema. She was a good wife and did not speak to me much on roaming so I could focus on work and not waste money and time. As she was quite busy, she never sought minor details of my travel itinerary, as long as I was available on the mobile, except flight timings. I spoke to her early in the morning or late at night when Seema was asleep. I excused myself to the men's loo to call her a couple of times in the day to keep her in good humour. "Don't bother about me. Impress your clients," she said.

Lata messaged which was not a problem, even with Seema in the vicinity. Cell phones made it easier for me to be with Seema outstation. Or else, Lata could well have called the hotel we were staying to ask for me. That could be very tricky.

"Why did you get involved with me knowing that I am a married man?" I gently asked Seema when she was in a good mood. She looked absolutely ravishing in a new two piece bikini I bought her at the Colva beach market.

"I was curious for sure. I wanted to know how it is to be with a guy. I was bored. I wanted a change. I liked your dimples when you smiled. I never thought of you as a married man. You look like an innocent boy. I felt comfortable."

The dimples had played their part. I repeated time in front of the mirror later figuring out their particular attraction. There was none.

On another occasion, when Seema was again in a better frame of mind, I asked about our future. "I have never been involved with anybody. I think my parents would not have liked it. I chose you because I love you. I want to get married to you."

"Don't you think things may get messy as I am already married?" I said, very politely, lest she smashed crockery around the hotel we were staying. I was in no mood to pay for the broken items, at five-star rates.

"That is for you to work out. You should not have got involved with me if you were not sure."

"I did not get involved with you thinking about marriage," I probed.

Fortunately, Goa and Vodka had sobered her a bit and she was amenable to speak her mind reasonably. "Everything in our relationship cannot be determined by you. You have got what you wanted -- sex with a beautiful girl and company that you lack in your existing marriage as your wife is too busy with work and kid. I want to get married to you. I too should get what I want."

"What do you want me to do?" I asked her.

"You will have to get a divorce."

I vacationed more with Seema to keep her in a happy state of mind. We went for more *bharat darshan* trips like IAS probationers, visiting Goa, Ladakh, Mumbai, Jodhpur, Jaisalmer, among other cities. During check-in at hotels, Seema told the front desk she was my wife.

"You should say the same," she said. Thankfully, they do not ask for a marriage certificate or passport at Indian hotels. Traveling abroad with Seema would be tricky.

Yet, some of the stress began to tell on me physically and also on my marriage. Although I kept myself fit by hitting the gym regularly, I fainted after sex with Seema. I climaxed and as I walked towards the bathroom of our deluxe room at Leela, Kovalam, Kerala, I fainted, collapsing on the floor.

This had never happened to me before. Seema rushed towards me holding my head tight against her breasts. Her tears flowed onto my face. I remembered my mother doing the same when I was unwell as a kid. I missed my mother lying in Seema's arms. Later, the MRI revealed nothing. Seema accompanied me for all tests, firmly holding my hand. The doctors said it was sudden low blood pressure.

I began to fight with Lata. My mother-in-law was the obvious target. I could not restrain myself anymore. I called her a mean-hearted witch. In anger I threw my cell phone out of the house on the road in front. It disintegrated into several pieces.

"I think you are stressed out working on your own. What is the use of earning more money when you are going to be unhappy? I think you should get back to a regular job," Lata concluded.

"I hope you are not getting involved with that girl who you claim is working for you. Don't think I am a fool. You have long conversations in the basement. I have heard you talk to her in the bathroom," Lata said another time. I was a little taken aback by her observation.

"All of this is bullshit. She works for me. Do I accuse you of affairs with people in your office? You just want to side-track the main issue that is affecting our marriage, which is your witch-y mother," I shot back. I think I was losing it.

One way out was to immerse myself in cricket. I wrote the following about T20:

It is T20 IPL cricket season in India again. Able bodied young, old, superannuated, dropped, playing cricketers from across the world have converged to try and hit the ball like Chris Gayle, the Don Bradman of capsule cricket, with added ability to do the Gangnam dance. T20 cricket has subsumed evening prime time at the cost of others that usually draw attention.

Thus, interest in Arvind Kejriwal's fast unto death has been as much as the recent test match in Mohali. The activist turned politician did not eat for many days, lost lot of weight, but had to pack up his few diehard followers to go home as his health deteriorated. Perhaps, Kejriwal should have stuck to being an activist. Indians in general don't like politicians.

Meanwhile, there has hardly been any analysis of one more speech by Rahul Gandhi that again underlined his ability to speak like a very intelligent undergraduate student. The guy is improving but needs to graduate to the next level.

Due to cricket, nobody has had the time to read between the lines of another Narendra Modi loud and aggressive speech that is supposed to subtly convey to his detractors in the BJP that he deserves to be Prime Minister of India because of his Gujarat performance.

If Sanjay Dutt were to be pardoned, the media play would probably be after Stuart Binny's blistering knock. I did not know who Binny was till yesterday. Now everybody knows he is the son of Roger Binny, a gutsy yesteryears cricketer. Dutt must be wondering in relief where the omnipresent TV cameras outside his house have disappeared.

Even Justice Katju has been uncharacteristically quiet. With his superior acumen he has probably figured out that he will be unheard in the din of cricket balls smashed around and sexy girls dancing and hip shaking between overs and sixes.

Given the new anti-rape laws one is unsure whether it is legal to ogle at the girls anymore. Or to stare at Katrina Kaif's flat tummy during her IPL inauguration aerobics routine in an exercise bra, that was passed off as a dance performance.

Could that be a non-bail-able offence? Could the cops suddenly appear at your house and say, "Sir, we have seen footage of an IPL match where you have been caught looking at young girls dancing in little shorts, which is illegal. You are under arrest and have to go to jail."

Better to wear very large dark goggles or else follow Shahrukh Khan cheering, dancing, hooting and hugging his kids as if he has personally dismissed Gayle for naught. Going by past behaviour, SRK should soon pick up a fight to add to the already large number of post-match IPL party brawls.

The IPL-T20 marketing strategy has been worked out. The assumption is like porn anywhere and masala Bollywood films in India, Indians can never have too much of cricket. There will always be enough watching the game anytime for everybody -- management, promoters, cricketers, sponsors and TV channels -- to make profits.

In order to garner local support and fervour, players have been advised to speak emotionally about their attachment to the city they represent.

For example, Rahul Dravid has spoken about his love for Jaipur as his wife shopped there some years back. Anil Kumble has spoken about the night he walked on Marine Drive when he realized he was a Mumbaite. MS Dhoni loves Chennai as he rode a bike there once. I love Timbuktu because the sky there is blue.

The cricketers are happy. It is very good money for a few weeks in office. Youngsters, pestered by parents to study, take up a job and stop playing cricket, are national heroes. Players in their rickety 40s such as Dravid, Ricky Ponting and Adam Gilchrist, who could be brushing up their

English to write cricket columns for leading newspapers, find their playing careers extended.

Only Sachin Tendulkar is doing what he is supposed to do in his 40's, enjoying the game, without scoring runs. Meanwhile, the commentators alternatively speak Hindi and English to address the equally important India and Bharat viewers.

This can be a little uncomfortable for some. The usually suave Harsha Bhogle has been trying to stick to rehearsed Hindi clichés like, anything can happen in cricket or cricket is a game of uncertainties.

For other parts of his Hindi analysis he smiles assuming that the viewer will be able to read his thoughts in English. Mohinder Amarnath has no such problems. Both his Hindi and English sound like Hindi.

Still, there is talk that IPL may be losing steam and the money making may not be sustainable. Like Tendulkar's retirement, maybe it will happen, maybe it will not.

The End

Seema went abroad. I wrote her a hefty cheque to finance her education. During her first few weeks in America, she wrote long mails on how much she missed me and that I should visit her. Then she was in touch with me less frequently as she got involved in her routine in USA, studies and more.

She could attract guys anywhere. Our interactions dwindled. Her family shifted out of Gurgaon as her father found new employment in Greater Noida, a new construction hub. I watched from the terrace as mover and packer trucks transported furniture from her builder flat, including the bed on which we made out once, when her parents were attending a wedding.

I don't know what's with her life now. We are not friends on Facebook although I can see her listed. We have not sent each other a request. I guess both of us realize this is the best way to keep overwhelming emotions at bay.

As for my parents, our relations continue to be cordial. They have chosen not to shift to the apartment where I made love to Seema for the first time. It remains unoccupied. I have decided not to let it out.

My parents are happy with their West Delhi community, comprising retired government officials. We meet during occasions such as birthdays, anniversaries and illnesses, at neutral public venues such as restaurants, parks and hospital turned resorts. My mother, being more flexible, visits us at my in-laws, but my father made of sterner stuff does not. My parents visit Sid in London, especially during summer months fully enjoying their time with his family.

I own more properties around Gurgaon, including commercial space. The rental money is good to supplement mine and Lata's professional income. I continue to own my plots now enclosed by a brick wall. Many houses have been built in the vicinity. The nomads are long gone.

I have remained monogamous since Seema exited. I don't feel the need to be with any other woman. I think my relationship with her was the most complete in terms of man-woman equations, emotions, ego, adulation, sex, stress and distress. I can take no more of this. I do miss her at times.

I love Lata too, and my two daughters. Alaynah has a younger sister. She was born in 2010, the same year as Sushmita's second child. Alaynah has a big role in keeping me straight and sane. I enjoy my unadulterated time with her that I have blogged about. The following are some entries:

Four Letter Word

So, my daughter has used her first four letter word. It was couched in one of the innumerable ditties that kids her age sing, invent and improvise for their games. They are generally good-humoured but the one that caught my attention went something like -- boys go to school, so they are fools, girls drink Pepsi, so they are sexy. Now, now what would a seven year old know about being sexy.

Matters around such subjects can be tricky. A year back she had asked why Shahrukh Khans *susu* part bulged when he danced in the movie *Om Shanti Om* that she happened to watch.

I recalled the video, Shahrukh in leather pants that did accentuate the private portion, probably done to please his many adult female fans.

Searching for a quick explanation, I told her that King Khan bulged because a man's *susu* part is different from a woman's. She promptly said she wanted to see mine. I told her that this was not possible as children should not see older people without clothes (though it is okay the other way round in the presence of parents. I wanted to extinguish another line of arguments to tackle).

But, it seemed Shahrukh had settled in her mind ... she insisted three, four times. "I want to know why Shahrukh Khan's pants at the *susu* part are round and not mine."

So I told her that men and women have different physical features, just like I have hair on my arms and her mother does not. As for a man's *susu* part, it is also different and looks like the trunk of an elephant, though much smaller.

I think she got some idea and has not spoken about the subject since though she could again. As things stand the sexy word has not jogged any curiosity in her mind. So, I have kept quiet about it. But I am preparing for the day when she may ask. I am still figuring out what to say.

I am Sorry

Well, Alaynah mediated the first fight between me and my wife.

It was actually one of those insignificant incidents between a couple that escalates into a verbal slanging and plenty of steam letting. The end result was that I threw a glass of wine into the sink and my wife sat outside the house on the stairs.

Alaynah intervened. I was brooding in the drawing room. "You should not have thrown the wine. You should go and say sorry to mama," she said.

Clearly she thought I was at fault. She looked me in the eye and spoke with a bit of authority that I have not noticed often in her voice. She meant what she said. I could not argue back. I went out and said sorry to my wife. She was surprised by the gesture as I have a habit of not saying sorry.

She instantly came back in and the New Year eve preparations continued. Later at night she checked with me: "Alaynah said she told you to say sorry."

"Yes,"' I replied. There were no further words spoken as we hugged and wished each other a happy new year.

Mother's Kitty Party

One fall out of working from home and a working wife is school and picking and dropping of my daughter. After a year, I have been invited to join the mothers' weekly kitty party, worked out by some mothers who have been interacting with each other and me for a while.

Needless to say the hour of the party will be immediately post-school, with each mom by turn hosting the lunch when the husbands are off to work. One mother has kindly agreed to supervise the lunch of my daughter, though I can manage on my own. Alaynah insists on having her meal herself whenever I supervise. She gives a tough time to her mother and grandmother.

The mom conversations, as is usual, will centre on interesting cooking recipes, clothes and the most dreaded figure, the "mother-in-law".

Don't mind it as it is a welcome relief from all the business, politics and strategy I am constantly updating. The mothers have also agreed for my turn, a restaurant would do, where everyone will go Dutch.

After contemplating a little I have decided to give the mother's kitty party a miss. Although I am tight for time, I could accommodate the weekly interlude, but it would be difficult to explain to my wife why the lone male kitty party attendee happens' to be me. I cannot keep this fact away from her as word will travel from daughter to wife or alternatively mothers to kids to my daughter to wife. Guess will have to wait for my daughter to grow a bit to have her on my side and keep secrets.

In reply to the invitation I have told the ladies it does not look good that I am the only guy around. They have all understood that I would have wife problems. After all they wouldn't let their husbands do the same.

Laughs

A few things I say and do that Alaynah liked and found funny, though not necessarily her mother:

@ If you happen to be at a volcano and it shows signs of bursting, then run away from the mountain and not towards the top as that is where the volcano is.

@ At the house of a viceroy (turned into a museum) I picked her up to a large mirror placed on a shelf she could not reach and said: this is a special mirror, if you look at it you see the face of the viceroy... her eyes gleamed with anticipation when I picked her up, though she saw herself only.

@ She learnt about Napoleon, how he could even sleep on a horse. I asked could he even do potty.

Terror

Terror does play on the mind of a seven year old especially after the November 26 Mumbai attacks. Alaynah has been learning about the seven biggest countries in the world, an order that I keep forgetting -- Russia, Canada, China, Brazil, USA, India and Australia. Hope I have got that right.

Today morning (most of our close conversations incidentally happen when we are in the car together, commute from school or tennis or other classes) she asked me about the top seven in terms of number of terrorists -- I named Pakistan, Afghanistan, Iran, Iraq, Saudi Arabia, India, Indonesia.

I realized in a bit her worry was about Gurgaon, where we live. She asked within India, which were the states with maximum number of terrorists? I named Uttar Pradesh, Bihar and also told her terrorists are bad creatures who could be anywhere. Then, came the clincher... "Are there any terrorists in Gurgaon?"

I said, "No."

She asked, "Are you sure?"

I said, "Yes."

The last thing I want her little mind to worry about is terrorists ... in some way I felt it would be a victory for these criminals if they also managed to scare Alaynah, given the innumerable lives and families already destroyed.

Yet, the way militants are striking crowded areas, the packed Gurgaon malls can be a prime target. I do hope what I told my daughter turns out to be true.

Obama Girls

Obama has written a letter to his two daughters that have been made public. He mentions about the change in his attitude about life from thinking about himself and his ambition to the world of his daughters and the infinite pleasures due to their little achievements.

What he says is true -- for me money, professional highs are important but others involving Alaynah take precedence, unlike earlier.

Among the infinite pleasures that I have derived include seeing her joy in managing the slide on her own at the neighbourhood park when she was 3 or so, swimming with floats on both her arms, then with one and finally without any and nowadays managing to get the shots right in tennis and even some golf.

I happened to watch the movie *One Fine Day* recently, in which Michelle Feiffer, as a working mom has to choose between an important client meeting and the football game of her son. She chose the latter.

Between a client mail or call and taking Alaynah to her tennis game, I too would choose the latter. That is the way life is, I guess.

Tennis Match

As I have said earlier Alaynah has been playing tennis for a few months now.

Mostly, it is a fun hour for her during which the coach has to repeatedly remind her not to chat with fellow kids. But, she enjoys and is beginning to hit the ball across, so I am happy.

Last month she played in her first intra-club match and lost, which I expected. She was a little disappointed and I told her that there is always the next time when she should try harder. This month, the matches are being played and I took her again.

I expected her to lose, but is seems that she had put a bit of thought into her game. She was placing the ball intelligently and was looking to win the points. The match was getting competitive. I had taken Aravind Adiga's *White Tiger* and did not read a page as I cannot recall a more involving tennis match ever.

Let me tell you it is quite a different feeling to watch your kid fight it out in a game. You want her to win, period. For a minute I understood the predicament of Father Williams when he speaks about all the nervous energy when his kids play.

It is tough. It was like meeting a stiff deadline, perhaps worse.

This is not going to be easy. Tomorrow is the second round and she is all keyed up. So am I, perhaps more.

Tennis Match 1

Continuing from the earlier blog, Alaynah lost her match. She did not stand a chance as she was up against Father Serena Williams. Alaynah's opponent was a little girl like her, but the Father treated the match as one more step by his ward towards winning a Grand Slam. He stood by the lines, argued with the referee and showed his disgust on missed points.

There are quite few such dedicated people around, who, for example plan the entry of their kids into IITs and IIMs from class KG. Alaynah's opponent has been enrolled for personal one to one coaching, undergoes video bio-mechanical training and carries a very fancy racquet. It shows in her game.

After losing Alaynah ran towards the corner I was sitting and repeated, "I lost," almost in tears. I told her, "Even Sachin Tendulkar loses matches and gets out on zero."

Of course Alaynah knows a bit about cricket because of me.

"Don't worry next time try harder, train harder, there is an improvement from last time when you lost the first match. So be happy," I told her.

Father Serena Williams, of course, was beaming.

Potty Washing

For any father handling a kid, potty training is mandatory. So it has been between me and Alaynah. Like terrorists, stock markets, road rage, the potty can strike anytime anywhere -- market, mall, pool, school, stadium, birthday party.

So, one has to be prepared about the process and also impress upon the kid that he/she should not hold it too long as it is not good for health.

Alaynah, however, is generally a magnanimous kid and has perhaps understood my reluctance, laziness or lack of natural ability to take on most assignments that are handled by her mother or other mothers of her friends in similar circumstances.

So she spares me the changing clothes routine at the swimming pool, eats on her own when we are together and we have long periods of silence in the car or at home when she senses that I am not in the mood to talk (because of work or whatever), which is not the case with her mom or grand mom.

However, in the case of potty she has been pretty steadfast in holding her ground. She insists that I do the washing, anywhere. Perhaps it is some kind of control she likes to exercise. In my opinion most women (perhaps even little girls) like to have their way in some matters with the men that matter in their life.

For me, for now, it is potty washing that I have to abide. So, the one question I ask before heading out: "Is potty coming?" It comes when it has to.

Mom & Pop

Mothers are different from fathers. It is apparent at Alaynah's school where the concerns of the mothers vary a bit compared to the fathers.

Mother's worries: Class teacher is not doing a good job; worksheets are not being sent on time; focus on extra-curricular activities is not there; child has to be taught at home to keep up in class.

Father's worries: Appreciating rupee is not good for exports; there is corruption in government; the school is making lot of money; Obama may be good or bad; anything can happen in the elections; there is a new insurance product; stocks have fallen; property rates are down.

The Specimen

A father involved with the routine of a kid (picking from school, birthday parties, sports, etc.) in the Indian situation elicits some reactions from people around and becomes a bit of a specimen, if I may use the word.

My impression is that busy fathers are intermittently involved with their kids, but a father (like me, being immodest here) involved almost daily raises some eyebrows among the sprinkling of grandparents and majority mother population involved in the hustle of kid routines.

As I work on my own and deal mostly with foreign clients I am able to revolve my routine amidst stiff deadlines. People who know me as somebody who manages work and kid compare. Some observations that I don't mind:

** You are so patient. I don't believe that you are so busy also. My husband would not wait for a minute (this is when Alaynah is busy at the school swings or an unending birthday party and I wait).

** You are never late to pick up your daughter. I have been noticing this and find it really admirable.

** You must be managing Alaynah's home work also (which I don't and cannot as it requires too much concentration and is handled by my wife and Alaynah's grand mom). When I say that I can only take care of the outdoor routine (it is also some time away from the computer screen and straining the eye), I get the feeling that some think I am trying to be modest, few also think that I hide how much work Alaynah is putting in (there is this undercurrent of competition always).

My wife is of the opinion that the above credits overrate my actual role as she is also working and involved with Alaynah in many more ways (like getting her ready in the morning, breakfast, home work in the evening, bath, dinner and reading to sleep). There is a flip side though. People (fathers and mothers) who don't know me think I may have lost my job or I am certainly unemployed to be able to follow Alaynah's routine diligently. If I happen to be unshaven the view is only buttressed.

Many are curious to know more and ask directly about what I do, perhaps unable to fathom the contented look on my face, when I am shaved.

In my opinion my efforts are actually minimal, though important, in the overall scheme of a child's development, but compared to others, I guess it must be more. At least there is more to show. I must add, though, handling a kid requires some patience. There is simply no choice.

Some Secrets

Of course there are some secrets that only I and Alaynah share, that could anger her mom, grandparents and perhaps a few others. It is some fun though...

** Driving the car at 140 kmph on the Expressway in exchange of claps and kisses (while driving) and hugs later. "Great driving," she usually squeals when I am at top speed.

** Not washing off the potty (her that is, if it happens to arrive) properly before jumping into the swimming pool. I tell her to do the breast stroke initially.

** Junking on a big packet of chips and coca cola, patties and visiting McDonald's for French fries – not too often, but once in a while.

** Getting her to taste chicken (I am a non-vegetarian), when the rest of the family, including her mother are hard-core vegetarians, and want Alaynah to be the same.

I don't know whether all of this is for the good or bad. I just don't think too much about it.

Playing Politics

7-year olds can be pretty smart about finding their way through the maze of parental and family roadblocks and permissions to issues that may be important to them. So is the case with Alaynah, who considers her mother (sometimes grandparents) to be the more formidable person to reason with, than me. So, her strategy at times is to extract a yes from me before moving onto a public debate.

She knows that parents are consistent people and when I say yes to her privately, I will have to defend her position in front of others as well.

One latest instance concerns an overnight school trip that me and my wife are not in favour of, as we feel that she needs to grow up a bit before such excursions.

Alaynah, of course wants to go. In the car (after school), where most of our one-to-one conversations happen, she told me that she wants to go for the trip and that I should say yes. My antennas were instantly up as I knew that this was building up for stage-2 with her mother: "Papa has said it is okay to go," she would begin.

So I replied: "We go for so many trips together, so we can go for another one and have some fun."

"I have fun with you and mama," she reasoned, "but with friends it is different."

"How?"

"Well, me and my friends, we can get up at night, switch on the lights of the room when the teacher is asleep and play games -- also eat chips," she explained.

"Ok," I said.

"So, is it a yes then?" she asked very innocently.

This was the crunch question, so I had to tread very carefully.

"I am not saying yes or no," I said, "Let us debate the issue with everybody and then decide."

"You mean you are saying yes, but others have to also say yes?" she asked.

"No," I said, "I am undecided and want to hear what others have to say."

"So, you are not saying yes or no," she said.

"True."

She knew I had guessed her game and would not give in.

But, it was well tried, Alaynah.

Time Management

Handling a kid with work requires some tough decisions. For example, if it is pick up/drop time and an important client mail needs attention or deadline looms, it is never very easy. On the one end could be a cranky or dissatisfied client and at the other the kid with near tears and worry in her eyes as she keenly awaits your arrival. Technology, including GPRS mailing, helps a bit with cell phones allowing one to parry a client situation for some time.

But, matters do need to be managed by the minute. Keeping track of time becomes important in the midst of bunched up deadlines and kid schedules.

For example, I do not like to send an important document close to kid pick up time as it can get nervy. Further, it is important to keep several time sources handy, without relying on any one: laptop, cell phone, table watches, car clock, at least one watch in the bath room, dressing room and bedroom.

One also has to account for traffic snarls, etc. A couple of years back the battery of my wall clock sank and it is not the best sight to see your kid waiting eagerly for you. But, things do get better as kids begin to borrow their teacher's/friends mother's/coach cell phone to make calls and find out.

"Sid, where are you?" Alaynah called the other day. "The party is over, please come and pick me up right now."

Perks of the Job

There are some inherent advantages in having a kid tag alongside, one being attention of comely women. For example, at my local gym where most of the bombshells who quickly slot you as the one who stares (at the mirror in front) while they jog on the treadmill, which I guess is a self-preservation drill given the generally sex-obsessed and starved population in India.

The ice was, however, broken following a couple of visits by Alaynah, who sat in the lounge area and read a book while I exercised.

The smiles and attention have not ceased. "What a cute child, your child, I did not know you had a child," one bombshell volunteered a conversation. I guess the fatherly image triggers a concomitant safe to talk to message to most of the opposite sex. Another pretty girl even asked me out for coffee at Café Day as she wanted to discuss the dynamics of setting up a business. This has never happened to me before. More are now my friends.

So I asked a long-standing friend the depth of such attention. "It's simple," she said. "You are like a lake and these women like little pebbles. They know that their entry into your life will only cause little waves, unlike a young bachelor who may turn obsessive, possessive, romantic and in love. So, they feel it is okay, they don't need to think too much while interacting with you."

For curiosity sake (???), I further asked whether such comfort levels can also result in more (you know what I mean).

"It can if the woman is not committed," my friend said. "She knows exit is easy, so why not try out something different, while the option is there, but I would strongly advise against such adventures as they can turn dangerous (she meant emotional)."

Well well, I am listening…

Hugs and Kisses

For a young guy a kiss can mean a lot. There was a time when I travelled quite some distance to meet a girlfriend. As my parents were against bikes and cars for being too expensive, I changed three buses, walked a bit in the heat to arrive at the residence of the pretty girl in question.

Then I took her out to the local market (no malls at that time) for *chaat*, walked her at her local park, praised her, her family and her dog expecting the big prize, the kiss in some corner for the efforts -- the girl of course thought she was doing a big favour still and sometimes refused, saying she was not in the mood.

So, one walked back, disheartened, hoping for another day and time.

Now, of course, I hanker for a kiss from Alaynah (a different heart soothing feeling), who has been quick to turn it to her advantage -- perhaps due to some female genetic intelligence flowing down.

So, it is no longer easy to get a kiss from her, unless she wants to. The other day she wanted me to wait another hour at a birthday party and promptly planted a kiss on the cheek. I complied. Off late, at the park, she kisses from a distance to negotiate more time. I have been complying, but feel short changed.

The only time I get many kisses for free is when I drive fast -- she likes it, so do I, but given the current traffic situation, the occasion is not often, even if I take some risk.

Technology and Kids

Kids growing up today are exposed to gadgets that did not exist during my time. At seven Alaynah is comfortable in handling the cell phone, dialling, taking a call, reading missed and received calls. She has a thing for cellular multi-media games nowadays.

She has learnt computer commands, including keying in passwords and can operate the paint brush which I cannot. She logs onto Google on her own, downloads and plays Barbie and Power Angel games online during holidays, mutes the sound when her time is over and has begun to use search words to read material.

What is a bit of concern for me, however, is the smut that is so easily accessible on the Internet. The transition from hearing about the word "sex" and knowing about it visually is very minimal. This is when I and my wife continue to stick to the story of fairies delivering Alaynah to us.

During my time it was never so easy to access sleaze, available at local video parlours -- one had to be a bit of a grown up (late teens I would say) to walk up to the guy at the counter and wink or point at the smutty stuff and pay for it.

The video cassette (including copies) had to be suitably camouflaged (among books for instance), smuggled into the house and hidden away so that parents, including very snoopy and suspicious mothers, did not find them.

Most adult shows were then group events involving several friends in the neighbourhood as word usually got round quickly about any household where parents happened to be out for a late night party or work.

Today a kid could easily surf a porn site, just one search word or URL away, within the confines of a muted laptop, even if the household is teeming with people. This is not a very palatable situation and I cannot think of any preventive solution that can be effective. Suggestions???

Phone Calling

Mother, girlfriends, wife and now it is the daughter. In hindsight, it was the easiest to handle calls from my mom as she simply believed all I said (or so I used to think) and never asked too many questions. This made it difficult to lie though I often did. After all, how could I tell her that I was too drunk to come home and had to spend the night at a friend's.

A better way to escape the situation was to speak about joint night study. Girlfriends, of course, one had to lie, especially when routines involving other girlfriends were concerned.

Over time, one has to handle the situation with the wife as well. For example a visit to the pub could be a client meeting or extra time at golf business development. However, with Alaynah things can be very tricky. What I do today will definitely be an example followed and practiced by her when she grows up.

For example, I have a problem about sticking to time… I lose track of it, especially when fun and frolic is involved. Off late, Alaynah calls to find out what time I am going to be home as there are some general knowledge games she has learnt that requires a quorum of people over the dining table.

"Sid," she says over the phone, sounding sometimes like my wife. "Just be home for dinner today, okay."

Thoughts cross my mind that a few years from now it is definitely going to be me who will be calling her to find out what time she is going to be back, given hectic social routines of teenagers. There is immense pressure on me now to do as I say. Parenting is a tough job. It teaches you to stick to time, for one.

The other day I told her while driving that I was going for a movie for grownups with some colleagues. "Stop the car, turn it around and come home right now as I want you to be home for dinner," she said.

I am struggling.

Car Phone

It has been a while since I wrote this blog... Alaynah has, of course, grown a bit ... one change is in the car after I pick her up from school ... she grabs the cell phone to speak to many friends similarly placed... Heading back home in their mode of transport, school bus or personal cars... Sometimes she speaks softly and I hear her say: "I don't want my father to hear this..."

Potty and Junk Food

This sequence goes something like this. Once, sometimes twice a week, from school I allow Alaynah to binge a bit on junk food at a local super mart -- it is usually a cola or a packet of chips. Of late, I have been running into a bit of an issue here.

Her argument is that I let her binge more on the condition that next week she would forego the high calorie, low nutrition intake, which I know will never happen. The next week would never come and be turned into a supposed sacrifice for the following week.

So, it has not been the best of times travelling back from school arguing about eating out. Of course, when I don't give in she snaps: "I will never talk to you again." "I will never give you a kiss again."

"I will never share chips with you again; not even a single piece." She knows that I have a weakness for any food.

Anyway, I have finally managed to come up with an explanation, though it does not sound very appetizing. I told her that eating junk food is like going for potty -- one can't do lots of it one day and not do it again for the next few days.

Similarly, one cannot eat lots of junk food in one go and then forgo it for many days. It is better to eat in bits over time as the urge to taste junk food will re-surface after a gap, just as potty does. For now, the explanation has worked ... our junk food arguments are over, though I have a feeling she may now say that "since potty is every day, why not junk food?"

She has not, until now.

Handling Candy

Girls like dolls, just as boys love cricket bats. Alaynah has many dolls. Candy is one favourite. I am supposed to be Candy's father as she is Alaynah's sister. So, if I push Candy away Alaynah reminds me, "you are her father, she is your daughter."

Alaynah loves to skate. We have found a stretch of road in Gurgaon that is smooth and isolated, where I take her sometimes. I watch and walk while Alaynah skates. I also have to hold Candy as Alaynah wants her to be part of the fun.

As instructed, I have to hold Candy with her face against my chest and other arm around her back so that people are not able to make out that she is a doll. Somehow, Alaynah does not want people to know about the real Candy. It probably embarrasses her. Alaynah keeps an eye from a distance, sometimes looking back while skating and waves to me in case I am not holding Candy the way she wants me to.

Candy is about three feet tall, head to toe, a bit big for a doll. She wears Alaynah's old shoes that dangle and beat against my body when I carry her. Alaynah also dresses Candy with clothes that don't fit her any more.

All of this is very well, except that on-road Candy draws many stares from people and passers-by who wonder why I am clutching the doll the way I do.

An elderly gentleman stopped by and said that when he saw me from a distance, he was worried that I was not holding the "baby" right. Later, he realized it was a doll. I have told Alaynah several times that we should leave Candy in the car.

She says that is impossible as Candy would cry all alone scared. I have told her that we could leave her sitting on the car dicky, watching her skate. She has a point that would be too dangerous and someone (other kids) might steal Candy.

Last week, I finally found a way out of my uncomfortable public situation. I told Alaynah that Candy has gone off to sleep in my lap so we should make her lie down on the back seat of the car so that she is comfortable. I lock the car so nobody can take her away. This has worked.

I don't have to carry Candy around, though Alaynah intermittently checks to see whether her "sister" has woken up. I say that she is fast asleep and we should not disturb her.

Hello Boys

Alaynah is over 8 now.

She has a set of "best girlfriends for life" who call on my cell phone to speak to her. They chat with me when I pick her at school or other occasions such as birthday parties.

Alaynah in turn talks to their parents. I guess all of this is also to impress the importance they attach to each other and their circle of girlfriends.

Some of her friends sometimes complain to me about a teacher and also ask whether Alaynah talks about them as much as they talk about her at home. "All the time," I tell them, which is the absolute truth.

Alaynah is, however, a bully when it comes to boys younger than her and constantly spars with boys her age (mostly classmates), which often extends to physical fights that can get ugly and bruising and sometimes requires the intervention of adults.

The story is a little different with older boys. In the recent past I have had to strike conversations with some, particularly requested by Alaynah.

One is a Class 8 football "star," the local Ronaldo whom the whole school apparently cheered during a high voltage inter-school competition in which he scored two goals; another was the leading protagonist at the school play, who I have now noticed usually has a set of "older girls" hanging around him and giggling all the time at his jokes.

Both are tall, fit and handsome young boys. Of course, Alaynah is too young for them to notice or acknowledge and this is how I come into the picture.

As per the instructions, I have to walk up to the stars, say hello to them, "shake hands" and then point at her and introduce, "this is my daughter." The boys are polite and good naturedly nod at her, even as she smiles back "star struck". She then runs to her friends to tell them that the famous "Mr Hooks" said hello to her.

Till date, I have said hello to four "stars". To the football "star" I said that I read about him in the school magazine and wanted to congratulate him for his feats. To "Mr Hooks" I said that I watched his act in which he was fabulous.

I am now prepared to speak to many more "stars" that I am sure I will have to.

A Better Husband

Alaynah often complains that I and my wife argue a lot, often on silly issues. She gets particularly peeved when we quarrel in the car. "It gets very boring," she says.

After one such prolonged squabble with my wife recently, I told Alaynah that I wish that she and her husband don't bicker. "I will get myself a better husband," was her prompt reply. My wife, of course, nodded in complete agreement.'